I0747183

TO SHATTER BONDS

LE SOMBRE
BOOK TWO

CINDY GUNDERSON

Copyright © 2025 by Button Press LLC

Cover design by Seventhstar Art

Character art by Parker Gunderson

All rights reserved.

No part of this book may be reproduced in any form or by any electronic or mechanical means, including information storage and retrieval systems, without written permission from the author, except for the use of brief quotations in a book review.

WITH GRATITUDE

Editing and Critique
Jordan Truex
Scott Gunderson, Sue Prince, Jami Thornton, A.E. King

Special Edition Art
Parker Gunderson

Cover Design
Seventhstar Art

Special Thanks
Stacey Wilson (assistant)

AUTHOR NOTE

I'm beyond thrilled to bring you book two in the Le Sombre series! This story has lived in my head for months, and yet it was surprisingly difficult to get down on paper. I actually took a month break in the middle of writing it because I there were a few things that needed to settle.

I think all of us want to live our life to the fullest, but it's difficult to always understand what that means. I wanted to play with this in a world where vampires wish for a death they can never have and the guardians can't escape rebirth even if their mortal journey ends for a time. *How do your actions change when you're caught in an endless loop? Where do we find meaning?*

There are a few things in this book that may be triggering to some, so I wanted to acknowledge that. There is depiction of violence between males, female oppression by a dominant male (nothing explicit or descriptive), and an instance of self-harm in the context of reincarnation. I felt these situations were necessary to the story and worked to treat them with sensitivity.

I hope this book grips you and doesn't let go. And that you'll then go back to the first book, To Vanquish Darkness, with new eyes...

xo Cindy

PROLOGUE

Theo's breath came in ragged gasps as he wiped the grime from his brow with a trembling hand. The hardened leather of his armor dragged on his shoulders, the weight of it making him stagger. The sun dipped lower, and the silence made a mockery of the carnage littering the earth. Blood soaked the dirt beneath his feet, the scent mingling with sweat and gore in the cool evening air.

"Etanos!" he rasped, forcing his leaden feet forward to help a fellow tribesman drag himself out from under a fallen warrior. The gritty soil clung to his boots, and the weight of his sword pulled at his side.

A strangled cry from nearby snapped his instincts back to the forefront of his mind. Theo whirled, scanning the ground. Etanos lay crumpled a cart length away, his tunic torn and darkened with blood. Theo surged forward, muscles screaming in protest as he gripped Etanos beneath the arms and dragged him from the mud.

The earth clawed at his feet as he hauled his friend's limp body toward the jagged shadows of a boulder cluster. Sweat caught dirt and blood as it dripped down his face, stinging his eyes. He blinked to clear his vision.

Theo grunted as he stopped and lowered Etanos's body to the ground. His friend's head lolled to the side, his face pale and slick with sweat. "Stay with me, brother," Theo murmured, dropping to his knees.

Now his eyes were stinging for more reasons than one. This battle had been foolhardy. Desperate.

Yes, they were protecting their tribe, but there was still no hope of resolution. They'd fought them off this time, but the Ariante tribe was twice their size. Probably more than that after their losses.

They would have to leave the land of their inheritance. They had no other choice.

Theo worked quickly, his hands steady despite his tremoring nerves. He tore strips from the cleanest parts of his own tunic, then uncorked his waterskin, pouring the precious liquid over the wound to wash away the grime. Etanos winced but didn't cry out.

"You're not dying here," Theo said through clenched teeth. He sprinkled crushed herbs from his pouch over the wound, the sharp scent providing a sweet respite from the fetid air.

Etanos's breaths were shallow but steady, his lips parted as he struggled to stay conscious. Theo pressed the strips of fabric to the now cleaned and treated wound, then nodded once, his throat too tight to speak. His gaze swept over the battlefield again, searching for any other signs of movement or life beyond those friends fortunate enough to still be moving about.

The moon rose over the horizon, its silver glow bathing the grasses and trees. Shadows stretched and shifted, revealing the dirt-streaked faces of the surviving warriors.

"Theo!" Barteron called.

Theo lifted his eyes, communicating silently with his chief. Yes, he understood. They couldn't stay here.

Etanos stirred, his voice a rasped whisper. "Theo, go. Leave me."

Theo's head snapped toward him, his jaw tightening. "Quiet. You're not dying here, and I'm not leaving you."

He tied his waterskin to his belt, then drew a breath before lifting into a low crouch. He rose slowly, his legs burning as he slung Etanos's arm over his shoulders. "Come on," he grunted, hauling him to his feet. Etanos hissed in pain but managed to stand, leaning most of his weight on Theo.

They moved slowly, following the others. The ground was uneven, the soil churned into a muddy mess by the chaos. Every creak of the trees made Theo's pulse quicken. His eyes darted in erratic circles, scanning the darkness for any sign of an ambush.

Etanos coughed. "You're as stubborn as an ass."

Theo huffed, adjusting Etanos's weight. "And you're about as heavy as one." A faint chuckle escaped Etanos, then dissolved into a pained gasp. Theo gritted his teeth.

The terrain became rougher as they climbed toward a ridge. Theo's muscles raged with the effort, his breaths coming in short, shallow bursts. They reached the top by some miracle, and Theo paused, letting Etanos lean against a boulder for support while he gathered his strength. The valley stretched out below them, cloaked in darkness. Smoke curled from distant fires, and the faint glow of their village flickered on the horizon. Relief warred with dread in Theo's chest. They were close, but it would still take most of the night to get back to their families at the rate they were traveling.

The warriors worked together to carry their wounded down the slope, one by one, then continued their trek northward. The air chilled, and all friendly chatter died by the time dew formed on the tips of the grasses.

"We're almost there," Theo grunted as Etanos stumbled. "A little further." Etanos nodded weakly, his eyes heavy-lidded.

Then, as they approached the edge of the trees, Theo froze. His senses prickled. As they rounded a bend, the faint glow of the village's fire pits came into view. Relief flooded Theo's chest, but it was short-lived. The fires burned low, their embers dim and lifeless. No voices carried through the air. No shapes moved within the flickering light.

Etanos's weight sagged against Theo. "Something's wrong," he murmured.

Theo nodded, his throat dry as Barteron's eyes met his. Someone should have put out the fires. They always put out the fires.

They entered the village to only the sound of crackling embers. No voices, no cries of children. The air hung heavy with the stench of smoke and iron, thick and cloying. Theo lay Etanos against a hut when Barteron cried out.

He surged forward, straining to see through the shadows. His family. He needed to cross the central meeting area and get to his hut.

The bite came so fast Theo barely registered the pain. Something slammed into him, throwing him to the ground, as sharp teeth pierced the flesh of his neck. He gasped, the hot, searing agony coursing through his veins like fire. His sword fell from his grip, and his vision blurred as a guttural cry ripped from his throat. He thrashed, kicking and clawing at the creature, but its grip was unyielding.

The world tilted. Shadows danced before his eyes, his strength waning with each beat of his heart. His pulse pounded in his ears, a deafening drumbeat, as warmth spilled down his neck, soaking into his already damp tunic. The scent of copper filled his nose, mingling with the acrid tang of smoke and rot.

The weight on his chest released, but he couldn't move. He was dying, he could feel it. His limbs were leaden, his breaths shallow. Darkness curled at the edges of his vision, threatening to swallow him whole. But even as his life ebbed, a single thought pierced the haze, sharp and unrelenting.

His family.

With a strangled cry, Theo forced his shaking hands to move, clawing at the dirt beneath him. His fingers dug into the ground, his nails breaking as he dragged himself forward. He had to hurry, to get to them before it was too late.

More choking cries, and yet he could see nothing. His vision was muddy, his hearing underwater. His chest heaved as he pulled himself up onto his knees then staggered to his feet. He felt as if liquid fire coursed through his veins, incinerating his body from the inside out.

Theo stumbled over a clay pot, its shards biting into the worn soles of his leather shoes, but he didn't stop. Not until he felt it. His home. He'd found it by memory, and recognized the soft scent of iris root his wife used in her oils.

"Dara!" He forced her name from his lips, the cry sounding more animal than human. He had to find her.

Theo scrubbed at his eyes, barely finding a way to distinguish between light and shadow. He pushed into the hut, stumbling forward and dropping to his knees, feeling along the packed dirt floor. He pushed forward to the pallet near the far wall, where his wife and daughter should have been sleeping.

His breath caught as his fingers met flesh.

Cold.

Unmoving.

His hands jerked back, his vision beginning to clear. A shadowed shape. Dark hair spread like a halo.

"No . . . no. Please." Theo collapsed over her, burying his face in her hair as a sob tore from his throat. His hand landed on the small bundle beside her, and his heart shattered. He looked up, blinking against the burn in his throat.

His daughter, barely a year old, lay lifeless, her tiny face pale and still. Blood stained the simple linen wrap around her, a black poisonous mark against the soft fabric. Theo's hands trembled as he reached for her, cradling her fragile body against his chest. Her warmth was gone, her laughter silenced.

The room spun around him, and he clenched his jaw, tears streaming down his dirt-streaked face. The bite on his neck throbbed, the heat of it spreading like poison through his veins. But the pain was nothing compared to the hollow ache in his chest, the crushing weight of his loss. He rocked back and forth, clutching them both, whispering prayers to gods he wasn't sure he'd ever believed in.

A scuff outside jolted him. Theo's head snapped with such force, he tasted blood.

A figure shifted in the doorway. A silhouette against the pale moonlight beyond the threshold. That old protectiveness surged in Theo even though the hole torn through his heart made it impossible to forget he had nothing to fight for.

"What do you feel?" The man's voice was low and calm.

Theo wanted to rip his throat out, but he couldn't force himself to loosen his grip on Dara. "Remove yourself from my home." The words felt like vinegar in his throat. Caustic and biting.

What home did he have? He'd fought, spent days in the woods, and for what? Was everyone they loved gone?

Theo's heart pumped faster as he thought of Etanos slumped against the hut at the edge of their village. Had he discovered his loss yet? Would he make it through the night if he had?

Or was it only his family that was taken?

"I asked you a question." The man took another step, his pale hair falling in loose waves around his severe nose and cheekbones.

Theo blinked, confused by what he was seeing. Moments before, he'd been peering through silted river water, but now . . . everything was clear. Sharp. It was as if the sun shone through the doorway, allowing him to see every detail.

"Is this your doing?" Theo demanded, the hairs on his arms lifting.

The stranger didn't answer, only tilted his head. Watching. Waiting for something. For—

The first crackling surge of strength began in his chest, a fire ignited deep in the furnace of his heart. He arched his back, throwing himself from Dara's pallet as every sinew in his body tightened. His muscles pulled taut as if a blacksmith were hammering them into steel beneath his skin. The pain was not a single flame but a wildfire, liquid bronze filling his veins, weighing him down until he thought he'd sink through the earth and be buried alive.

"There, there." A voice floated above him, low and melodic. "I can help you. If you'll let me."

1

Aurelia
213 BC
Ancient Gaul

Aurelia pressed her cheek against the smooth bark of the beech tree. It was her favorite, not because it was the most majestic or beautiful, but because it was the most impossible.

Before her rebirth, likely before her parents were reborn, the tree had been struck by lightning and split nearly in half down to the roots. Yet somehow, it still stood, and its branches spread farther and wider than any other tree in the forest behind their village. Nobody could explain how it was still standing.

The branches were so lush and heavy and reached at such a severe angle, they should have snapped free from the trunk.

Aurelia hated when children climbed on it, worried that even an insect landing on its secondary branches would be force enough to make it crack. But somehow it stood seasonring after seasonring.

Each year at the arrival of sunlasting with the first sweet blossom of the Hawthorn tree, Aurelia stood on this very spot. It was where she encountered her first fox, her first butterfly. Where she hid when the tribes marauded through with their wares. Where she played with Fiona and her siblings.

In the past, when she stood with her eyes closed and chin lifted to the leaves shaking off their blanket of dew in the sunrise, her heart had been full to bursting. Today, she wanted to slash it out and bury it in the ground.

"I could run," she murmured, as if this tree or any other in the thousand-year-old forest would care about one girl in a village on her eighteenth seasonring. She'd been dreading this moment and had tried for the entirety of their last lunar cycle to make the time pass more slowly. Yet somehow her efforts only had the opposite effect. It was as if she blinked, and this morning had jumped out of the shadows, elated to catch her off-guard.

Aurelia couldn't have been the only guardian who fantasized about living a different life, but today of all days she had more reason than most to consider it. To think about disappearing into one of the tribes, preferably a nomadic one that would move far from Magos as soon as the seasons shifted.

She was of age. She had a duty to fulfill, a sacrifice of her blood to offer. *She was of age.*

The words thudded through her like a drum beat. How many times had she imagined binding her hair and working as a druid or human healer? Nobody would be the wiser. Her family would miss her, but as a middle child, they had other daughters and a son to fulfill their covenants. They would get over it eventually, wouldn't they?

"Aurelia!" Her mother's voice sounded, weaving between the trunks and branches. It was far enough away, she was likely calling from just behind the house. Aurelia drew a deep breath, absorbing the scent of decaying wood and damp earth.

She closed her eyes and exhaled, knowing full-well she was an ungrateful wretch. And yet, acknowledging it did nothing to assuage her guilt or motivate a new course of action. She should have been satisfied. Her sisters had been through this before and neither of them had griped.

But they hadn't been hovered over their entire lives. Her mother had treated her more harshly, expected more, pushed her harder, and she still didn't understand what she'd done—or not done—to deserve it. This was yet another opportunity to be a disappointment, and she would avoid it to the last second.

"Aurelia?" Her mother's voice moved closer, the sound of her footsteps padding along the soft, spongy forest floor, growing heavier by the second.

Her toes twitched. She could run . . .

But she wouldn't.

Aurelia exhaled, her shoulders drooping. As much as she dreaded this day and as much as she enjoyed her fantasies, her life wasn't something she could claim. She was a small flicker of light in a robust and intricate tapestry. As much as she played pretend, it was never a question of whether she'd fulfill her covenants or not. As unremarkable as she was, she was still a guardian. Who else could she be if she walked away from that calling?

The footfalls stopped, and Aurelia knew exactly what she would encounter when she turned—her mother standing with her hands planted on her hips, her long, dark hair pulled into a twist at the back of her head, a stern expression on her face.

Aurelia drew a deep breath and pushed back from the smooth, crisp bark of the tree.

"I know you heard me calling." Her mother's face was pinched, her skin looking more flushed than normal against her azure tunic and skirt. She was a beautiful woman. Fair with fine features. Often, Aurelia had inspected other women in the village and hoped she would grow to be like her mother and not any of them.

Now, at eighteen, she was her mother's spitting image.

The frown Aurelia knew better than she knew her own face tugged at her mother's lips. "You have no reply?"

Yes, Aurelia had heard her. She'd heard everything her mother and father had said over the years. She'd read and re-read the prophecies and instructions in the scroll of the guardians, *Dugionos Ambacton.*

Her parents were the Bearers of the Balance. The intercessory between the guardians and the creatures on the hill. Now that she was of age, she would be brought into that inner circle. Allowed to take on responsibilities and assist them with their tasks as her older sisters did.

But that meant at some point, she would have to stand face-to-face with one of those creatures. She wasn't looking forward to that either.

Aurelia wriggled her toes against the soft, stretched leather of her shoes. "I wasn't ready to answer."

Her mother tsked. "We're already late."

Words bubbled to her lips, but she yanked them back. There was nothing she could say. No words she could conjure, no arguments or rational rebuttals she could give to sway her parents in this matter. Her fate was sealed.

Aurelia brushed her long dark hair over her shoulder and

shivered. "Why are we attending today? It makes no sense. I wasn't born until the day after—"

"You know the tradition, Aurelia."

She did know the tradition, though nobody in her family had ever been asked to participate. Alain, the only vampire she or anyone else in the village had ever seen, appeared in shadow on the dais of the temple. He selected from the guardians who came of age that season. An honor. One that she wouldn't receive.

"He doesn't even know me. How could he miss me?" she teased.

Her mother said nothing. Aurelia's jokes were not appreciated this morning. She sighed and took a step forward, and her mother nodded in approval.

"Good. I was wondering if I would have to call your father and have him haul you out of here."

Aurelia gave a small smile. "I should have waited. That could have been fun."

Her mother's lips twitched, but she didn't respond. She simply turned and retraced her steps along the well-worn path in the forest underbrush. Aurelia followed her like a duckling. Or perhaps a more fitting metaphor would have been a baby lamb. She was dressed and cleaned for the slaughter.

Goodbye.

The word trickled through her mind, and her stomach churned. This wasn't a finale. She didn't need to say goodbye. The ceremony would take a few minutes at most, and then she'd be back home. Back here by the tree if she desired. But a pit still opened up inside her, empty and cavernous.

She would not be the same.

None of them ever were after their first offering.

Her mother sighed, picking her way over a fallen branch. "We will walk together to the temple. Your father and I will wait on the steps until you return from the ceremony. Then we'll meet with Brennos and Lita and the others." Her mother tromped ahead, but Aurelia's eyes snagged on her fingers, twisting in the fabric of her tunic. They were tight, her knuckles pale.

"Mother." Aurelia slowed. When her mother didn't answer or turn, she called again. "Mother, please—"

Her mother spun, her expression still wound tight. "Aurelia, I told you, we're already—"

"What is it like?" She swallowed hard, working to clear the lump in her throat. The leaves rustled, the cool morning air pressing against her cheeks. The reality of her life as a guardian stretched before her like the vastness of the stars. Forever. She was chosen by the Goddess to serve as a protector, to fight back the curse of Le Sombre and the dark creatures he created.

Forever. This life. Her next, and the others after that. Her throat thickened as her ribs cinched around her middle.

Her mother sighed. "We've talked about this."

"No, I'm not asking about generalities." Aurelia took a step closer. "What was it like for you to offer up your blood?" The first time. Did her mother even remember? Her parents served diligently in the temple every few days and they never spoke of what happened there, not the specifics.

Aurelia reached out and gripped her mother's wrist, turning it over. The two marks on her skin from the day prior were barely visible. By the time she offered herself again, they'd be fully faded. "Is it always here that they bite?"

Her mother pursed her lips. "It depends."

Aurelia's eyes flicked up. "On what?"

"On . . . whom."

Aurelia's mouth went dry. "What if . . . what if I don't want—"

"We're late." Her mother clicked her tongue and turned, pulling her along.

As they climbed the low slope leading to the house, the smell of roasting mutton filled the air like perfume. It did nothing to calm her nerves. She was sweating, and her hands were shaking as they approached the front door.

"You don't have time to wash. But please do something with your hair." Her mother dropped her arm.

Aurelia bit back her argument and stalked through the door. She was glad she didn't have time to wash. Why take so much care preparing for something she wouldn't participate in? She would stand in front of everyone with a false smile on her face as she watched one of her peers ascend the steps of the temple, extend their arm to Alain, and feign composure as he drank their blood.

The whole tradition was barbaric. Then she'd have that image fresh in her mind as she entered the temple and offered herself, thankfully never having to set eyes on the creature who fed from her. As it should be. They fulfilled their duty, but vampires didn't need to be idolized.

Aurelia pulled on her ceremonial tunic, then trained her hair into a plait. When she returned to the front door, her father and mother stood waiting for her. She glanced around the room. "They're not coming?" She didn't mean her younger brother, of course, but her two older sisters had already gone through their own ceremony. They attended the Day of Light selection every year.

Her father shook his head, his gray eyes flitting to meet her mother's. "Your mother thought it would be best if it was only the three of us." He ran thick fingers over the scruff of his beard, waiting for her reply. Where her mother was order and expectation, her father was tenderness. At least with the three girls. He was harder on Matthias, but that was to be expected.

His soft words and hopeful expression made it impossible to snip. Aurelia gritted her teeth as she nodded and fell into step beside them.

Neighbors and friends looked up from their hearths and washing as they passed. Aurelia was used to it. Not only because of her parent's station, though that played a part. From the time she was little, she'd heard the murmurs and noticed the glances that stuck to her like pine sap. *Not worthy. Not chosen.* But none of that had been close to what she'd experienced over the past weeks as her seasonring approached.

Eighteen years ago, the entire village of Magos had tipped their heads heavenward in awe when the sun forgot to sleep. It had happened. A day of light, just as the prophecy proclaimed. They watched for the second promise, for a guardian child to be born during the night, to usher in the end of the curse.

Her mother was the only woman due to deliver. But Aurelia came hours after the sun finally set. Hours after what was supposed to be their miracle. Before she'd even opened her eyes, she'd failed them.

Druids and philosophers had theories as to why the sun stayed hanging in the sky, none of which had anything to do with a prophesied guardian child. The Day of Light was a sign of divine favor, a moment when the veil between the mortal world and the divine realms was thinnest. Or it was the triumph of the sun god *Belenus* over the forces of darkness, signifying renewal, fertility, and protection. Astronomers were convinced it was an anomaly in the natural order, a harbinger of change in the cycle of seasons.

Humans gave sacrifices in their own rituals for the Day of Light, and Aurelia had always wished to see them. To see the celebrations in person. To wear a golden flower wreath and hold a shimmering shield. It was frivolity. Ritual. Celebration.

Exactly what it should be.

But she wasn't supposed to interact with humans on her own, though now that she was of age, that rule didn't technically apply. If they dressed the same, there was nothing about their physical appearance that would expose them. Humans and guardians looked identical on the surface. It was only their blood and the power that came with it that set them apart. None of which humans could tell from their senses.

Besides, the prophecy wasn't fulfilled, so why did it matter? It was better to believe in the human explanations than take to heart what traveled in the whispers. That she had displeased the Goddess. That her family wasn't worthy. That the guardians would have to wait hundreds, if not thousands of years for another chance as outlined in the Dugianos.

Until the Day of Light, guardians will wait. They will serve. They will protect. And when she who is sent to bind appears, they will follow.

For over a thousand years, guardians and vampires had lived protecting the delicate balance of shadow and light. It had been eighteen seasonrings since the sun hung in the sky.

Vampires still lived in the shadows.

Guardians still offered up their blood.

The Day of Light had come and gone, and the prophecy was still dead.

Aurelia stumbled when her parents stopped in front of her. She gripped onto her father's arm and righted herself, then lifted her chin. Somehow they'd already made it to the bottom of the bleached stone steps. The crowd around them chattered in excited anticipation.

"Go on." Her mother reached out and nudged her shoulder. "Your father and I must meet him inside."

Aurelia's heart stuttered. She scanned the crowd and found her peers standing to the left of the stairs in their ceremonial tunics.

"Aurelia—"

"I'm going," she hissed, then crossed her arms over her chest and walked forward.

2

Aurelia took her place as a hush settled over the courtyard like mist before dawn. Above, banners fluttered from the spires—sunbursts and crescents embroidered in golden threads that caught the light. Their edges snapped gently in the breeze.

She wished the wind would reach her there with the others at the base of the stairs. Sweat had already begun trickling between her breasts. The ceremonial tunic—cream silk, stitched by her mother's hand—clung damply to her back. Why did they hold this as they approached the heat of the day?

The scent of crushed herbs and smoldering wood hung thick in the courtyard, rising from the braziers that lined the perimeter. Tallin leaned over. "You couldn't be on time?"

She rolled her eyes. "Does it look like Alain is on the steps?"

He smirked. "I'm surprised you came at all."

"As am I."

Renna caught her eye from the other side of their group and gave a small wave. She smiled back. She tried to still her breath, but it kept fluttering shallow and fast in her chest.

This moment was supposed to be sacred. A celebration of balance between the dark and the light, between predator and protector. Curse and blessing. Every story, every lesson since she was old enough to stand pointed to *this*.

And yet—

Her stomach churned as the great archway doors swung open, and there he was. Alain. The leader—or figurehead?—of the coven. She'd never had the gumption to ask her parents more about him, though she'd gathered they met together often.

Aurelia shivered as he stepped forward. He wore black threaded with gold, his cloak trailing behind him. He was unnaturally beautiful. His features were perfectly symmetrical, and his hair shimmered like sunlight.

On either side of him walked her parents—the Bearers of the Balance.

Her mother strode with the grace of ceremony, the golden circlet glinting against her brow. Aurelia's pulse thundered. Alain paused at the dais, hands folding loosely in front of him as her parents stepped past him, claiming their places at the center of the dais.

Her mother raised a hand. "Friends. Family. We gather on the Day of Light, as we have for a hundred seasonrings, to renew the sacred vow between dark and light. Between vampires and guardians.

"Our ancestors made this covenant in blood," she continued, "not to war with one another, but to preserve the fragile equilibrium of our world. Without light, the shadow devours. Without shadow, the light would be unnecessary."

Aurelia clenched her hands at her sides. She'd heard this speech before. Every seasonring. She knew the words like she knew her own name. And yet, now, standing in the late morning sun, sweat cooling between her shoulder blades, she felt each one land inside her like a stone.

Her mother's voice rang over the courtyard. "The Guardians offer strength and service, their blood a gift freely given. The Nightkind, in turn, vow restraint and respect, their bond forged not by chains, but by choice. Tonight, that vow is renewed."

Her mother turned, casting her gaze over the small gathering at the base of the stairs. Her eyes flicked over each of them—then paused, for the briefest second, on Aurelia. Heat bloomed in Aurelia's chest, instant and sharp. She wasn't sure if that look was filled with pride or shame.

Let it be her. Aurelia silently prayed to the Goddess. She didn't wish to make a spectacle of herself, but the idea of walking up those steps. Of being chosen. No longer the girl who wasn't worthy of the Goddess's favor. The idea was intoxicating.

"My honored Guardians." Alain stepped forward, his voice velvet and smoke. "Your presence here humbles me." His gaze passed over them like a blade drawn gently across skin. Not cutting, but enough to leave a scratch.

"You are the ones who stand between chaos and order," he continued. "You are not only protectors of the innocent—but of us as well. You keep our hunger in check, our instincts honed, our covenant intact. Without you, we are monsters."

A soft murmur rose from the crowd.

Alain smiled. "With you, we are balanced. Whole."

Aurelia's throat tightened. What would it be like to despise your own instincts? To see yourself as a scourge? She couldn't help but feel compassion.

Choose me. The words unspooled like a prayer. She'd already made her choice. When she followed her mother from the woods. When she slipped on her tunic. It was too late to be chosen of the Goddess, but she could be found worthy by Alain.

Aurelia glanced around, counting the others in her season. Calculating her chances. She straightened her posture. Not too stiff. Chin up. She watched him, her gaze steady.

Please.

Alain turned toward them. He descended one step. Then another. Aurelia's pulse crashed against her ribs. He paused before them, eyes gliding down the line—lingering for the briefest moment on Tallin.

Then—

Her.

For a heartbeat, their eyes locked. His silver gaze shimmered, unreadable, and her breath caught. But he turned his head. Reached for Renna.

Aurelia blinked. Renna stepped forward, letting out a shaky breath. Her mouth curled at the edges as she gripped his hand, ascending the steps.

Aurelia's feet rooted to the stone. She stared straight ahead, past the curve of the staircase, past the marble columns, unfocused. A flicker of movement caught her eye—her mother, standing on the dais. She didn't glance down.

Aurelia's skin burned. At the top of the stairs, Alain turned to Renna, murmuring something too soft to carry. She smiled, nodded once, then held out her arm, flipping it to reveal the inside of her wrist.

Alain stroked the underside of her arm, then cradled her elbow. He bent, and Aurelia flinched as his mouth met the inside of her friend's wrist. Renna sucked in a breath, then her lashes fluttered, her lips parting on a soft gasp.

Time oozed like tree sap. The world seemed frozen, pinned up, until Alain lifted his mouth from Renna's wrist. A single drop of crimson lingered at the corner of his lips. He brushed it away with a slide of his hand, then licked it from his finger.

It was done. Aurelia let out a slow breath, her disappointment lingering like stale sweat. She hadn't been chosen—of course she hadn't. Why had she even allowed herself to hope?

Renna blinked her eyes open as the crowd hummed their approval. Alain whispered something to her—soft and reverent. The ceremony bell chimed once, and Aurelia's mother stepped forward. "Guardians of age, begin your ascension," she called.

Aurelia's stomach sank. Right. It wasn't over. They had not been chosen for the ceremony, but they were still expected to fulfill their duty. She moved forward with the others, her heart jolting. She pressed a hand to her chest, the urge to turn and sprint back down the packed dirt road so strong, she worried her legs might explode in the other direction without her permission.

Her father met her eyes, and that was what propelled her up the first step. *She could do this.* Her entire family line had fulfilled their duty after the age of eighteen, and none of them seemed to regret it. Though perhaps that was because they never spoke of it.

They were changed after the ceremony, yes, but what did she expect? To be a child forever? Her mother had married at seventeen and had her first child within the year. By this time next year, Aurelia could be standing here wearing a torc around her neck.

Her cheeks heated as she climbed another step. Would Caelan offer her one? He'd said as much when she'd let him hold her hand after they swam in the river the week prior, but men said plenty when they were getting what they wanted.

Did she desire to be bound to Caelan? He was handsome enough. Strong and capable. Why hadn't she thought to ask him about his ceremony? He probably would've told her anything if she'd offered to kiss him again behind the rushes.

"Don't get sick on my robe," Tallin whispered.

Aurelia turned her head to find him grinning at her. "I'm fine."

He winked. "Sure. You seem fine."

She pursed her lips. "Will we all go in together?" In past years, the guardians who'd come of age all entered the temple as one group, but she'd never thought to ask what happened after that.

"I don't know. Would you like me to hold your hand, though?"

Aurelia rolled her eyes. She caught her breath at the top of the stairs and forced herself toward the arch. She counted her steps, measuring the last seconds before she passed between the pillars and into the shadow of the temple. She'd walked past this building thousands of times, but had never entered. Her curiosity almost overpowered her paralyzing fear.

"Aurelia."

She turned to find her mother striding toward her. Tallin gave her an odd look as he walked ahead. Aurelia moved to the side. "Is something wrong?"

Her mother smiled. "No, of course not. I only thought—there's a large group today, and since your day of birth isn't until—"

"Is this your daughter?" A shadow fell over them, and Aurelia looked up to see Alain standing at the door.

Aurelia's mother straightened. "It is. My third."

Alain gave a small bow. "Had I known, I may have altered my choice."

Aurelia forced her face to remain calm. Something about his comment felt patronizing, though his expression was sincere. "The Goddess chooses, does she not?"

"You are right, of course." Alain sighed. "One can only suppose her reasons." He glanced at the entrance to the temple. "You are not attending with the others?"

Her mother gave a small laugh. "Of course she is. I only wanted to speak a few words of comfort."

Alain nodded. "As any mother should." He moved to the side, holding out an arm. Aurelia glanced back at her mother's tight smile. There hadn't been any words of comfort. If she'd heard her right, her mother had been asking her to wait. *Had she misunderstood?*

Aurelia nodded once, then stepped over the threshold. Her breath hitched as the cool shadows of the temple embraced her. It took a moment for her eyes to adjust. Sunlight spilled through narrow slits carved high into the curved walls, illuminating the temple in slender, golden beams. It was as if shards of the sun itself had splintered off and embedded in the stone.

Massive columns, carved to resemble twisting branches, rose to the domed ceiling. The echo of her leather shoes brushing against the stone floor mimicked the rush of wind through wheat grass as she hurried to catch up to the group.

At the center of the room stood Elder Eron. His robes were bone-white, trimmed with black and bronze. His silver hair lay braided down his back. "You will enter one at a time."

Aurelia's fingers curled into her robe. Her feet edged half a step back. Just enough to hide behind the others. Tallin went first, of course. Zero hesitation, winking as he passed.

Eron escorted him down the hall. When he returned, Davi caught his attention and whispered, "Is this always how it is? One at a time?"

Eron smiled and shook his head. "No, only the first. You will receive more instruction in your classes next week once you understand the ritual."

Aurelia's jaw tensed. So secretive. Why? Why could they

not sit everyone down and explain exactly what happened within these walls? She understood not discussing details with children, but if they were old enough to conceive, shouldn't they be informed before stepping beyond the pillars?

Tallin didn't return. One by one, the others walked with Elder Eron out of the atrium, and as their group dwindled, Aurelia's pulse quickened. She hadn't intended to be last, but each time she considered stepping forward, her feet didn't want to obey.

She was lost in the flicker of the candle on the wall, breathing in the soft scent of melted beeswax when Eron touched her elbow. "We've anticipated your arrival."

"You were so sure I'd come?"

His grin widened. "I know your mother." The fabric of his robes caught the faint light, the white shifting to almost iridescent with his movement. Eron inclined his head, then turned and gestured to a doorway on his right.

She walked through ahead of him. The corridor beyond the main chamber narrowed, and the light grew dim. Aurelia's palms were clammy. She clasped them behind her back. When the hall opened into a small, circular room, she stopped and swallowed hard, taking in the view in front of her. What was she looking at? Dark shrouds hung from the domed roof, creating a half-circle, like when she was a child and lifted up her mother's skirts to hide inside.

Eron pointed straight ahead, and Aurelia took a hesitant step. Were they all different? Depending on where she entered, would she find a different experience? A different . . . creature. *It depends on whom.*

"Should I—?" she started to ask, but Eron pointed again. There, she saw it—a slight rustle of the fabric. Her heart leaped into her throat.

If she'd felt the pull to run in the woods, the tug against her spine now felt like a rope tied around her middle. *Do your duty.*

She clenched her jaw, forcing her feet to move. Her hand was numb as she reached forward to part the shroud. As she stepped inside, she was enveloped in shadow. Blackness all around her.

A soft beam of light slipping through the crack she'd left in the fabric was the only way to make out her surroundings. Another ripple, this time to her right. And there, a second gap in the shroud.

This was the only instruction her mother had given her. She was to slip her arm through. Aurelia started to sweat.

Unworthy.

Her teeth began to chatter. The nails of her left hand bit into her palm, and she thrust her hand forward.

3

The ancient, worn fabric of the shroud was rough against the tender skin of Aurelia's wrist. Her hand shook as it passed through, and she cursed herself. Her parents had prepared her for this since she was young, and she hadn't been afraid then. Not until she was a bit older. When she heard the stories.

The summer of her twelfth seasonring, all of her friends had heard the story about Maera's aunt who disappeared one night after supper. Maera insisted she went to the temple and never came back. She was sure her aunt had been taken by *them*. Claimed or consumed by the creatures hidden in shadow.

The Shadow Fangs. Blood Drinkers. Children in her village had a handful of names they used when trying to terrify each other during daily chores. But Maera's story expanded by the day, the details bloating like a dead fish. She had always been one to seek attention.

Still. The story troubled Aurelia.

When she'd admitted this to her parents, they'd listened

and nodded, then reminded her of the truth. That Le Sombre, the god of shadows, cursed men to be his companions in the darkness. In his selfishness and cruelty, he'd caused them to transform, to feed on the blood of humankind, to live forever as the damned.

It wasn't their fault. They didn't choose it.

Which was why the Goddess Soléne had balanced Le Sombre's curse with a gift. The guardians. Humans with her bloodline. They would not die when bitten, and it was their duty to provide sustenance for these creatures.

There were many reasons a woman would go missing. Plenty unrelated to the creatures behind the wall.

Vampires.

Aurelia sucked in a breath as smooth fingers encircled her wrist. She forced herself not to yank her hand back through the shroud or fall to the floor weeping. His hand was large, his grip firm, but not cruel. He could snap her bones in an instant. Pull her through the shroud and devour her whole if Maera was to be believed.

"You're frightened." His voice was low and soothing. "I won't hurt you."

Aurelia exhaled with a low shudder, heat rising to her cheeks. She didn't want him to speak. It would be easier to pretend there wasn't a living, breathing creature next to her. "That's what they say." *Please. Just take my blood and let me leave.*

His thumb brushed over her skin. "You believe the rumors, then?"

She shivered. "I've heard enough to make up my own mind." Why had she admitted that? Why was she talking with him at all?

The vampire didn't respond. Aurelia's palms started to sweat, her wrist still tipped up at his mercy. When she thought she might burst, he finally lifted her hand, and his breath whispered against her skin.

Aurelia tensed, her skin prickling as she let out an audible puff of air. "Do you require our services often?"

The fingers on her wrist stilled. Aurelia swallowed. *Idiot.* She shouldn't have spoken. While she didn't know exactly how this was supposed to go, she was fairly certain conversation wasn't part of it. But her heart beat in her chest at the speed of a frightened rabbit, and the idea of him pressing his lips against—

The vampire let out a low chuckle. "I'm always amazed at how little you know of our kind."

Aurelia set her jaw. "How would I know more? I'm barely of age."

She held her breath, her lungs burning, as his thumb brushed over her wrist. "Right. I'd forgotten. This is your first time." It wasn't a question.

Aurelia stiffened. Forgotten? Did this day—the ceremony —mean nothing to them? Though, why would it? Whoever this was, it wasn't Alain, and she hadn't been chosen. "Yes," she whispered.

"Your hands are trembling."

A small sound bubbled up her throat. *She couldn't even do this part right.* "I'm sorry. I'm trying to keep them still."

"Don't apologize. I meant what I said. I won't hurt you."

She nearly bit her lip. "I've seen the wounds left on my mother and father's skin. That can't be pleasant."

When the vampire spoke again, his voice was closer, as if he'd passed through the fabric and hovered over her. "They haven't told you."

"Told me what?"

He pressed his thumb into her palm. "Do you believe the gods would curse you to a life of servitude and pain?"

Aurelia considered this. "We are guardians, protectors—"

"Yes. You protect the humans. But your blood was a gift, not only for us, but for you as well."

Aurelia sucked in a breath. "A life of servitude. I would not call that a gift."

He chuckled. "Perhaps you're right."

Questions exploded in her head. She'd read the book. Vampires were created by Le Sombre—they'd tried to change other humans and discovered their power was depleted when they did. How could he or her parents continue to insist any of this was a blessing?

"Was that all it took? Me agreeing with you?" He traced her fingers with his, and Aurelia blinked. She'd stopped shaking. "Tell me your name."

She hesitated, then obediently answered. "Aurelia."

"Aurelia. A name of love and light."

"My mother thought it was pretty," she snapped, her skin beginning to itch. Could they have given her any name that was more of a shameful reminder for both of them?

The vampire laughed. "You do not?"

"It's only a name. Do you admire yours?"

"Is that your way of asking for it?"

"No, I—"

"My name is Theo. So you'll know whom to blame if you have any complaints."

She opened her mouth to speak, but all thoughts evaporated like smoke as pressure and heat hit her wrist. She whimpered at the sharp sting that followed, and then her head tipped back involuntarily. A rush of pleasure surged through her, tugging from her center and filling every inch of her to bursting. She couldn't stop a sigh from hissing through her lips, and couldn't think fast enough to clamp her free hand over her mouth to hide it.

Aurelia was no longer aware of her body, not in a physical sense. She was floating. Expanding. Blending with the air around her, becoming energy and light and everything *good*. It was like standing at her beech tree at sunset, being bathed in warm water from the springs, letting honeycomb melt on her tongue.

And then, all at once, the gap that had yawned wide snapped closed. Aurelia slammed back into herself at dizzying speed. She jolted and probably would've fallen had an arm not been clamped around her waist. Had her back not been pressed up against a solid chest.

He was holding her. The vampire. *Theo.* Her arm was still invisible, hidden behind the shroud, and she could see nothing of him behind the black fabric, but she could feel . . . everything.

"I'm sorry." He panted, his voice coming from just over her head. "You started to slip, so—"

"I did?"

He swallowed, his breath still coming in short bursts. "You did."

She struggled to fill her lungs, still sinking into him, not trusting her own legs. A gift. Had that been what he meant? That feeling? That ecstasy? "They didn't tell me. I didn't know . . ."

She trailed off, not sure how to finish that thought. How could her parents or anyone else for that matter have prepared her for what she just experienced? How could they have explained? Even if they'd tried, she never would've believed them. That a feeling so euphoric could come from a wound—a bite from one of *them*.

But Renna hadn't made a sound. Renna hadn't slipped.

"Are you able to stand?" Theo's voice was more solid now, his body no longer slumping forward, curling around her.

Shame flushed her cheeks. "Yes." She pulled away from him, and he dropped his arm. But as she tried to pull her arm through the shroud, he held fast. Aurelia wet her lips and stammered, "I-is there anything else you require of me?" It was a very adult question. Mature. Wise.

Theo cleared his throat, now more distant. His grip loosened, and she pulled, her eyes searching for marks as her forearm and hand reappeared. There they were. Two perfect incisions directly over the pale blue lines of her veins.

"Thank you. For your service," he murmured.

Aurelia didn't see him go, but she felt it. The sudden lack. She closed her eyes, holding her arm to her chest. She should go. She needed to walk back through the curtain and out into the hall. To face the elder and walk back out into the light, down the steps—

She blanched at the thought. How could she look her parents in the eyes after that? Her body felt liquified, mixed up and unsettled. Like she'd been taken apart and put back together. Her heart thrummed, and blood rushed in her ears. Low in her belly, there was an ache—a yearning.

Her throat thickened with shame. She wanted to experience that again. Longed for it.

She wanted to cry out and beg for Theo to return, but as her lips parted, a thought hit her square in the chest. Someone could be returning. A vampire could be walking in at this very moment, and she would still be standing within the shroud.

Aurelia pushed out through the fabric, stumbling forward into the light. *It depends on whom.* No. She didn't want just anyone, she wanted him. She wanted to skip back in time and experience that all over again for a second time, a third. To live in that moment until she could wrap her mind around it.

She struggled against the lump in her throat, her eyes stinging with tears. Would she ever find it again, or was this why there was sadness in her mother's eyes each time she left for the temple? Was it like this for everyone? Did they experience their first and spend the rest of their lives chasing an experience they'd never have again?

Aurelia straightened, blinking back her tears and smoothing her tunic. She needed to leave before Eron came looking for her, before her parents started to worry. She schooled her expression into something she hoped looked stoic, then strode into the corridor.

Eron wasn't there, nor was there another elder to guide her. Which direction was she supposed to go? The others hadn't exited through the atrium, but perhaps since she was the last—? She couldn't stand still another second and rushed down the corridor.

As she entered the main room, she strode directly for the arch and passed through into the sunlight. Everything was as she'd left it. Guardians waiting on the steps, her parents now standing on the path below her. Their eyes widened as they saw her, and all heads turned her direction.

Wrong direction, then.

She ignored them, lifting her skirt and descending the steps until she stood in front of her mother and father.

"It is done?" her mother asked.

Aurelia nodded, noting the slight fall of her mother's face. Had her time in the temple not been long enough for her to hide her disappointment? Her mother reached for her wrist, flipping it over and inspecting the marks. She stared, unblinking.

Aurelia pulled her hand free, pressing it to her side, and the three of them turned and began their walk home. Aurelia trained her eyes on the path, refusing to look up and acknowledge any of the onlookers.

"Brennos and Lita will arrive at midday," her mother

started, detailing the rest of the afternoon's celebration. Aurelia tucked all that had happened in the temple in a box to open and dissect later. For now, she would grab this distraction by both horns.

For all her apprehension, this was the part of the day she had been looking forward to—when her service was over and they could enjoy bread, cheese, fruit, and roasted meat as a family. But now, the thought of it left a sour taste in her mouth.

She rubbed the inside of her wrist, pausing over each raised mark. No wonder her sisters were never the same. After that, how could she be?

"Aurelia, are you listening?" Her mother stopped, putting a hand on her shoulder.

She slowed and turned. "Yes, of course."

Her mother's eyes narrowed. "Then what would you prefer to do first?"

Aurelia pursed her lips, scrambling for the last vestiges of their conversation. Before she could answer, her gaze snagged on a flash of spring green ahead of them on the path. She exhaled with relief. "Mother, it's Fiona . . . may I go to her? I'll be quick, I promise."

Her mother exhaled, then pressed a finger to her temple as she nodded. Aurelia smiled, then scurried off before her mother could change her mind.

4

urelia and Fiona walked far enough that the risk of being overheard was slim. At this hour before the midday meal, any pestering siblings should have been occupied, but it never hurt to be cautious.

They sat down on the grass at the edge of the woods, and Aurelia curled her fingers against the cool earth. "How did you sneak away?"

"I told my parents I was sick." Fiona waggled an eyebrow, her eyes dancing. Paired with the golden sun glinting off her fair hair, she looked almost angelic. If angels were prone to lying.

Aurelia's hand flew to her breast as she feigned shock. "You misled your parents?"

Fiona laughed and rolled her eyes. "I haven't been dishonest. I've felt unsettled on and off for weeks now."

Aurelia grimaced. "So it hasn't gone away?"

Fiona shook her head, and Aurelia's chest tightened. They'd discussed this twice before, each time hoping her symptoms had been due to lack of sleep or something she ate. By the silence that stretched between them, they were both toying with the same thought.

"Do you think it's possible?" Aurelia reached out and held her friend's hand.

Fiona drew a breath and exhaled slowly. "Yes. I feel . . . different."

Aurelia's stomach sank. Fiona was so young. Guardians never knew if or when they would be chosen to bear a child. Their lives ended and they were reborn, given immaculately to women who were worthy.

Fiona had been chosen. It should be cause for celebration. But something twisted in Aurelia's gut. She'd hoped they would have partners before they conceived, but now here Fiona was, barely a seasonring older than her and going to be a mother.

"Have you told them yet?" Aurelia asked.

"I think they already know," Fiona blew out a breath. "My mother is watching me like I'm a vine of grapes about to ripen. It's been a few weeks of her hawkishness."

"Are you worried about waiting too long before cleansing?"

Fiona shook her head. "I want things to be as normal as possible for as long as they can be."

Aurelia pulled her friend against her side, wrapping an arm around her shoulders. She thought about walking into the temple, about how frightened she'd been standing in that circular room, staring at the shroud, then about stepping past the fabric—and what happened next.

"I think there are many things we don't understand."

Fiona raised an eyebrow and turned her head. "Does that comment have any reference to the ceremony?"

Aurelia couldn't help the flush that rose to her cheeks. She dropped her arms and stepped back. "I wasn't chosen."

Fiona shrugged. "Neither was I."

"Well, the Goddess seems to favor you now." Aurelia motioned to the hand still sitting on her friend's belly. She drew in a breath and held it a moment. "Why didn't you tell me?"

Fiona frowned. "What is there to tell, really?" She twisted her hands in her lap.

Aurelia nodded once. "I don't know . . . how we walk in one at a time. That would've been helpful."

Fiona's mouth quirked. "Right, I forgot about that."

Aurelia gave her a look. "How could you forget?" Aurelia wouldn't forget any of it. Not the candlelight, the slow shift of the shroud, the sound of his voice. "I do understand . . . it would be difficult to describe."

Fiona's brow twitched as she looked up. "Not that difficult. It didn't seem especially noteworthy. I was mostly relieved it didn't hurt."

Aurelia tried not to show the confusion on her face but failed. "Didn't hurt? That's an understatement."

A slow smile crept onto Fiona's face. "You liked it, then?"

Aurelia nudged her playfully. "I was surprised, that's all."

Fiona's smile widened. "You already want to go back."

Aurelia opened her mouth to refute the statement, but she couldn't. She did want that. Out of curiosity, confusion, or wonder—maybe all three—melding together into one intoxicating stew. "Is it the same the second time?"

Aurelia didn't realize she'd spoken the question out loud until Fiona answered. "Yes. At least it was for me. Every time it's similar. A short sting and then pleasantness."

Aurelia blew out a breath. "Pleasant? Is that how you'd describe it?" Her heart picked up speed.

Fiona pondered this. "Maybe 'peaceful' or 'calm' would be a better description."

Aurelia held her tongue. That was the opposite of what she'd felt. A storm had raged inside her as Theo had taken her blood. She'd been on fire, lit up from the inside out. There was nothing peaceful or calm about it.

Fiona put a hand on her knee and leaned in with a conspiratorial glint in her eye. "I think we should go."

Aurelia frowned. "To the temple?"

Fiona's face split in a wide smile as she whispered, "No! To the celebration."

Aurelia's eyes widened. "With the tribes?"

Fiona nodded. "It's your birthday. I'm going to be a mother in a few months' time. If we don't go now, when will we?"

Aurelia worried her lower lip. Although she'd considered running free as recently as that morning, the idea of actually leaving the village sparked fear in her heart. *Could she do it?* "Do we know where they're gathering?"

Fiona nodded. "I heard my father talking. With the lowering of the river, they'll be in the valley at least until the quarter moon."

So what harm could it do for them to join in one night of celebration? To be observers?

A wave surged through her like a tide pulled by an unseen moon, inexorable and wild. It climbed higher, filling her lungs, her veins, fusing to her bones. A moment of decision flared. Aurelia teetered on the point of it. "If we get caught—"

"We won't." Fiona shrugged as if she had the gift of foresight. "Meet you at your tree after sundown?"

Aurelia's heart picked up speed. It felt like pretend. Like their childhood fantasies. Maybe that's all this was. They'd meet at the tree and laugh about how foolish their idea was.

Would they actually make the trek? Once they were under the cover of night, she doubted it. There was an equal chance that they'd walk a ways and sit under the canopy of tree branches and stare at the stars like they had as little girls. "I'll be there."

———

Aurelia ducked inside the family longhouse, the cool evening air still clinging to her skin. The space was already alive with the sounds of laughter and the crackling fire in the central hearth. Smoke swirled upward, curling through the thatched roof's smoke hole. The earthy scent of the packed dirt floor mixed with the tang of spiced meat and the faint sweetness of baked apples made her sigh.

Aurelia hurriedly washed her feet, then pulled on her slippers and strode past the tapestries and hanging dried herbs. She took her place around the large oak table, polished from years of use and laden with bowls of stewed turnips, wild greens, flatbreads, and a platter of slow-roasted mutton.

"There she is!" her father bellowed, his deep voice booming like a drum. Gone was the somber mood of the morning. Now he was seated on a carved chair near the hearth, just beneath the heirloom sword he prized so much, his wide shoulders wrapped in a heavy woolen cloak. He beckoned her over with a grin, his calloused hand waving eagerly. "Almost wondered if you'd miss your own feast."

Her mother waved him off. "You knew she was with Fiona."

"Exactly why I was worried." He grinned, then stood and wrapped her in a hug.

Aurelia turned to find both Vala and Nora watching her, their gazes shrewd. *They knew.* They had to know. Both of them had been through their own ceremony in prior years, and Aurelia was suddenly desperate to ask them about it.

The way Fiona described her first offering and subsequent visits sounded nothing like what she'd experienced. Was it vastly different for everyone? Or had it only been different for her?

Nora stepped toward her, sweeping her golden hair over her shoulder. "You have trees in your hair." She plucked a leaf from Aurelia's braid, holding it up for everyone to see.

Aurelia flushed. That had likely been there since the morning. "I took a walk."

"Ah, and here I thought *they* sent her back looking like that." Vala leaned casually against the table, her dark hair braided with copper bands that gleamed in the firelight. "I was sure they'd keep her as a pet."

Aurelia blanched, and their mother tsked. "That's not funny." She handed Vala a clay carafe of water and shooed her back to the well to fill it.

Aurelia glanced at her wrist, the twin half-moon marks still raw and vivid against her skin.

"Sit." Her mother set a steaming bowl of stewed barley in front of her. She brushed a tendril of gray-streaked hair from her cheek. "Let us eat."

Aurelia sank onto a bench, her legs trembling beneath her.

Her cousin Elric, seated nearby, grinned as he tore into a chunk of bread. "Did you faint?"

Aunt Lita glared at her son. "Until you go through with your own ceremony, you are not entitled to comment."

"I heard Menau fainted," he murmured, reaching for a piece of flatbread.

"Enough, Elric," Uncle Brennos grumbled.

Aurelia worked to swallow. She needed water. A full plate. Anything to keep her mind from wandering back to the darkness behind the shroud. To the feel of Theo pressed up against her, his arm circling her waist.

Lita glanced between Aurelia and her mother as Vala returned with the water. "Was there . . . anything out of the ordinary?"

Aurelia frowned and waited for her mother or anyone else to answer. What kind of question was that? When nobody jumped in, she said, "I wouldn't know. I have nothing to compare it to."

Lita smiled. "Understandable. But your mother—"

"No. It was exactly as it should be." Her mother started scooping mutton onto plates and passing them around to anyone who would take it from her.

Again, the sting of her mother's disappointment hit her like a leather strap. The prophecy. *Born on the Day of Light.* Aurelia's cheeks burned. "I'm going to get some air." She pushed to her feet before anyone could stop her.

She stepped outside, the cool evening air a relief against her flushed skin. The longhouse was set on a gentle rise overlooking the forest, the trees dark silhouettes against the fading sky. The celebration carried on inside, laughter and clinking clay cups spilling out into the quiet night. She pressed her back against the timber wall, her fingers brushing the marks on her wrist.

She would go tonight, and she didn't only want to walk in the woods. Fiona was right. Their lives were changing, and if they didn't have a little fun now, when would they? The promise of a small rebellion settled her stomach.

How long would she have to bear this shame? When would her family and their village forget? She couldn't wait until she knew the answer to start living. Aurelia was of age. She could make her own decisions now, and she refused to be hampered by the expectations of an ancient, possibly false, prophecy.

The voices inside grew louder, and she pushed away from

the wall. She would go inside. She would put on a good face so neither of her parents would suspect she had plans after dark.

Aurelia slipped back into the house. She found her seat again, trying to avoid the questioning looks from Nore and Vala. She plastered a smile on her face. One she hoped would communicate *I'm only tired* and not hint at her true emotions. The feast carried on around her, but she barely touched her food, her appetite lost to the tangled mess of her thoughts.

As the evening wore on, Aurelia didn't have to feign exhaustion. When her father stood and invited her to follow him down the hall, she had to rub her eyes, forcing them to perk up even though she'd been excited about this moment for months.

Being of age meant she would now reside in a private alcove. Her father, uncle, neighbors, and friends had worked on the addition for weeks. Building the wooden frame out of timber, weaving together branches for the wattle, creating the mud daub walls, and finally, binding reeds for the thatched roof.

Aurelia followed her father in. A single lamp sat on a small table along the wall. She stood there a moment, taking it all in, then walked forward and ran her fingers over the intricately carved wooden bedposts.

She turned back to her father. "When did you have time to make this?"

He beamed at her. "I always carve my children's beds."

Aurelia laughed, her eyes beginning to burn. "I know, but I didn't ever see you working on it."

Her father stepped closer. "There are many things you do not see." He dropped a hand on her shoulder, then kissed her forehead. "I will leave you. Happy season of birth, my love."

She brushed a hand over his cheek and nodded her thanks, unable to form words. He slipped out through the woven curtain, and Aurelia was left alone. After so many years of sleeping in the same room as her brother, it felt strange, almost foreign. *But tonight it would be convenient.*

Aurelia pushed all thoughts of her parents and the prophecy out of her head as she readied for bed. She couldn't think about the feast or her new living quarters. Otherwise, the guilt of sneaking out with Fiona would eat her from the inside out, and she wouldn't be able to escape into the woods.

She didn't want to be secretive, but her parents would never allow it. Even when she was no longer living under their roof, unless she was called to work in trade or mentorship, it would always be frowned on to visit the tribes. Guardians worked with humans, protected them, but they did not fraternize.

It was too dangerous. They had covenants to keep. They couldn't afford to be distracted or drawn away from the village. It was one of many things her parents taught that didn't make sense. If they faltered, wouldn't the Goddess simply take their lives and allow them to be reborn? To try again?

Aurelia waited until the house stilled. Until the lamps were blown out and no more light filtered under the curtain to her room. Then she laced up her leather shoes and crept to the doorway. Her hand brushed the curtain, and even though the fabric was nothing like that in the room of the temple, her mind tumbled into the memory.

It already felt like a lifetime ago. Like a strange and disorienting dream. She had been there. She had given her blood.

My name is Theo. So you'll know whom to blame if you have any complaints.

Aurelia shivered. She should've asked her sisters. She needed more than one experience to compare hers to, but that wouldn't happen until tomorrow if she wanted to meet Fiona on time.

She steeled herself and slipped through the fabric. Holding her breath, she tiptoed through the main room then threw on her cloak and opened the heavy wooden door. She tugged it closed behind her, careful to gently lay the latch.

The night air landed crisp and cool on Aurelia's flushed skin as she stayed low, following the house until she was under the cover of the woods. She crept down the hill and made her way to her tree. Fiona was already there. She held out the candle-lit lantern between them.

Aurelia pressed her back against a solid trunk, her fingers trembling as they smoothed the rough-spun tunic over her hips. It was one of her sister's, handed down, and its loose fit made her feel less like herself. Less . . . obvious. "I had to wait until everyone was asleep." She drew a deep breath, working to calm the flutter of nerves in her stomach.

"I figured." Fiona rested a hand over her belly. The movement seemed subconscious. Protective. Aurelia hadn't been old enough to remember when her mother was pregnant. Her little brother was only two years younger than her.

Fiona set the lantern on the ground and rubbed dirt into her hands and cheeks, softening the natural sharpness of her features. Her dark curls, usually pinned back, tumbled freely.

Aurelia dirtied herself up, too, then reached out for the lantern. "Here. I can carry that."

They started off, and the forest came alive in the silence. The sounds of life flaring into existence when they were so often missed in the light and noise of day. A frog's croak, the snap of an insect's wings.

With each step, Aurelia waited for Fiona to suggest they stop and sit, but the suggestion never came. They walked, whispering to each other about any thought that popped into their heads, and eventually, Aurelia forgot her hesitance.

"Will you choose someone. Commit to a union?" Aurelia asked.

Fiona shrugged. "My parents will insist."

"But?"

She blew out a breath. "Who would I choose?" She walked on a moment, considering. "Honestly, I don't know why I'm with child and not you since you have someone already. Even if you did barely come of age."

Aurelia was glad for the cover of darkness to cover the blush in her cheeks. "I don't *have* him."

"You would if you wanted to."

Aurelia snorted. She didn't want to admit that she'd thought of it. Of Caelan and a potential union, wearing the torc around her neck as a symbol of their commitments. "Be careful." She pulled Fiona closer, avoiding a patch of feathered plants along the path. Hellebore. It looked close enough to wandering sage that she'd picked some once accidentally when gathering herbs for dinner. Thankfully her mother had known the difference or they would've all been heaving their guts. The itching hives between her fingers was enough to make her never forget the experience.

"All the more reason to make it official." Fiona turned her head, and even in the dim candlelight, Aurelia could make out her cheeky expression.

Caelan. Right. She changed the subject.

They talked of the weather, responsibilities at home, and dreams of the future. Anything to keep their minds and mouths from moving toward eligible men. Eventually, the faint glow of bonfires ahead painted the underside of the canopy in flickering oranges and reds, and her task became simple. Neither of them spoke. Aurelia pulled her cloak around her, beginning to tremble.

It was one thing to imagine breaking the rules, wandering

into a human camp. It was another thing entirely to step out of the shadow of the wood and show her face.

Smoke, rich and sharp, drifted through the air, carrying with it the mingled scents of roasting vegetables and meat. Guilt gnawed at her for the second time since sunrise. Her family had prepared a feast for her, and here she was, betraying their trust. "Fiona, I—" she started to whisper, but was cut off by the sound of a steady drumbeat. The resounding thump was deep and resonant, reverberating through her bones.

Fiona turned back, her eyes wide, as if she'd just found the first ripe pomegranate. She pulled the hood of her cloak lower and darted from the trees. Aurelia lunged for her, but wasn't fast enough. She cursed under her breath, then bolted after Fiona's mulch brown cloak before she lost her in the crowd.

She kept her head down, only looking up far enough to keep her friend in her sights. Laughter and singing threaded through the air, weaving a tapestry of joy and frivolity. Aurelia's heart raced, heightening every one of her five senses. She was walking among humans. Would they know the difference? If they caught sight of her face, would they be able to tell instantly that she wasn't one of them?

Aurelia lifted her eyes, trying to catch sight of someone—to inspect them in the firelight and decide for herself. She hesitated when she saw a woman, bare chested, her head thrown back, her eyes closed as she gyrated her hips in rhythm with the drums.

"Keep moving," Fiona whispered, grasping onto her arm and pulling her forward through the crowd.

At the edge of the camp, they paused, crouching low behind a thicket of ferns. Aurelia could finally watch unabashed as the scene before them unfurled like a dream. The clearing was ablaze with life, firelight licking at fabric, hair and skin, shadows twisted and stretched across the ground, distorting the figures of the revelers as they whirled and leapt around the bonfires in various states of undress.

Aurelia narrowed her eyes, trying to make sense of the vivid spirals and patterns of blue woad drawn on their skin. The designs crawled up arms and legs, encircling necks and stretching across bare shoulders like vines. Bells tied to their wrists and ankles glittered and chimed. Women twirled with their hair loose and unbound, and men watched with hunger in their eyes, stamping their leather-clad feet against the matted grass.

Fiona perked up, like a rabbit catching the sound of a fox. She pointed to a few different groups scattered through the clearing. They wore cloaks like the two of them and stood gathered around the fire. Fiona turned to her, raising an eyebrow.

Aurelia nodded, her throat tight. She squared her shoulders, her fingers brushing the novel scabs on her wrist. It was a habit she'd formed since that morning. She wasn't sure if it would fade even when the marks did. Together, they stepped out of the treeline and into the frenzy of the celebration.

The heat of the bonfires hit her, a wall of dry air that made her cheeks flush and her skin prickle. They kept to the edges at first, weaving between clusters of villagers who were too engrossed in their revelry to notice two strangers slipping through the crowd.

Then it was the smells infusing her senses. Spiced meat sizzling on spits, the sour tang of fermented drinks sloshing in clay cups, the earthy sweetness of herbs being burned in offering bowls. They were halfway to the closest fire when a hush fell over the clearing and the drumbeats faded away.

Aurelia gripped Fiona's arm, pausing as a procession of robed figures emerged from behind the largest of the tents.

They carried between them a struggling goat, its bleats of terror piercing the sudden silence.

This was what they'd come for, hadn't they? To see the human traditions. To be a part of their celebrations.

Aurelia wanted to look away, but couldn't. The goat's cries reached a fever pitch as the robed figures stretched it out across a flat stone altar. A glint of sharpened stone flashed in the firelight, and Aurelia's stomach churned.

She squeezed her eyes shut, remembering the sharp sting of the vampire's fangs piercing her skin. The delirious bliss of her blood being drawn out surged unbidden to the forefront of her mind. She swayed on her feet, dizzy, as the first drops of the goat's blood spattered across the altar stone.

Fiona's arm clamped around her waist, steadying her just as shouts rang out at the other end of the clearing. Aurelia's eyes snapped open. They sounded frenzied, pained.

Her heart jumped into her throat as she searched for the source of the cries, but more shouts rang out. Movement. Blurring shapes.

"What's happening?" Fiona murmured, and Aurelia shook her head. It didn't seem like it was a part of the sacrifice.

Tent poles toppled, landing in the fire and sending sparks and embers cascading across the trampled grass.

"Nosferatu!"

"Blood drinkers!"

Shrieks and cries rose around them, and the air grew thick. The sounds and smells slowed to a lazy drip, blurring at the edges. Blood drinkers. The words refused to coalesce in Aurelia's mind. What could they mean? Why would humans be running and screaming in fear? How could—?

"Run!" Fiona yanked on Aurelia's arm, nearly making her drop the lantern. "We have to run, now!"

Aurelia stumbled after her friend, still searching for some

sound or image that would make sense of the scattering figures and growing flames. They plunged into the forest, heedless of the branches that snagged at their hair and clothing. Behind them, the sounds of carnage grew fainter, replaced by the rasping of their own gasping breath.

Snatches of terrified shouts drifted to Aurelia's ears as they ran, the voices of the tribespeople raised in panic and despair.

Nosferatu.

Blood drinkers.

A numb horror settled over Aurelia, sinking into her skin. Was it possible? How did the humans know of vampires if for hundreds of years they had no reason to fear them? And why would they invoke their name during a celebration?

Aurelia spun, dragging Fiona to a halt. "We should go back."

"Did you not hear what they said?" Fiona hunched over, sucking in a lungful of air. "We cannot be seen."

Aurelia shook her head. "There are no vampires there! That isn't possible."

"Are you certain?" Fiona straightened, her hair wild around her face, one hand on her belly.

Doubt pricked her mind. *Was she certain?*

How could she be? The humans spoke the words, but did they understand their meaning? Were they making sense of the threats of their world just as they sought to explain the appearance of the sun?

But if they were right. If vampires had left the wall, if they hunted here . . .

No. Her parents would know. They maintained the covenants through their council, and they would never allow something like this to happen.

Aurelia glanced down at her friend's swollen belly. She couldn't put Fiona in harm's way, but she couldn't leave this place and wonder. Aurelia handed Fiona the lantern. "It doesn't make sense. Why would vampires hunt when they don't have to? When human blood is less desirable than ours?" The hairs pricked at the back of her neck, and she turned, searching the shadows behind the trees.

"Aurelia—"

"Stay hidden," she hissed. "Don't move until I return."

5

Aurelia crept forward through the scrubby underbrush that sprouted up between the wide trunks at the edge of the woods. The bonfires still burned, but the clearing was eerily silent now that the humans had scattered back to their tents. Somewhere across the grass, a sob broke out, but was quickly hushed.

There was no need to be silent. If this was an attack by a vampire, they could scent living things from across the river. But why would they attack humans? Guardian blood was their preference, and they were given it freely.

Aurelia felt emboldened with each step. Vampires wouldn't come here, and that meant there was something else threatening the humans. Something she needn't be afraid of. Guardian lifespans were double that of humans. While she looked like them, her blood held healing properties that protected her from ailments and injuries. Yes, she could die under extreme circumstances, but as long as blood ran in her veins, her body would restore itself.

Her leather shoes barely made a sound as she kept to the

shadows, scanning the ground lit by the flickering flames for anything she could use to make her case. Paw prints in mud or a tribal arrow would've been ideal. Something to prove that this was a case of human assumption and not a shattering of the covenants between guardians and vampires.

The thought brought her comfort. While she never enjoyed hearing about tribal conflict, that was common. Especially this time of year when the water was low. It would make far more sense than—

Aurelia froze. A human male lay on his back ahead of her, his skin glowing pale blue in the moonlight. She crept closer, noting the torn fabric of his shirt, the unnatural angle of his left arm.

She dropped to her knees and crawled across the soft mulch. She paused, squeezed her eyes closed, and drew a breath to calm her stuttering heart. Then she moved the final few paces forward to discover the wound that took this human's life.

At first she saw nothing. No blood on his clothes, no tear in his skin. And then her eyes snagged on two dark marks on the man's neck. The shape of tear drops. Black as night.

Aurelia blinked, hoping the marks would magically transform in front of her. She glanced down at her wrist, then back at the man on the ground. The marks were the same.

Dread flooded her from head to toe, her stomach twisting in knots. It didn't make any sense. *How could this happen?* Why would it happen? Why would a vampire leave the haven of Magos for inferior blood?

She reached out a hand, pressing her fingers against the man's cold skin. It gave way under her fingers, sallow and tacky with sweat. Anger built like storm clouds in her chest, making her nose sting as she scrambled back.

She should leave. Immediately. Find Fiona in the trees,

rush home, and pretend she'd never seen a thing here in the valley. Perhaps the light was playing tricks on her, or maybe there were other creatures whose bites looked similar?

Aurelia forced herself to her feet and planted her hand against a tree trunk, waiting for her head to stop spinning. When her vision finally settled, she turned and started back through the trees. There was some other explanation. There had to be.

The covenants between guardians and vampires were binding. Nevermind her parents or the council, Soléne, the Goddess herself, would never stand for this. If she could strike down a guardian, why not a vampire also?

Aurelia slowed, catching her breath as she trudged up the incline. *But those marks.* Her stomach sank. She'd seen them. She knew what they were, and no amount of internal argument could make the image of that man's blood-drained flesh disappear from her mind's eye.

She stopped turning back and looked down the slope. They would never believe her. If she told her parents what she'd seen here, they would demand proof—they'd need it before they could take it to the Monopteros. And if they did take it to the vampires? Why would the coven have any reason to believe her?

Hope sparked in her chest. That was it. She needed to provide proof. Then her parents would give her an explanation. If they couldn't, when they talked with the coven, they would have more than just her word. Maybe the coven didn't know of this betrayal. If she didn't say something, would this terror persist?

She drew a breath, clenching her fists. It would mean admitting she'd left the village. She would probably have to furrow planting rows for a week.

Aurelia started back down the slope. She found her way

back to the dead man and tried not to focus on the sight or feel of him as she wrapped her hands under his arms and yanked. She fell back, landing hard as the body flew with surprising ease toward her. It weighed less than she expected. Moved easier than a sack of garden roots.

She clenched her teeth and scrambled back to her feet, trying to keep her stomach from heaving. The body was drained of blood. Sucked dry. The man's limbs felt like bones coated with soft leather. It made her dry heave as she pushed to her feet, hunching to drag him back into the trees.

There had to be a better way to do this. Aurelia dropped the man's arms and straightened as soon as they were both in shadow. But not as dark as it had been. She looked up, glimpsing the lightening blue on the horizon, and cursed under her breath. How had they been gone all night? The sun would rise soon, and they still had the uphill walk through the woods back to Magos.

Her parents were going to send her to her second life. *But not if she had proof.* Aurelia steeled herself, assessing. The man was tall, but perhaps if she put him over her shoulders—

Her vision exploded in bright lights. She was flying backward, a hand clamped over her mouth. Aurelia's hands flew up, instinctually fighting to pull the fingers from her nose and mouth so she could draw breath.

"Silence." The voice was low, a man's breath whispering against her ear. She clawed at his hands, barely recognizing that there was something about his tone that seemed familiar. Her senses were so scattered, she could barely tell the ground from the sky.

Aurelia froze as a branch broke ahead of them, past the body she'd left sprawled out over the damp, fallen leaves. Was that one of them? A vampire still slinking through the woods? She stilled, her hands clamped around her captor's wrists.

Where was Fiona? Aurelia prayed to the Goddess that she'd stayed back, far from the clearing. She needed to break free, but the man's grip was iron.

His chest rose and fell against her back, his heart beating against her spine. Was he human? Did he think *she* was? She'd thought they were all in their tents. *Stupid.* She'd been dragging a body through the underbrush, probably making as much noise as a wild boar hunting for roots.

The hand slipped from her mouth, and she greedily sucked in fresh air. Her eyes darted, scanning the dark underbrush for any hint of movement. The air soothed her lungs, but before she could plan her escape, a soft blanket of calm wrapped over her.

Her hands relaxed, her shoulders dropped. This was better. She was safe, wasn't she? The threat must be gone. But something about these thoughts rankled. How was it possible that this human male saw more than she did? Why would she feel so comfortable in his arms?

She was safe. The thought pulsed through her again, rooting her down into the soft earth. There was no reason to fret.

And yet she was in the arms of a *human.*

This was wrong. She shouldn't feel at ease. Her mind was frazzled, mixed up. Aurelia pushed past the fog in her head and the man's arm. He released her without protest, and she stumbled to the side, refusing to show her face. She needed to run before he discovered that she wasn't a part of his tribe.

But she still needed proof.

Her heart beat against her ribs. She kept her body turned, her head lowered.

The man cleared his throat. "You should not be alone in the dark."

Another twinge of recognition. *What was it about his voice?* She couldn't turn to see if she recognized him. Most likely, he was someone she'd met when walking the merchant tents with her parents.

"It's no longer dark." She masked her voice, making it lower than it normally was. Perhaps he was doing the same.

The midnight-blue sky receded, the stars winking out. Mist rose from the ground as the first rays of sunlight flicked over the hills. There would be no vampires in the light, but their path home wound through the woods where there would still be shadow.

Aurelia stepped toward the body, then froze as the man's boots rustled the leaves behind her.

"Leave the body and go," he growled. "Do not speak of this."

Aurelia's throat thickened as she searched for some excuse—some reason why she would need to take it with her. The tribes were not strangers to their village, they knew Magos. But they did not understand its purpose or the magic held within it. Sowing crops and building permanent structures, both of which they did, was foreign to the tribes. Dangerous. More than once she'd heard elders call her father a fool. There would not be enough food, or they were scarring the earth.

The tribes knew the guardians to be kind, but there was already too much skepticism. If word got around that a woman from Magos had taken a body of one of their tribe members after an attack like this, who knew what rumors would spring up.

The man stalked forward into the light, and she turned further toward the trees until all she could see were the dead man's bare feet. "This was an attack. By the Nasferatu." She used the word she'd heard yelled in the clearing, her hands beginning to tremble.

She needed to get home. Her parents would wake soon, and

while they wouldn't come looking for her immediately, they would start to wonder if she wasn't out to help with first meal.

Just as she opened her mouth to continue her line of reasoning, to explain how she wanted to show their elders, warmth spread through her. It started at the crown of her head and moved through her chest, her limbs.

What had she been worried about? It was sunrise. She was safe. The humans were no longer under attack, and this man had saved her life when she'd been rash—impetuous.

"Thank you." Aurelia lifted her head, no longer worried about him seeing her face, but the man was turned. He was tall with broad shoulders, his dark hair mussed.

Odd. He wasn't dressed as the other villagers. He wore dark pants and a tunic, not colorful or cloaked for celebration.

"Go quickly," he murmured.

Aurelia blinked. Her brow furrowed as she searched for the argument that now seemed just beyond the stretch of her imagination.

"Now," he commanded.

That time, Aurelia listened. She couldn't remember why she'd been dragging the body in the first place. Of course her parents would believe her. They had to. She'd seen the marks on the man's neck, and she wasn't one to fabricate stories.

She dodged tree trunks, easily flying up the low hill that she and Fiona had been so careful to descend in the dark.

"Aurelia!" Fiona gasped, jumping out from behind a tree and throwing her arms around her, nearly knocking her over. "What took you so long? I was about to come after you, and . . . " Her friend trailed off, frowning as she inspected her face. "What is it?"

Aurelia shook her head, her brow furrowed. "I don't know." She turned to look back toward the clearing. She was too far to see the man hunched in the dirt, or the body. Blood rushed in her ears as she panted from her run.

Her thoughts seemed to emerge from muddy water, and at the same time, she could no longer remember what the man had said to her. How he'd convinced her to leave.

"Did you find anything?" Fiona searched her face.

The man on the ground. The marks on his neck. All of it flooded back into her head. "I saw a man. Dead."

"And?"

Aurelia's hands began to shake. "Fiona—"

Fiona sucked air through her teeth. "Did you see one? A vampire there? Amongst the humans?"

Aurelia started to shake her head and stopped. That feeling . . . that voice. *What had he said?* The skin along her wrist began to tingle. It was familiar. The sound—

"Aurelia!" Fiona gripped her shoulders and shook. "Are you hurt? What is—?"

"No. I only saw marks on the man's neck." She had not seen a vampire. She'd heard a stick break in the woods. Been held back by a man—a man who'd walked away from her freely into the sunlight.

"Marks like ours?" Fiona's eyes widened.

Aurelia nodded, pressure building behind her eyes. "But there could be another explanation."

Fiona's lips drew into a thin line. "We have to tell your parents."

"Or we could—"

Fiona snatched her hand and started running.

6

Aurelia burst through the front door of the longhouse, gasping for breath. She didn't try to be quiet or hide that she was coming home in the wee hours of the morning. That was a decision she and Fiona had made just as they passed the beech tree. There was too much at risk. They had to tell them the truth and hope for the best.

A clatter broke the silence as her father exploded into the entryway, holding a wooden post. His eyes widened. "Aurelia? What—?"

"There was an attack." Her voice was raw, and she tasted iron in the back of her throat.

"Humans?" Her father's hackles rose like a wolf.

She nodded, then realized her mistake by his expression. "No, humans didn't attack. There was an attack *on* the humans."

Her father tightened his grip on the post, his brows drawing into a deep furrow.

Her mother rushed in, still tying her robe. "What is happening?"

Her father held up a hand to silence her. "What are you doing fully dressed and tromping through the woods, Aurelia? What kind of attack?"

Images flashed in Aurelia's mind. The golden flicker of flames, humans sprinting to their tents. The shrieks of terror, the eerie silence that followed.

The body on the ground.

Pale. Hollowed out.

Two marks on the side of his throat.

She pursed her lips. "I'm not sure. I—"

"What did you see?"

Aurelia's mouth opened and closed like a fish. "There is probably some explanation I missed. I—"

"Aurelia," he growled.

Aurelia's eyes snapped to his, and by the cold glint in her father's eyes, she suspected he knew before she said the word. "Vampires."

———

Aurelia sat in a chair before the fire, her father's thick woolen blanket wrapped around her shoulders. Her parents, as Bearers of the Balance, would not forget that she had snuck out in the middle of the night. She and Fiona would have to take responsibility for their actions in front of the council, but for now, they escaped chastisement and punishment.

The trade-off wasn't worth it.

Aurelia ran her fingers over the rough fibers of the blanket, mesmerized by the flickering flames. As far as the guardians knew, there hadn't been a vampire attack in over a hundred years. The fact that there had ever been one was news to her.

Now her parents spoke in hushed voices as Aurelia stared

at the flickering flames. Was she wrong? Was she creating a stir out of nothing?

It had been dark. Had she seen what she thought?

The image again flickered into her consciousness. Yes. She'd seen it.

Her mind spun with sinister possibilities. Was this the first? Had this been happening all along? Though her parents spoke with tribe leaders when possible, the tribes were always coming and going. Had they been moving on faster than usual?

"Aurelia, come." Her father appeared next to the hearth, his coat in hand.

Her head snapped up, and she pulled the edges of the blanket closer around her. Clouds had rolled in just before she reached the house, and the dampness in the air smelled of rain even though she hadn't heard drops yet land on the thatched roof.

The weather didn't seem to be a deterrent. There was no use arguing when his jaw was set like that.

"Grab your cloak," he instructed, then stalked toward the door.

Aurelia still had her boots on. She draped the blanket over a chair, then scooped up her cloak from the floor and fastened it around her. Her mind fluttered with questions, but she bit her tongue. There was only one place her father would insist on going after her report.

But her sisters were already awake. Why would he ask her to accompany him instead of going on his own? She'd already told him everything that happened.

Aurelia stepped outside to see her mother already standing on the road. "What about the morning meal?" Aurelia asked.

Her mother's lips pinched. "Your sisters will handle it."

Aurelia's pulse raced as they trudged through the gloomy streets, passing a handful of guardians moving about in the slow drizzle. She'd never been to the Monopteros. Would a vampire be waiting there? Did they appear at any instant? *Were they always watching?*

She shivered and pulled her cloak closer, the mist chilling the tip of her nose. They passed the square and the steps to the temple, where she had been the previous morning. When they passed through the cluster of houses at the other end of the village, Aurelia began to tense. This was the wrong direction. The Monopteros was east and this . . .

"What are we doing?" she whispered, unable to stop the words from spilling past her lips.

Her mother's eyes flicked to hers. "You are of age," her mother said.

"And you are the witness," her father added.

Aurelia's eyes widened. "We are not—that is not allowed," she stammered. "And we don't know whether the attack came from this coven."

"Alain is the only one who speaks with the other covens. I am not seeking to condemn. I am seeking answers." Her father kept his eyes trained on the path ahead. "This cannot wait. If what you say is true—"

"Of course what I said is true, but we mustn't go beyond the walls!" Aurelia hissed. How could her parents even consider this? Her knuckles burned, her clammy hands twisted in the fabric of her cloak. Was there another explanation? Aurelia scrambled for any possible option.

Her father's shoes skidded on the stone as he pulled her to a halt. "We must defend our covenants." His jaw tensed, the light from the candle glinting off his grey eyes.

Something inside Aurelia's chest constricted. That look. The widening of his pupils, the slight part of his lips. She hadn't seen that expression on her father's face since last light season when her brother was swept away by the river. They'd found him at the inlet, coughing and spluttering.

Seeing her father just as frightened now sent a chill down her spine. He dropped her arm and continued down the street. Aurelia forgot her aching legs and trembling fingers. She forgot about her brother sleeping warm in his bed, about her sisters preparing the morning meal, about Fiona and the life growing inside her.

She walked. One foot in front of the other.

Finally, when her father slowed, she lifted her head. Her heart jumped into her throat as she took in the broad, blackened gates. The wood looked as if it had been charred, still coated in ash.

"Why would they answer?" she whispered.

Her father lifted his hand and slammed his fist against the door. "They don't sleep as we do."

"And you've done this before?" Aurelia clung so tightly to the edges of her cloak that her fingertips began to go numb.

"We appear at our scheduled audiences in the Monopteros," he said. "But there have been occasions where we have appeared at the walls."

When? How had she never paid attention to where her parents went or who they were meeting with? Aurelia opened her mouth, then nearly swallowed her tongue as the blackened wooden door scraped open.

It loomed above her, the iron studs glistening with dew in the dim light from her father's lantern. The wood was rough, the grain raised and splintered with age, but it was nothing compared to the ancient breath that washed over them. The scent of honeysuckle enveloped her, and the hairs on her arms prickled. It was both lovely and laced with a sense of wrongness that curled through her senses like smoke.

A figure stepped from around the pillar. The woman's skin

was porcelain, her hair so light it seemed to glow as it cascaded in waves over her shoulders. But it was her lips that Aurelia couldn't drag her eyes away from. Blood red when the candle-light hit them and nearly black in the shadow.

The only vampire she'd ever set eyes on was Alain at the ceremony each year. She'd never imagined the others could be even more beautiful.

"Welcome." The vampire's voice was smooth, like the finest silk brushing against her skin. Aurelia forced her lungs to fill, her thoughts and emotions churning in a toxic stew. She didn't want to be here. She never should've left her home in the middle of the night, and yet, if she hadn't?

Her father stepped forward, his voice strong and commanding. "We have an emergent concern and must speak with Alain."

Alain? Aurelia's eyes widened. Could they do this? Walk in and demand an audience with their leader?

She thought of his speech on the dais. He always seemed grateful and willing to help. Perhaps it was that simple.

They are not the enemy.

The words pulsed through her like a prayer. How often had her mother repeated that sentiment? She blinked as a thought burrowed through her fear and nestled in.

Don't jump to conclusions. What if the vampires didn't know that one of their own was breaking the covenants? Perhaps the humans were suffering and guardians and vampires needed to come together to find a solution. Perhaps they would be amenable to a discussion and intent on carrying out justice.

The female vampire's gaze washed over them, and Aurelia's breath whooshed out. "Of course." Her smile widened, her teeth flashing white against her crimson lips. She looked almost human. A perfect version of flesh and blood. It didn't seem possible. Vampires had immortal strength and speed, and yet their bodies looked as if the same laws of mortality should bind them.

Aurelia exhaled, her shoulders slowly lowering. While she had no desire to take on her parents' responsibilities, she did care about her family. About all guardians. Shouldn't the vampires be concerned, as well?

The ghost of a whisper heated the skin of her wrist. The temple. The shroud. Theo's touch. Soft. Warm.

She remembered his name.

The female vampire turned, gliding over the cobblestone path. "Follow me."

7

Aurelia trailed her parents through the door, drinking in every detail of the trees and courtyard beyond. All of it felt foreign. She'd only come this far outside the village once as a child, but the experience was fused to her bones. The slight cooling of the air. The stilling of the breeze. Looking up at the ivy-covered wall, too scared to reach out and run her fingers over the pockmarks in the stone.

It had been a stupid joke. A dare from which she hadn't backed down.

Guardians weren't taught to hate vampires, but the secrecy was enough to strike fear and confusion into all of their hearts as children. If they weren't dangerous, why were they separated? Why didn't they see the vampires their parents served? And most importantly, why didn't the vampires serve them in return?

That was what had never made sense to Aurelia. If this was a mutual relationship, what were they gaining from staying rooted to their village and obediently appearing at the temple each week?

Again her wrist tingled. Was that her reward? The gift of pleasure? Relief? The knowledge that their sacrifices protected the human tribes?

It was eerily quiet, the sound of their footsteps disappearing too quickly, like it was smothered with a blanket. The hairs on the back of her neck prickled as if eyes were on her, but when she turned her head, she saw nothing.

The pale-haired vampire glanced over her shoulder, her glittering eyes landing on Aurelia. "Don't be afraid," she purred.

Aurelia bristled. They passed the corner of the stone house in front of them, and the churning in her gut was overshadowed by morbid curiosity. There were more houses, all made of stone with thatched roofs and . . . openings in the outer walls. They were covered by sturdy wooden shutters, but still. How were they keeping their homes warm if there was a gap that large in the stone?

Perhaps they didn't have to keep their homes warm. The thought sent a shiver through her. *I'm always amazed at how little you know of our kind.* Theo's words rolled through her. Did anyone in the village ask questions? Had she avoided learning more for a reason?

Now she wished she'd paid more attention. Without realizing it, she'd created an image of this place beyond the walls. Dead and cracked. Sapped of all color and life.

The reality was nothing like she'd expected. It was beautiful. There were trees and flowers, vines and shrubs, their colors made even more vibrant by the gray morning light. The path was clear and edged with stone, all of their surroundings well cared for and organized. It was the most lovely place she'd ever been, and had she found this anywhere else, she would have stopped and stood gaping.

But the movement through the courtyard hammered home

exactly where she was. Vampires moved through the streets under the cover of clouds. Some had dark hair and eyes, while others had light features, like their guide. All of them were tall, lean, and stunningly beautiful.

Their eyes flicked up as they passed, and Aurelia clutched her cloak, feeling suddenly like she'd just stepped out of the river without her tunic. It hadn't occurred to her that just behind these walls lay an entire bustling community. There were so many of them. Aurelia tried not to stare but failed.

They reached the middle of the square, and Aurelia's breath caught in her throat. A central building with arches and spires rose above them, set on a wall of steps. Ivy clung to the walls, its tendrils weaving in and out of crevices, softening the harsh lines of the stone. Dozens of vampires were gathered there, all standing at attention. She scanned the group, obscuring herself behind her father's broad shoulders as their guide stopped, lifting her gaze.

Alain stood at the top of the steps. He wore all black, his skin standing out like pale petals against the dark fabric. He tilted his head, his sandy hair falling out of place as their guide ascended to stand beside him and whispered something in his ear.

A smooth smile spread across his lips. "What is so urgent that you had to travel to us?" Alain flicked his cloak away from his body so the hem settled against the back of his leg. Her eyes narrowed. That fabric. The darker dye. It wasn't anything like what he'd worn at the temple. Had he gotten it from the tribes? It looked oddly similar to the clothing of the man she'd seen in the woods.

Aurelia scanned the small group in front of them, noting that every article of clothing seemed to fit each person perfectly, as if it had been tailored specifically to their proportions.

"Yes," Aurelia's father stepped forward, moving his hand to pull her mother behind him protectively.

Did they trust him? Beads of sweat stood out on her father's forehead. Aurelia moved closer to her mother.

"We've received word of a vampire attack amongst humans at the Day of Light celebration," her father continued.

The corners of Alain's mouth lifted as he took a step closer. He descended to the first stair, his dark eyes still fixed on them, unblinking. "Did you see this attack?"

Her father's jaw clenched. "Not personally. As I said, we received word—"

Alain held up a hand. "Humans make up any number of fanciful tales to suit their purposes. It serves them to create stories of villains and creatures to keep their tribes committed and strong."

"This was not a story told around the fire," her father retorted, and Aurelia stepped forward, speaking before she could think better of it.

"I was there. The humans ran in fear. I saw—"

"Your council allows you to fraternize with humans?" Alain raised an eyebrow.

Aurelia's father scooped her back behind him like a hen covering her chick. "It does not matter what we allow or disallow. Are you aware of this breach of our covenants?"

Alain's smile withered and closed like a flower at sunset. He descended another step, and then another, but did not drop to stand fully in front of them. "I'm pleased you wish to speak of them. Our covenants are binding."

Her father's throat bobbed. "You say this as if we are barely of age."

Alain's eyes shifted to Aurelia. "One of you is." He paused a moment before continuing. "I was there when our covenants were forged. Were you?"

Again, her father swallowed hard. "You know I wasn't."

Alain finally broke eye contact with Aurelia, and she blew out a shaky breath. "All of you were reborn into this circle of trust, of protection. Yet you come to accuse?"

"We come for answers." Aurelia's mother spoke up. "If there is a member of your coven who is breaching our agreements, we can work together to—"

"A member of my coven?" Alain's voice was low.

"Or others," her father amended quickly. "You know of these things, we do not."

Alain's lips twitched. He didn't speak for a long moment, then let out a sigh. "I hoped you'd come to this on your own, but it seems I'll have to lead you to it."

Aurelia's heart quickened. He was treating them like the enemy, like they had done something wrong in seeking his help.

Alain's expression hardened. "I find it interesting that you stand here and speak of covenants when you have broken yours."

Aurelia's father tensed, his arm growing rigid against hers. "We have done nothing of the sort."

Alain's attention shifted to Aurelia. He stood eerily still. "Have you not?"

Every cell of Aurelia's body seemed to stretch, pulled tight enough to snap. What was he talking about? Her parents were Bearers of the Balance. They led the guardian council. They were diligent. Obedient. They would never knowingly break a covenant with the vampires or the gods.

"You will follow me." Alain turned when he descended the final step and walked toward the south side of the stone structure ahead of them. The female with the pale hair followed and the other vampires dispersed from the square. Alain was powerful. Aurelia could clearly see that. Her parents held power in their village, and yet the guardians did not move around them like frightened fish. If anything, guardians swarmed them whenever they left the longhouse.

Alain and the female kept a few paces ahead of them no matter how they tried to keep up. Finally, they passed under a stone archway and into a small building sitting adjacent to the main structure.

Aurelia's heart picked up speed as they passed through a door and into a darkened room, lit only by a candle. It smelled of beeswax, smoke, and . . . something she couldn't place. Something sour. A tang of metal or—

Aurelia's eyes adjusted, and she sucked in a breath. A male vampire, shirtless, stood with his head lolling over his chest, his arms stretched high, wrists bound with thick rope slung from a hook in the ceiling. Strange markings swirled over his skin—his chest, his shoulders.

Alain and the female didn't give him a second look as they entered. She took her place beside Alain as he sat down at a small writing desk. "Now that we are in a more private setting, let us speak of covenants." He glanced up, his eyes locking on Aurelia. "Your daughter is of age."

Her breath caught in her throat and her mother lifted her chin. "Yes. She came of age, and we presented her at the temple."

"Oh, of that I'm quite aware." Alain motioned for Aurelia to move free of her father. Her heart hammered against her ribs like a baby bird trying to break free of its shell.

"How long did you think you could keep it a secret?" Alain's eyes grew cold as he appraised the three of them. "Eighteen seasonrings and not a word."

Her father's breathing quickened next to her. Aurelia's

blood ran cold. *What was Alain talking about?* Eighteen season-rings . . . since what? The only impactful thing she could think of was the Day of Light. Did the vampires foolishly believe in the prophecies as the guardians did? But what had that to do with their covenants or with her?

Aurelia couldn't keep her eyes from darting back to the man hanging from the ceiling. He was moving now, his feet shifting on the stone.

Then she saw it. Blood. Dripping down his side, soaking into the waist of his trousers. Bile rose in her throat.

"There has been nothing to report," her father snapped. "We watched, and there was no sign of—"

Alain laughed out loud. "This celebration you speak of, the one your daughter attended, what was it for?"

"You know very well what it was for." Her father's voice was low and hard.

Alain didn't seem to notice his tone. He smiled. "The Day of Light. So monumental. The tribes all over Gaul celebrate, make sacrifices, and pray to the gods each year in the hopes of finding favor, and yet you do not consider this enough of a sign?"

Aurelia looked to her parents, flummoxed. Of course, it had been a sign to them. A sign of failure, of their lack of worthiness.

Alain rounded the table and approached with such speed that Aurelia stumbled back. "Not one birth." Alain's face was an inch from her father's as he drew out each word. "I asked for the records, and not one birth was reported on that day."

Her father's brow furrowed, his face reddening. "Because there were none to report—"

Alain held up a hand, turning toward Aurelia and then to her mother. "He seems convinced." Aurelia's mother stiffened, and Alain's smile only widened. "How did you manage it?"

Aurelia scanned her mother's face, noting the muscle tightening in her jaw. The pinch in her mouth.

"For eighteen seasonrings, you kept her." Alain lunged closer, his speed unnerving. "For eighteen seasonrings, you spat on our covenant, and now you dare to show up before dawn accusing me. Accusing our coven?"

Aurelia gripped onto her father's hand. He was shaking. How dare this vampire make such accusations? She wanted to yell in Alain's face. To push him back, to force him to apologize. But power rolled off him in waves.

They were not safe here. She would never forgive herself if she did something to anger him further, and her parents paid for it. So instead, Aurelia worked to keep her anger from boiling to the surface.

"She was born after the sunset," her father snapped. "She is not the one spoken of in prophecy."

The words hit Aurelia like a slap.

Alain stepped back, a cruel smile spreading over his face. "Not the one spoken of." He held perfectly still, watching them. "In. Prophecy." He clasped his hands behind his back and paced, as if waiting for the barbs to sink deeper into their flesh.

What was he trying to insinuate? Did he not realize that the guardians had waited for the prophecy to be fulfilled? That they would be the first to declare a miracle if it had happened?

Alain's arm shot out like lightning, his hand gripping the dark hair of the vampire bound in rope. He forced the male's head up, and Aurelia's world tipped on its head.

The vampire stared directly at her, his eyes a deep, endless black. Even battered and bruised, his features were flawless. Symmetrical. Sharp and angular.

It seemed as if the room between them was folded up and pressed together at the ends until they stood directly in front of each other. His breath seemed to whisper over her cheek, the beat of his heart sounding in her chest.

Was this how their glamours worked? Was it through their eyes that they drew you in like a moth to a flame? Holding you pinned?

Nasferatu.

Aurelia tried to tear her eyes away, but couldn't until Alain snapped his fingers, breaking the spell. The female beside him snatched a swathe of dark fabric from the back of the desk chair. She threw it over her shoulder and strode forward, slipping the rope used to bind the vampire's hands from the hook on the ceiling. The male dropped to his knees, bracing himself against the stone floor with trembling hands.

Aurelia thought she was going to be sick. He had long gashes across the flesh of his back, dark crimson blood coating his skin, snaking through the marks over his waist and side. Who could do such a thing? And why?

Alain prowled forward, placing two fingers under the male's chin and lifting his face to the soft glow of candlelight. "Put on your shirt."

The male jerked his chin away, then pushed himself up from the ground. He was unsteady as he took his tunic from the female and pulled it over his head, grimacing. Aurelia held her breath. She'd seen male bodies before when swimming in the river or helping raise a longhouse. But this male . . . he was beautiful. She couldn't pull her eyes from his lean, muscular body. From the wounds inflicted there.

It was an illusion, she reminded herself. Part of Le Sombre's curse. It was why guardians met vampires only at the temple, behind a shroud. Beauty was not reality. It was a dangerous lure.

A distraction. This was why they had their rules and kept their covenants.

Alain was wrong. Whatever he was accusing her mother of, he was mistaken. She was devoted, committed. She would never willingly break a covenant with the Goddess.

Alain glanced up, looking pleased as the male straightened next to him, his lip cut, his eye nearly swollen shut. Alain held Aurelia's eyes for a moment longer, then turned to the vampire, leaning in to whisper, "I hope I've made myself clear, Theo."

Aurelia's heart jolted in her chest. *Theo?* She blinked. How common was that name? Or had she heard wrong?

She stared at him, drinking in every detail and comparing it with her memory. He kept his head bowed as he buttoned his shirt. He didn't glance up, didn't give any indication that he knew or cared who she was.

This was the vampire from behind the shroud? Who'd gripped her when she'd faltered?

The female vampire crossed the room, moving between Aurelia and her father and opening the door. "Come."

They followed, Aurelia's heart hammering against the backside of her ribs. This felt wrong. Something was wrong.

They stepped out onto the stone, and Aurelia blinked. The clouds had shifted, and the sun peeked out, burning through the mist. The female kept to the shadow of the building, as did Alain and Theo.

Why was he here? It couldn't be a coincidence.

"Go ahead. Show them." Alain crossed his arms over his chest.

Theo shot him a look of disdain, but didn't hesitate. He strode away from the building. The female vampire sucked in a breath as he crossed over into the sunlight and—

Nothing.

Nothing happened.

Theo stood there a moment, lifted his hands, then turned to face them. His eyes seemed to glisten.

"Would you deem that worthy to proclaim?" Alain's voice lifted from behind them.

"Impossible." Her father clutched a hand to his chest.

Alain laughed, the sound caustic and snide. "Yes. Impossible." He strode forward, the vampires again shifting around him like a school of fish. "And yet you can see it with your own eyes."

He paused, his jaw working as he fingered the edge of his cloak. "Does your daughter understand why this is cause for such commotion?" Her mother whimpered, and Alain's eyes glinted like struck flints. "No. Probably not. Considering you have kept everything of importance from your family."

"I didn't keep—" her mother started, but Alain held up a hand.

He turned to Aurelia. "You see, my dear, vampires cannot come out in the light. The sun burns our flesh. For over a thousand years, we have been relegated to darkness, to shadow. And yet, there Theo stands without consequence."

At the sound of that name, it felt as if a knife slid between Aurelia's ribs, piercing her so deeply, she couldn't breathe. *A thumb grazing her wrist. Breath on her skin. Liquid fire pulsing through her veins—*

She blanched, and Alain practically salivated. "You understand, don't you? It was your blood—"

"Do not speak to her!" Aurelia's mother stepped forward, her face twisted in anger.

But Alain didn't flinch. He didn't look away. "Would you like to tell them, or shall I?" When Theo didn't respond, Alain rounded the three of them. "Not impossible, it seems. Theo fed at the temple yesterday. He drank the blood of one of your guardians. Can you guess who it was who offered herself?"

Blood drained from Aurelia's face, and the edges of her vision clouded. *Not a coincidence.*

A whine sounded deep in her mother's throat as she took another step. "You have no proof—"

"It was her." The vampire wiped his mouth with the back of his hand.

"How could you know that?" Aurelia's father spat.

Theo's lips twitched. "Because I watched her leave."

8

No. Aurelia opened her mouth to protest, but Alain's voice snapped like a whip across the stone. He pointed at another vampire approaching. "You. Take his place."

Aurelia struggled to breathe. Her lungs felt punctured. Shredded to ribbons.

Theo stepped back into the shadows, his movements calm and measured. Another vampire, clad in a thick-woven tunic and slacks, hesitated at the edge of shadow and light. Finally, he extended his arm into the sunlight.

The reaction was immediate. His skin sizzled and cracked, dark marks spreading like inky fingers across his flesh. With a hiss, he retracted his arm, the acrid scent of burning flesh filling the air. Aurelia's stomach churned. *This* was what she'd expected, what she'd been taught since she was a child.

Yet Theo stood unharmed, his face and hands fully exposed to the sun.

"You may retreat," Alain said smoothly. The sunburned

vampire bowed his head and returned to the shadows, his breath coming in short gasps.

Aurelia's chest constricted, and her legs wavered beneath her. She wanted to scream, to run, but her body betrayed her. She stood catatonic, rooted to the stone beneath her feet. Was it possible that her blood had done this? That Theo, just by drinking, had been released from a piece of his curse?

Anxiety crept up her spine, a dark shadow tightening like a snake coiled around her neck. She felt like the goat being dragged by its legs through the clearing. How was this possible? How could her blood have this power?

Aurelia clenched her fists at her sides, nails digging into her palms. "Father—"

"Silence." Alain stilled, his eyes hard as he nodded to Aurelia's mother. "You're a Bearer of the Balance. And yet you lie to your own family?"

Aurelia looked from Alain to her mother, waiting for her to say something, but she didn't open her mouth. Her lip trembled, her eyes filling with tears.

"Is it true?" Her father's voice was a whisper.

Aurelia's mother reached for her, but she pulled away, tears stinging her eyes as she pressed back against the wall. What had her mother lied about?

Her father's face crumpled. "Lara, you didn't—"

"I would not condemn her!" her mother choked out. She turned to face both of them, tears now spilling freely over her cheeks.

Aurelia stood in stunned silence. Condemn her? What was she talking about?

Her father dropped his face into his hands. "Who else knew?" he murmured. "Who else—"

"I'm sorry. I had to—"

"Who else knew?" Her father dropped his hands, shaking with anger.

Lara trembled, her eyes glossy and pleading. "Tayara. She's the only one."

Her father cursed under his breath, and the air whooshed from Aurelia's lungs. Tayara. The midwife. She'd helped with nearly all the births in the village, including her own. *Who else knew?*

Aurelia's mind reeled. Her birth. Her mother had lied.

Bile rose in her throat. "You told me we were deemed unworthy." Aurelia's mother clapped a hand to her mouth, her face twisting in anguish. Or possibly regret? But Aurelia couldn't stop the river of words flooding her mouth. "You told me the prophecy was unfulfilled. You let everyone believe—"

"I'm sorry!" Her mother gasped.

Aurelia's chest was so tight, her lungs fought for space in her chest. *Her mother had lied.* To her, to her father, to their entire village. Aurelia's whole life, every reading of the Dugianos, every lesson with her tutors. All of it, a lie.

"Why?" The word slipped out of her on a breath. If vampires and guardians were meant to fulfill each other, why would they keep this a secret? Wouldn't both vampires and guardians be looking forward to the day their curse would be broken, when the light and dark would be bound eternally? Wouldn't her mother have been honored? Been shouting it from the rooftops?

Her mother let out a broken sob. "Because—"

"To seal the dark, the light must submit!" Alain's eyes burned. "You speak of prophecy, of covenants—"

"That is *your* prophecy, not ours!" Her mother's voice shook with contempt.

Alain ignored her, circling the three of them like a wolf. He motioned to Aurelia. "Step forward."

"No!" Aurelia's mother threw herself between them.

Alain's smile was cold. "You have now seen proof, and yet you wish to pretend she is not the one sent to bind?"

Proof. Aurelia began to hyperventilate. All these years—all their talk about waiting on the Goddess, on the prophecy.

Her mother's voice trembled. "She is barely of age. We must have more time—"

"You had eighteen seasonrings, and you have broken my trust," Alain snarled. "I will lay my claim, and if you dare oppose—"

"She is not yours to claim!" her father roared, but with one flick of Alain's hand, he was thrown to the ground, his face pressed into the dirt.

Aurelia's mother gasped, dropping to the ground beside him. "Stop this! We do not yet know—"

"I know everything I need to know." Alain crouched to look her in the eye. "As do you. Or you wouldn't have kept this secret from me. From your family."

Alain motioned for the female vampire still standing near the door, but before she could yank her mother from the ground, Aurelia cried out, "Stop! Please!"

Alain stood, his eyes dark and cold. "I have every reason to deal with your parents harshly."

Aurelia's breath came in quick gasps. She didn't understand the covenants they spoke of. She didn't know the vampires were aware of the prophecy, but if her mother had hidden the true nature of her birth, there could only be one explanation.

She was afraid. Despite all her talk about looking forward to the day it was fulfilled, she understood something that she was not willing to inflict on her own flesh and blood. *I would not condemn her.*

Aurelia did not understand. But she knew her mother. "I

have committed to keep the covenants of the guardians. What do you desire of me?"

"No! Aurelia you mustn't—" Her mother's voice cut off as the female vampire tore her from her knees, twisting her arms behind her back and making her cry out.

"Stop!" Aurelia begged. "What do you desire of me?"

Alain considered her. "You've seen what I do to those who withhold information. Who break their covenants." He flicked his eyes at Theo, who now stood brooding in the shadows. Aurelia's throat tightened. What had he done? He'd stood in the courtyard and named her. He must've told Alain everything for them to be in this situation in the first place.

Alain lowered his voice. "I would be willing to show mercy."

"If what?" Aurelia gasped. She could not allow him to touch her parents, to do whatever he'd done to Theo. *Theo.* His voice rang in her head. *I watched her leave.*

Alain wet his lips. "You will remain here—"

"She will do no such thing!" Aurelia's father struggled, but the vampire's knee only dug harder into his back.

Tears welled in Aurelia's eyes as she fell to her knees next to her father, the ground slamming into her bones. "Someone in your coven broke their covenants! I saw the attack! You are not innocent."

"You saw it?" Alain's eyes narrowed.

"W-well, no, I saw the marks—"

"Where is your proof?"

Aurelia gritted her teeth. "I tried to bring it. I was stopped by . . . a man."

"A human male?" Alain smirked.

Aurelia's cheeks burned. She opened her mouth to argue, then clamped it shut. What could she say? That she had been disoriented? Confused? That would not help her case. "Please. Let them go."

The vampire holding her father down only watched her, his dark hair pulled into a braid, his hazel eyes unflinching.

Aurelia bowed forward, pressing her forehead to her father's cheek. What could she say? That she was sorry she left the house? Alain knew about her before they'd arrived. Had they not come here seeking answers, how long would it have taken before he came for her?

She fell forward, barely catching herself with her palms as her father was ripped up from the ground.

"This was not your fault, Aurelia," her mother hissed. "I only wanted to protect you. I didn't—"

"You will stay." Strong hands gripped her waist, pulling her upright. Alain lifted her from the ground like she was a fallen leaf. "And in exchange, I will allow them to leave."

"Do not try to ingratiate her!" her mother spat, pulling against the vampire who held her. "You abuse your power!"

Alain laughed. "Do not allow your envy to speak for you."

Aurelia pulled against his iron grip and cried out, reaching for her mother and father as the vampires dragged them further down the path, her cries turned to wracking sobs. "I love you!" Her throat was scrubbed raw, her words barely lifting into the air before falling flat on the stones and packed dirt.

"Aurelia!" It was her mother's voice she heard last. Her mother's strangled cry before all went silent.

"You will be kept safe." Alain's voice whispered against the shell of her ear, and she jerked her head away from the sound, from his breath. "Your blood is more valuable than gold, and you will be treated as such a prize."

Aurelia's stomach twisted. She would be *kept*. Her tears turned bitter, her grief igniting into anger. "Let go of me," she growled. "I've read the prophecy. Even if I am who you claim, you have no right—"

Aurelia sucked in a breath as her feet left the ground. The lightening sky whirled through her vision, and then she was planted again, this time with new arms and hands binding her. *That scent.* Was it only from the temple that she knew it? Or had there been somewhere else?

She slumped momentarily before forcing her spine to straighten.

"I believe our new guest is exhausted." Alain stood in front of her now, his eyes fixed on the man—not man, creature—pressed against her back. His eyes hardened. "You understand the importance of her safety."

Theo spoke, his voice rumbling through her like thunder. "Of course."

Safety. The word was laughable. "Please," she whimpered, hating herself for being so weak. But what else could she do? She couldn't break free. She couldn't fight. A vampire smaller than Theo had knocked her father to the ground faster than she could blink.

How was this a fair partnership? Every caustic thought she'd had since she first learned of their covenants ignited until the flame in her middle licked through her limbs, threatening to engulf her.

Guardians weren't gifts. They weren't servants of Soléne or protectors of humans. If vampires could snatch them from the streets, from their lives, at any moment, they were no better than slaves.

Aurelia's knees buckled, and she fell toward the earth, her chest heaving. But she didn't hit the ground. Theo pressed her to his body like a sword being sheathed. That's what she was, wasn't she? A weapon?

If her blood allowed vampires to walk freely in the

light, there was nothing to keep them from walking through their village or standing among humans. Though . . . what had been keeping them from doing that in the dark all along? Did they walk among them and she'd never known?

Questions and possibilities she'd never considered swirled in her mind like poison as Theo rounded the stairs. Aurelia worked to keep her feet from dragging. His strides were so long, she had to take two steps to match one of his. *What did the vampires want?* Alain had quoted prophecy, but not anything from the Dugianos. Her mother recognized it. *What else had she hidden?*

Theo gripped her like a sack of carrots from the market, and even with his fingers pressing into her skin hard enough to bruise, his scent made Aurelia heady. And then everything tumbled into place.

"It wasn't a human male outside the village. It was you," she hissed. His hands, his scent, his clothing. She tried to wrestle from his grip. "Stop. Right now."

He grunted as she stumbled on the incline. "You heard my orders."

"You're using your glamour, and I can't think straight—" She sucked in another breath, her arms weakening.

Theo let out a puff of air. "Is that what you call it?"

Aurelia's head spun. He must have followed her from the temple. Her blood had allowed him to step into the sunlight. "You witnessed what I did, and yet you're protecting your kind? After what Alain did to you?"

Theo said nothing as he hauled her along. That made her want to jab him in the stomach. "You said nothing. You know the covenants were breached—"

"It is not my place."

She scoffed. "Not your place?" They finally reached flat

ground, and the light of sunrise bathed the alabaster stone in pale peach. "Do you not enter into the same covenants?"

"Your mother had no problem ignoring hers."

Aurelia gritted her teeth, but she had no response. "I've never heard of a promise to turn over one of our own."

"Because she never told you that either."

Aurelia fumed as they passed through the first arch and turned right, biting her cheek to keep from breaking into sobs a second time. She regretted everything. She should've disappeared into the forest that morning, ran while she had the chance. Perhaps all the hesitation she'd felt before her ceremony had been a premonition.

Aurelia focused on taking one step at a time. The vampires she'd seen when they'd crossed through the blackened gates were nowhere to be found. The paths were empty now that the sun was fully up, and despite the light, the silence was almost more unsettling.

They passed through a set of wooden doors and entered a second courtyard. Aurelia gasped despite herself. Flowers of every color and variety bloomed in carefully tended beds, and trees with broad leaves provided shade from the early sun. How could such beauty exist here?

"You cultivate life, even though you can't enjoy it," Aurelia murmured.

Theo hesitated, then changed directions, leading her out into a shaft of sunlight that broke through the tree branches. He said nothing, and Aurelia had no response. Her mind raced with what she'd seen that morning. Could he walk outside of the shadow forever? Did it only take one drink for him to be released?

That last thought brought her hope. If all Alain wanted was for her to feed his vampires, to allow them to walk freely, would she have to stay here long? Perhaps she'd only need to endure it for a time—once they'd all fed, she would be free to leave.

Theo led her inside, and she blinked, waiting for her sight to adjust to the dim interior. The hallway was shiny and clean. She put out a hand and ran her fingers over marble columns that stretched upward to a vaulted ceiling, then gaped at the intricate carvings and colors adorning the walls.

She didn't realize they'd slowed until her breathing returned to normal. Her skin flushed. How obvious her awe must be to Theo. She didn't want him to think she was impressed.

His hands no longer clamped around her. Instead, his arm looped loosely around her waist as he shifted to the side. That only made her blush deepen. They must look like two lovers walking arm in arm.

He paused, turning her to the right. Aurelia peered beyond the arched doorway, gritting her teeth against the tightening low in her abdomen.

What was she supposed to think? Ahead of her lay the most lavish bedchamber she'd ever seen—rich fabrics, hand-carved furniture, and one of those windows she'd noticed in the habitations they passed. One of the shutters was propped open, letting in a stream of morning sunlight. A fire already burned in a low hearth. Even from the doorway, the room felt cozy and inviting.

She bristled, taking a step back.

"I don't want it."

Theo remained silent. So eerily quiet that she wondered if he'd heard her.

"I said—"

"I know what you said," Theo snapped.

Aurelia pushed at his hand, but it didn't budge. "You expect me to step inside and gratefully accept this offering when I have been told nothing of what's to become of me?"

"It will be better for you."

She let out a caustic laugh. "You know this from experience?" Theo stiffened, and for a moment, she almost felt pity. It evaporated the second he readjusted his grip. "Is this how it works for your kind? He beats you, punishes you, and you jump to do his bidding?" Aurelia shoved against him again, but his grip only tightened.

Theo lowered his head. "Had your parents told the truth about you, I wouldn't have been in a position for punishment."

Aurelia stilled. It was her fault? Had Theo been punished because he'd discovered this secret? But why would Alain take anything out on him when he'd only been going to feed as he should?

She swallowed hard, sorting through the meager information she had. Alain wanted her blood. Or thought she was a fulfillment of prophecy. Or both?

Aurelia wavered on this point. If Alain had wanted her blood, he could have taken it there in the courtyard. He could have required her to go to the temple to serve him. But instead, he had her escorted to private quarters.

Realization clicked. Alain's anger. Theo's punishment. He didn't just want her blood. He wanted to make sure he was the *only one* who had it.

Aurelia cleared her throat. "There's no need for you to stand guard. Do you think I'm stupid enough to run?"

"Yes." Theo answered with no hesitation.

Aurelia scoffed. "I'm not a child. I know what your kind is capable of."

"I'll let you go when I've seen to your safety."

"You're standing right here."

"You have not entered your room."

She set her jaw. "I do not wish to enter my room."

Theo exhaled. "Alain asked that you clean up. You only have a short time to prepare for your first meal."

Aurelia laughed out loud. "I will not attend."

Theo shrugged out of what seemed like utter boredom. "In the courtyard, you could barely stand from fatigue. So, whatever you decide, I will hold on to you until I am sure you are comfortable."

"I will never be comfortable here."

"That is by your choosing."

Aurelia stopped fighting. Exhaustion tugged on her heart like an anchor. That was what he expected of her? To accept this new reality in an instant and be grateful for the accommodations?

Tears pricked her eyes. "Please. Let me go."

Theo didn't reply. They stood there at the entrance to her room in silence for what felt like an entire rise and fall of the sun. How long would he do this? How long would he hold her? Bind her? Stand in this place for his entire coven to see when they woke? Surely, he had other tasks to attend to.

He couldn't be patient for long. Especially when the flesh on his back was torn and he was covered in his own blood. So. She would wait until his frustration got the better of him.

But if he was called away, would another vampire take his place? Could she, with lesser strength, force them to tell her what she wanted? Or force them to compromise and allow her to salvage some semblance of her old life?

What of her sisters? Fiona? Caelin? Would she ever see them again? Grief gripped her by the throat as the ramifications of Alain's pronouncement peeled back layer by layer.

"What if I promise?" Aurelia whispered.

Theo sighed. "I am not one you can make promises to."

"You haven't even heard what my covenant would be—"

"It doesn't matter."

Aurelia's heart sped, blood rushing in her ears. This could not be the only option. "But if I covenant to come back—"

"He will not accept it."

"You know this for certain?"

"Did you not see? The light has no power over those who feed from your blood," Theo explained blandly.

"You don't know that. You're the only one who ever has. Maybe it's not my blood, but something else, something within you."

"It is not something within me, and Alain knows it. So does our entire coven. What do you think will happen to you? If I let you walk out that gate, go home to your parents, your friends?"

"Wouldn't your friends obey their master?" Aurelia spat.

Theo's words came out clipped. "You claim you saw an attack. So what does your heart tell you?"

Aurelia worried her lower lip. At least it was easier talking to him like this when she couldn't see his face, but she didn't appreciate that he was making a good point. "What if they didn't know? Alain could let me out in secret."

"There are no secrets here."

"Clearly," she snapped. It felt good to argue. To fight. Although she recognized it was a pitiful rebellion. Panic rose in Aurelia like the river after rain. *She had no power here.* "Why did you watch me? You are not supposed to lay eyes on guardians just as we are not supposed to lay eyes on you."

"If your mother hadn't lied, it wouldn't have been necessary."

She scoffed. "That's your excuse?" Her eyes narrowed. "I don't understand. If you were the one to tell Alain about my blood, why were you hanging from the rafters?" Theo stiffened, and a strange sense of sadistic pride flashed through her. When Theo didn't answer, she pushed harder. "How did he earn your loyalty? To be a willing pet after he bound you like—"

"Let's have a seat, and I'd be happy to tell you." Theo snapped, shifting his grip.

Aurelia's nostrils flared. "I will do no such thing."

"Fine."

She gritted her teeth. "You are ashamed to explain?"

"I said I would. If you take a seat." His breathing was calm and even, his tone suspiciously loose.

Aurelia recognized the ruse and prodded from a different angle. At least growing up sandwiched between siblings had taught her some useful skills. "Is that your job then? To break me? To make me see the light? Believe that everything that happened has been a gift?"

That word ignited something in her middle. This life was a gift from the Goddess Soléne. Their strong bodies and good health, a gift. Their peaceful life and happy circumstances? *A gift*. And now this.

Born on the day of light.

Taken as Alain's pet.

He wasn't as he seemed. Nothing in her life was as it seemed.

Some ancient core within her tightened, solidifying like cooling iron, and Aurelia could not budge. She could not give in and take a seat on the upholstered chair. She would stand there as long as it took, and—

Aurelia gasped as Theo began to move. "What are you doing? I told you I would not—"

"You wasted your time allotted to freshen up. Alain will not be pleased."

9

Theo didn't release her when they stepped into the stone corridor or when they reached the stairs. He kept her close, his grip firm, even though he had to know he could counter any escape attempts with zero effort.

Was he being careful with her because he was commanded to? Or was this some kind of posturing? Aurelia's jaw clenched. She needed to understand more about this world. To know how much power Alain had over him.

They reached the landing, and Theo continued, the sound of their footsteps brushing against the walls. Aurelia glanced at the stone columns, the arches, and engravings of vines winding their way to the ceiling. Never before had she seen a building so large. So grand.

Aurelia's heart thundered in her chest as they reached the end of the hallway, and Theo paused in front of a set of double doors. She didn't want to cower in her room, but appearing in front of Alain was almost enough to make her reconsider.

Theo was a vampire. The woman at the gate was a vampire. And yet the man they called Alain felt like a creature unto himself. Somehow more than the other two. Cold. Calculating. Sinister.

When Theo looked at her, she felt pinned to the spot. When Alain set his gaze on her, she felt flayed open.

Theo pressed the latch. Aurelia's heart squeezed like a pomegranate under the wheel of a cart. The door swung open.

Gold gilding on the walls sent shimmering light in every direction. An enormous chandelier hung in the center of the room, with shimmering gems dripping like icicles from its branches. Aurelia's fear was momentarily eclipsed by wonder.

She didn't know how they'd found materials like this, or that they existed in the first place. If the guardians knew—if they saw how the creatures on the hill were living as they toiled each day to put bread on their tables—she doubted a one of them would bare their arms in the temple.

Alain stood in front of a throne-like chair at the head of a long, polished table, and when his eyes fell on Aurelia, Theo dropped his arms.

Cool air swept in around her body, and she shivered at the loss of him. Aurelia crossed her arms over herself, pretending not to be wholly unnerved. All of the kindness, the gratitude, was erased from Alain's features.

Aurelia turned her head, allowing her gaze to wander over the intricate tapestries hanging on the walls, their rich hues of crimson and gold illuminated by flickering candles and light from the now unshuttered windows. Anything to avoid the cold eyes in front of her.

Her mind flashed back to the marketplace she'd walked through with her father. Seeing the humans of the tribes, their colorful garments flowing as they bartered for fabric and spices. The air filled with the scent of sandalwood and cinnamon.

Aurelia stilled when she saw the woman who'd met them

at the gate. Her hair was even lighter in daylight, flowing in amber waves down her back. It was nearly impossible to look away, especially because the vampire who'd knocked her father to the ground stood at attention beside her.

Aurelia's stomach twisted with rage when she saw him. He was shorter than the others, but his stance was aggressive, his features brutish.

"Thank you for joining me this morning." Alain stood like a god made flesh. His olive skin gleamed in the flickering candlelight, his black eyes fixed on Aurelia with a quiet intensity that sent a shock down her spine.

He motioned at the table between them. It seemed to groan under the weight of roasted meats, ripe fruits, and golden goblets brimming with deep red wine. The heady aromas made her stomach twist with longing, but she forced herself to ignore the pangs of hunger clawing at her insides.

Theo stood a step behind her, his silence unnerving. Would he force her? If she refused, would he bind her again and whisk her to a chair?

"Aurelia." Alain gestured to the chair at the head of the table, its gold accents catching the light. "Please. Sit. Dine with me."

Had she told him her name? Had her parents?

There was that smile. That dip of his head. Her jaw tightened. She wished she could speak, to outright refuse his invitation and eloquently express the reasons why. All she could manage was a rigid shake of her head.

A flicker of amusement crossed Alain's face, his head tilting slightly as though he'd encountered a rare bird. "You test my patience, dear one," Alain murmured, taking a single, deliberate step toward her. His movements were liquid, effortless, predatory.

Aurelia's fingers dug into her palms until the bite of her nails grounded her. "I'm not your guest. And I'm not hungry."

The blonde vampire laughed softly, the sound like silk brushing against steel. "Hmm, Alain, she's decided to take a stand," she purred.

Alain's smile widened, though it didn't reach his eyes. "It's rare," he murmured. "And it pleases me."

Something twisted in Aurelia's stomach.

Alain tapped a finger on the table. "No matter. There are others who will enjoy this feast." He turned to the male behind him. "Fetch them."

The vampire nodded, his eyes flicking to Aurelia before he turned and left the room.

Alain's gaze returned to her, the smile already back on his face. "I've been brash, and I apologize. This must be frightening. It's difficult to remember that amid all this excitement." He turned to the female. "Clémentine, fetch the prophecy."

Clémentine's eyes widened. "But—"

"I did not ask for your opinion."

Clémentine snapped her ruby red mouth closed, then hesitated for the briefest of moments before nodding and sweeping from the room. *Not full obedience, then.*

Alain turned back to Aurelia, his eyes gleaming. "I believe you'll come to find our arrangement mutually beneficial."

Aurelia swallowed past her swollen throat. "I want nothing from you."

Alain chuckled. "We shall see."

The door opened, and the male returned, followed by three figures. Aurelia's eyes widened as they entered the room.

Not humans. Guardians.

Aurelia frowned, realizing she didn't know them personally. *Strange.* Her family knew most everyone in the village, and yet these faces were unfamiliar. Their skin was flawless, their eyes bright. If vampires were otherworldly perfection, guardians were the picture of health. Human but . . . not.

Aurelia's heart pounded as they moved to the table.

"Please, sit." Alain gestured to the chairs, and the guardians did as they were told, their eyes trained down on the floor. Alain glanced up, rubbing her nose in their obedience.

Aurelia swallowed hard. Guardians should not be in the company of vampires. But here they were, sitting at Alain's table, about to partake of his food.

Before they could fill their forks, Clémentine returned, a scroll in her hands. She moved to Alain's side and handed it to him, her eyes flicking to Aurelia before she stepped back. What power did he have for everyone in his company to bend to his will? Weren't all vampires powerful enough to be their own masters?

Perhaps it was as the stories said. That vampires like Theo or Clémentine had turned others and lost swathes of their power. The sound of Theo's breath behind her made her stomach churn. Had all of them done it at one point in their history? Hunted? Killed?

Alain unrolled the scroll and held it out to Aurelia. "This is the prophecy. The words that foretold your arrival."

Aurelia stood rooted to the spot.

"Here. Will this make you more comfortable?" Alain set the scroll on the table, then held up his hands and walked back, planting himself behind the three guardians who still sat, their hands poised over polished forks.

Her curiosity got the better of her. *That is your prophecy, not ours.* Her mother's voice from the courtyard rang in her head.

Blood rushed in her ears as she stepped forward to scan the parchment. Alain's distance shouldn't have put her at ease. He could snatch her up in a breath.

She forced herself to drop her gaze and attempt a read-through of the ancient script. Her mind struggled to translate.

When the earth sighs with shadow,
She shall rise, born of light eternal, marked by dawn that never sets.
Her blood shall flow as the river binds the forest and the mountain,
Uniting what was severed—
Light and darkness bound as one,
Blood to blood in death,
Blood to lips in life.
To seal the light, the darkness must know itself;
To seal the dark, the light must submit—

Alain's fingers brushed against her, and Aurelia jumped, dropping the scroll onto the tabletop. He caught her wrist. "You see?"

Bile rose in her throat as her fingers iced over. "It is the same prophecy of the guardians in different words."

He looked amused, his hand still gripping her arm. "Then you understand."

She shook her head. "I do not." There was nothing in the prophecy that justified this action. To rip her from her home, to force her here where she didn't belong.

"I am darkness, and I've lived long enough to know myself well," Alain whispered. "I am darkness, and you, having been born on the day foretold, are the light spoken of here. Which means all you must do is submit."

His words spread through her like poison, paralyzing each

muscle, making her skin burn. Aurelia stared back at the scroll. *The light must submit.* Her mouth went dry, her pulse a war drum.

Had this been what her mother understood? Had she hidden her birth for eighteen seasonrings because she knew this prophecy and believed it? If it was nonsense, wouldn't her mother have ignored it?

Or . . . did she know of the dangers here? Did she hide her birth because she disagreed with their interpretation and didn't trust them to listen?

In that moment, she couldn't know her mother's intentions. Would the Goddess be further displeased if she did not do as she was instructed? Or was this a test of her strength against the shadow?

Aurelia drew a breath. "These words—I do not know them. I must speak with the Bearers of the Balance—"

His free hand snapped to her jaw so fast, she saw stars. Alain caught her as she reeled, then forced her eyes to his, his glamour washing over her, making her body feel as if it were tied to stones.

His lip curled. "Your mother had her chance to explain. It is what was prophesied." Alain leaned closer, and Aurelia's body began to tremble. Her shoulders curled inward like a parched leaf.

She had no leverage here. He was too strong. His grip was iron, his fingers like leather cords The realization of her own powerlessness coursed through her like spoiled wine.

Aurelia's pulse throbbed, her blood rushing and skittering beneath her skin as his thumb brushed over her inner wrist. She gritted her teeth against the shame that swirled within her. They were watching. All of them. Clémentine, Theo, the other vampire and the guardians. She was nothing more than a puppet on a string.

Alain tugged her closer, his fingers digging into her flesh. "You're tense." His voice was a low purr, a vibration against her skin.

Aurelia kept her chin held high, but she couldn't stop the shudder that rippled through her. *Make it stop.* She wanted to cry out, to beg, but who here would acknowledge her supplication?

Alain's loose white shirt, unbuttoned at the collar, gaped as he curled over her. His blond curls, sharp features, and square jaw could've been handsome—if not for the monster hiding beneath his skin.

That's what he was. She was sure of it. The words that came out of his mouth, the light tone of his laugh, none of it covered up the cold, heartless look in his eyes.

"Relax," he whispered, his breath hot against her temple. "This is supposed to be pleasant."

This. What was this? What was he going to do with her?

Aurelia swallowed, her throat dry as sand. She willed herself to focus on the room, on the wooden table, the finely upholstered chairs. Anything to take her mind off his lips tracing the curve of her ear.

"Theo, you didn't mention her scent. Were you holding back?"

Aurelia nearly choked on her tongue. Theo had spoken of her? What else had he shared? Had he disclosed her weakness? Falling against him, nearly dropping to the floor?

She blinked back the tears beginning to sting her eyes as she forced her head to the side to look at him. Theo. Standing at the edge of the room. He stood straight now, no sign of his injuries besides the blood staining his shirt.

For the briefest moment, her heart stilled, a strange pause in the middle of her panic. His dark eyes burned like coals in the firelight. His jaw was set, his hands clenched at his sides.

Disgust radiated from Theo like a beacon, but she didn't know whether to cling to it or allow it to bury her alive. Did he hate this grotesque display of power, or did he hate that he wasn't the one with his hand clamped around her wrist?

She gasped as Alain twisted her arm, then whimpered when he held it aloft, straining her shoulder. He held her there, stretched out, facing Theo before his lips curled into a smile.

And then he struck.

Aurelia bit her lip, the sting of his fangs piercing her skin. She braced herself for the rush of euphoria, the heady sensation she'd felt when Theo had drunk from her. But it didn't come.

Instead, a sickly warmth spread through her veins, bubbling and churning. She gasped, her head thick as Alain's tongue and lips suckled against her skin. The sound made bile rise in her throat, and her knees buckled. Alain's grip tightened, holding her flush against his hip as he drank. She squeezed her eyes shut, wishing she could shred to pieces and cease to exist.

And then, as quickly as it had started, Alain pulled back, his lips stained with her blood. He licked them clean, his eyes half-lidded with pleasure. Aurelia yanked her hand back, but Alain's grip was like a vise. She couldn't break free.

He leaned in, brushing his wet lips against her cheek. "You will see me very soon," he murmured, his breath hot against her skin. "Whether you decide to eat the food I prepare for you or not."

10

Aurelia stumbled as Alain released her. She took a step back, her vision blurring. Theo was there in an instant, his hands on her shoulders. She flinched, but he didn't let go. He guided her out of the room, his grip unyielding.

As soon as the door closed behind them, Aurelia's legs gave out. She collapsed to the floor, her breath coming in desperate, furtive gasps. "Don't touch me!" she shrieked as Theo again reached for her.

Theo knelt beside her but, thank the gods, kept his hands to himself. "Aurelia."

She shook her head, her mind splintering like pottery crushed under the head of an axe. She wouldn't do this—couldn't do it. She couldn't sleep in Alain's bed, eat his food, only to be used as his plaything. It was clear that's what she was. He'd shown her the prophecy, told her exactly what he expected.

She was a guardian. But how could she protect anyone when she couldn't even protect herself? And what of the prophecy? She'd read the guardian scroll more times than she could count, but never did it say she who was sent to bind was to yield, to submit. Is this what Soléne intended for her?

"Get up," Theo growled.

Aurelia's eyes snapped open, and she glared at him through her tears. "You think I'm doing this by choice?"

Theo's jaw clenched as he pressed his palms into the stone floor. "You need to move. Unless you'd like to be sitting here when Alain passes through the doorway."

"Why do you care if I stay or not?" she spat, wiping her nose on the back of her shaking hand. Theo again reached out, but Aurelia curled her arm into herself. "I said, don't touch me."

"You need help."

"I don't want your help." Aurelia snapped her jaw shut, clenching her teeth so hard, her ears started ringing.

Theo's nostrils flared. He let out a slow exhale. "If you fight it, he will punish you."

Aurelia twisted to sit, pulling her knees against her chest. "You would know." Theo stiffened, and she gave a cruel smile. "I'm sure you'd enjoy watching another performance."

"Absolutely. In less than a day, you understand us perfectly. Torture is our favorite pastime," Theo snapped. His lips curled into a snarl. "If you insist on being a stubborn ass, there's nothing I can do for you."

Aurelia wiped her tears on her tunic, pressing her back up against the wall. "And what can you do for me exactly?"

Theo pushed up, standing in the hall as he ran a hand through his midnight hair. "There is no reason for you to die here."

"Only reason for me to suffer?" She drew a deep breath and forced herself to stand in front of him. "If you have such a soft heart, take me back to my family."

"I cannot."

"Why?" She shoved against his chest. "I cannot go back to him."

Theo's expression hardened. "You will."

Aurelia's pulse raced, and she opened her mouth to argue, but a cry cut through the silence. She froze, her breath catching in her throat.

Theo's head shot up as he turned, his eyes scanning the corridor. "You will return to your room." He glowered at her. "You can come willingly or I can carry you there. Whichever you prefer."

Aurelia wanted to slap him across the face, pummel his chest with her fists. But any movement she made would result in his hands on her, and she didn't think she could survive that. Her skin still crawled from where Alain had touched her.

She nodded once, then walked forward. This was not a battle she could win, at least not at the moment. But she would tear this puzzle apart until she found another one she could beat.

As they moved through the hall, Aurelia's senses were on high alert. Theo flanked her, his anger radiating off him in waves, his muscles coiled like a spring.

The sound came again. A muffled cry, followed by a low moan. It was closer now. Aurelia's blood turned to ice.

"Keep moving," Theo hissed.

Aurelia nodded, but she couldn't focus. Was this what happened in these rooms? Were there guardians like her who were being held? Used?

A thought flashed through her head, and she nearly gagged. *Were there humans here?* How much was being hidden from the guardians? From her parents and the council?

As they rounded a corner, the cries grew louder, and Aurelia's heart raced. It wasn't only a cry for help, but deep, guttural sobs.

Theo moved to her side, lengthening his strides. The door was visible now, a heavy wooden slab with iron bands. The blood drained from her face as she remembered Alain's breath on her skin, his hand clasped around her wrist, the sound of him drinking, sucking—

Aurelia stopped and lunged for the door, shoving against it with all her might. It flew open, and Aurelia hit the wall so hard that her teeth rattled.

One moment, she was pushing through the door, and the next, there was a hand around her throat. She gasped in a breath as the fingers pressing against her windpipe were ripped away. She struggled to gain her bearings.

Her eyes flew around the room, trying to make sense of what she saw. A woman was on her knees. A girl with long, dark hair lay in her lap. There was a smashed writing desk. A vampire baring his teeth at Theo.

The vampire growled through gritted teeth. "What in hell's gate are you doing in my room?"

Theo's back was to Aurelia, his blood-soaked shirt stretching over his broad shoulders. She couldn't see his face, but from his hunched posture and clenched fists, she doubted his expression was pleasant. "If you ever put a hand on her again, I will have you on the racks."

The vampire turned his attention to Aurelia as he scurried up from the floor. "Perhaps you should be more worried than I. Gallivanting through the halls with Alain's new pet."

Aurelia clenched her jaw, trying to hold back the tears stinging her eyes. The skin of her wrist was rubbed raw. It had only been a brief second, but her mind couldn't release that feeling of helplessness.

She'd never felt so small, so insignificant—like he could

have crushed each of her bones in an instant if he wanted to. Was this why the Guardians never left their village?

Theo's arm shot out so fast, it blurred in her vision. The vampire hit the wall, his head cracking against stone. Theo didn't respond to the vampire's comment, merely turned to survey the scene behind him.

Nosferatu.

The cries of the tribes rang in her head. Here she was, a guardian with superhuman strength and healing ability, magic in her blood, and she was no better than a beetle, easily crushed under a leather shoe.

The woman in front of Aurelia forced herself to her feet, pulling the girl on her lap to stand with her. The girl was young, probably only twelve or thirteen, if Aurelia had to guess. Her hair hung straight down her back, but she refused to lift her head.

The older woman's arm remained clamped around her shoulders as she kept her eyes on Theo and pushed the girl from the main room into an antechamber. Aurelia's stomach twisted as they disappeared behind the wall.

Something was wrong. That woman had been crying—screaming.

And then it clicked.

The woman and the girl . . . they weren't vampires. They were like the others in the dining room. Like herself.

"Who are they?" Aurelia snapped, still pressing her back against the wall.

Theo turned his attention to her, still blocking her view of the other vampire. "Get out," he growled.

"Why are my people being held here?" Aurelia demanded again, blood rushing in her ears.

Theo didn't give his command a second time. He tore her from the wall, throwing her over his shoulder like a petulant child and moving so quickly down the corridor she could barely catch her breath before he dropped her—not lightly—onto her bed.

"I said don't—" she started, but Theo's hand clapped over her mouth.

"I heard what you said, and I don't give a damn. You are a stubborn, reckless—" He clenched his jaw, his nostrils flaring as he drew breath. "You will do as Alain commands."

Aurelia's back stiffened at his words. She wanted to spit in his face, to scream and claw at him until he released her. But she knew it would do no good. She was trapped, a pawn in their twisted game.

She swiped his hand from her mouth, regretting it instantly. His scent enveloped her, a heady mix of something earthy and almost floral. How did he affect her like this? Alain's glamour left her feeling empty and nauseous, but Theo's . . .

"Why?" Aurelia hissed, working to avoid her eyes rolling back in her head. "Why would I bow my head and open my veins for a creature like him?"

Theo's anger seemed to drain out of him as he braced himself with his arms, his body still curled over her. His eyes softened, his lips parting for a brief moment, before his jaw clenched again. "You will do as you are asked, or I will do it for you. Those are your choices."

Theo reached out a hand to brush loose tendrils of hair from her face, but Aurelia jerked her head away from his hand. "I would rather die."

Theo dropped his hand back to the bed, then leaned in, his breath hot against her ear. "Be careful what you wish for." In an instant, he straightened. Her skin still burned where he'd touched her. She forced her hand to stay flat on the quilt beneath her.

"There is a servant prepared to bathe you." Theo stepped back and regarded her with a cold, calculating gaze.

Aurelia lifted her chin, her eyes blazing. "I don't want to see anyone."

Theo smirked, and he gave a mock bow. "As you wish."

He turned and strode to the door, his movements fluid and graceful. Aurelia's eyes followed him despite herself, her body humming. She hated him. Hated all of them. She hated that after all her protestations, she was now in her room reclining on a bed Alain had prepared for her.

Theo paused at the threshold and looked back at her. "I will be right outside."

It sounded more like a threat than a comfort. Aurelia glared at him, her hands clenching at her sides. "How very kind of you."

Theo's eyes narrowed, and he nodded once before stepping out and closing the door behind him. Aurelia broke, curling into herself, the instant he was gone. She sank into the luxurious pillows, her breath coming in ragged gasps.

Every fiber of her being rebelled against this, and yet . . . there was a small part, the part she despised most, that felt a modicum of relief. Of vindictive pride.

Were her parents disappointed now? Were they glad that she had, after all, shown some sign of power? The guardians had expected a savior, and she'd provided them nothing.

Could this have been what Soléne intended? For her power to be used to benefit these creatures? For her to be forever in their servitude?

How could this ever serve to bind the light and the dark if she were a slave to it? The prophecy spoke of restoration, of peace. An end to their suffering.

But had it said anything about the cost? Of her own sacrifices?

Aurelia dragged herself up, swiping at her cheeks before crossing to the small table in the corner of the room, her legs still trembling. She picked up the decanter of wine that sat there and poured a glass, her hands shaking. She drank it down in one gulp, the liquid burning a path down her throat, not caring whether it was good for her or not. Let it be poisoned.

She poured another and took it to the window, staring out at the trees, at the edge of the courtyard and the street beyond. It was quiet and still. The sun sat higher in the sky, and the leaves rustled lightly in the breeze.

Aurelia set the glass down and wiped her mouth with the back of her hand. She glanced around the room. The soft bed with its silk sheets, the thick rugs underfoot, the intricate carvings on the wooden furniture. It looked even more opulent up close.

Her eyes landed on the small door in the corner, and she crossed to it, opening it to reveal a privy. She'd never seen such luxury. A carved seat of wood was placed over what had to be a pit like the one her father had dug at home. There were silken cloths and a vase of clean water for wiping.

She crept in, her abdomen aching, both with hunger and her need to relieve herself. The last thing she wanted to do was accept Alain's offerings, but as she lowered her undergarments and sat on the seat, a resolve hardened within her.

Not for long.

What were her options? She could try to escape. That thought made her regret her stubbornness. She could have been demure with Alain. Let the servant bathe her, reveled in any kind of pleasure offered, and played the part. But now it was too late. Theo wouldn't be convinced after their conversation in the hall.

Aurelia used a cloth to clean herself, then picked up the vase of water. Fired clay.

Option number two. If this was a test—if Soléne wished her to stand against the shadow—what would make more of a statement than taking what they wanted?

Cracked pottery would work if she made enough cuts. Guardians healed quickly, but their blood could not regenerate if they experienced too much loss too quickly. She'd learned that last summer when Fiona's cousin got into a fight with a thieving tribesman.

Seven. He'd been cut seven times by the man's knife. The Elders hadn't been able to save him.

But could she do it? Could she cut deep enough?

Death, along with birth, was not the same for guardians as it was for humans. They were eternally bound, reincarnated each time they passed from the mortal realm.

Those left behind did not veil their faces or sit in shadows when a guardian took their last breath. Even when their hearts were broken. Even when they missed them so much, they couldn't think past the ache in their chest. They focused on the promise of rebirth, and they moved forward.

Her heart skittered as she set the vase down on the shelf. Option number three. If this wasn't a test . . . if Alain's prophecy was correct. She swallowed hard and stalked across the room. How could the Goddess ask this of her?

The window to her room sat open. There were no restraints. Alain wasn't concerned about her stepping outside. Aurelia leaned over the ledge and peered out, her heart twinging at the thought of what she would normally be doing on a sunny day like today.

Her stomach grumbled, thinking of the food her family would still be celebrating with at home. A tear slipped onto her cheek. What were they doing at this moment?

All her life, the guardians had spoken of the prophecy, and her mother hadn't said a thing. Would her father be angry?

Would the rest of the village? Would they strip her of her title, or would her father now hide her secret? Would they tell everyone where she'd gone?

Her throat thickened as she wrapped her arms around herself, remembering her mother at the temple. She'd known. She must have understood that Aurelia's offering could expose the secret in her blood. She tried to stop her, to put it off, yet when Alain appeared, she'd allowed her to enter.

Though what was her other option? Aurelia was of age. She might've saved her from that day, but what about the next? The one after that? Eighteen seasonrings she'd kept her secret, but she'd been backed up against the wall.

Aurelia swiped at her cheeks. She should've told her.

Truths came to her mind one by one, digging their pointed tips directly into the softest folds of her heart. Her father hadn't known either. Would he have done the same? Would he have told the coven immediately?

Her mother cared about the prophecy, about their duty. Had she acted out of love?

Aurelia thought of the guardians here. The attack on the tribes. The way her father had marched directly to Alain, demanding answers.

There had to be more transpiring between the guardians and vampires than she knew. It was the only explanation that made sense. They didn't agree on their interpretation of the covenants, that much was obvious, and while her parents and Alain presented a united front at the temple, they'd seemed like enemies behind the walls.

Aurelia reached out and slammed the heavy wooden blinds closed, then stalked back to the bed. She stared at it, then pressed her back against the wall and slid to the floor, curling her knees into her chest.

She worked to calm her breathing. There was no escape

from this. Even if she made it back to her home, what could her parents do? Even if she stayed in broad daylight, the night would come. And Theo could walk up to her with no consequences, regardless. Because of *her* blood. She clenched her hands, twisting her fingers in the finely spun fabric of the quilt.

She closed her eyes, wincing at the raw sting. Her whole face felt raw and swollen. She drew a deep breath, trying to lessen the pounding in her head.

Images flashed behind her eyes. The flickering bonfires. Long, stretching shadows. Crimson blood pooling in the grass. Sallow skin with scabbed marks. Golden morning light over stone. Strong, linear muscle bruised and flayed. Bound hands. A curling smile.

She trembled as her mind recycled the loop, playing it over and over. Alain would not let her leave this place.

Her eyes lingered on the bed and its crisp linens in front of her. She swallowed hard. When did vampires sleep? They could not go out during the day, and she clung to the hope that their cycle of wake and rest was the opposite of hers. Though she'd seen a vampire in the halls, and the sun was already up . . .

She could not get in that bed.

Aurelia choked back the sour taste at the back of her throat. She *would not* get in that bed. She pulled deep breaths through her nostrils. She would have to stay awake. Stay alert. Not that she could do anything if Alain appeared here. He'd already taken her blood. With his strength and power, he could force her to do whatever he wanted.

And her family . . .

Aurelia's throat thickened. She would stay awake. She would . . .

11

There was a tap.

Then another.

Aurelia furrowed her brow, wincing at the cold, hard surface against her cheek. Another tap. She blinked her eyes open, her surroundings fading into view. A ruffle of cloth. A strange square of polished wood. A post of some sort.

"I provide you with food, and you do not eat. I provide you with a soft bed, and you choose the floor." A man's voice. Cold. Angry.

Aurelia's chest constricted, her eyes dilating until the light around her was almost too much to bear. She pressed against the hard surface beneath her, forcing her body upright. Now that she was staring from a vertical angle, the world in front of her made sense.

A bedpost.

The room seemed to crash in around her, burying her in timbers and stone. Her arms and legs shivered. Her whole body chilled.

She was in her bedchamber. She'd fallen asleep. But light

still poured from between the shutters on the window. She turned her head and found Alain seated in the chair at the writing desk, his fingers gently tapping on the surface.

"You do not wish to be here." Alain's eyes were fixed on her.

"No," she croaked. Her throat felt dry and cracked as air whispered through it.

Alain gave her a pitying look. "I understand it has been quite the shock, but you know I cannot alter course." Aurelia frowned, and Alain's eyes glinted. "You told me so outside the temple. It is the Goddess who chooses. I have no say in the matter."

Aurelia's teeth clenched, making her jaw ache. Chosen. She'd wished it, hadn't she? As a child, she'd been ashamed that her birth was late. At the bottom of the steps, she'd sent up a silent prayer of hope. How Soléne must be laughing.

According to her birth, she was the "curse-breaker" the guardians had waited for. According to prophecy, she was supposed to strip the power from Le Sombre, not enliven it. But had they misunderstood? Was her blood to be used to bring vampires out of the shadows? Could both their prophecies be correct?

But this was only one coven. Her entire village worked to support the vampires here. How could one person, one body, be enough? It didn't seem a question she would have to ask since Alain seemed intent on keeping her to himself.

He tapped his fingers on the desk. "What are you thinking in that fragile head of yours?"

A thought crashed against her mind. Was this his room? His bedchamber? She started to hyperventilate. "I would like to see my family."

Alain dropped his hand from the desk and leaned forward in the chair. "You still do not understand. Keeping you here is a kindness. Protection. You're lucky we discovered your gift before someone else did. I'm sure you perceive my methods as brutal, but Theo tried to keep it for himself."

"What?" Aurelia's brow furrowed. Theo watched her leave. He was in the woods near the tribes. *Why was he there in the woods?*

"He would have come for you, used you, and made it impossible for the prophecy to be fulfilled." Alain exhaled, running a hand through his hair. "I saw you enter the temple, and when Theo didn't return, I was concerned for your safety. There are times when . . . well, I'm sure you've heard of strange occurrences. Just as guardians break rules, vampires are not immune." Alain looked up with an apologetic smile. "I'm glad we discovered his deception. He has been punished, and now that you're here, he will not harm you."

Aurelia thought of Maera. Of her stories. Yes, she had broken the rules and attended the celebration with Fiona. That wasn't the same as harming a guardian. "Yet you assigned him to watch over me?"

Alain's jaw tensed, and something flashed in his eyes. "He must understand his place." He dropped his hands to his knees. "The guardians here have chosen to stay. I'm sure you wondered. Our way of life may be different than what you're used to. I don't pretend to be gentle. It's not in my nature. But I care about the prophecy. I desire the same thing your parents do, or . . . I thought I did. I've questioned everything since discovering your mother's secret."

Aurelia's chest tightened, her ribs squeezing around her lungs so tight that her shoulders curled to keep the pain from showing on her face.

Alain rose from the chair, walking toward her. Aurelia pulled her knees into her chest. He stopped a few paces ahead of her and crouched until their eyes were almost level. "You may believe me a monster if you wish, but any blame for your predicament need not be laid at my boots. Your parents kept their secrets, and their selfishness has delayed the true power of Soléne and Le Sombre."

He reached out a finger, and Aurelia turned her head, her small act of rebellion snuffed out as Alain snapped her gaze back to his. He gripped both sides of her jaw between his thumb and forefinger.

"Do you wish to be as selfish? I understand you're angry with your family. Probably angry with Soléne. You are young and have yet to understand that her ways are not ours. I offer these luxuries to ensure your body and blood will remain strong. I only wish to do what is best for both our kinds."

Alain dropped his hand and stood, stalking toward the armoire. He retrieved a finely cut riding coat and slid it on, adjusting the lapel and sleeves before turning back to face her. "Warm yourself under my quilt. It would be a disappointment if I had to do it myself."

12

Hours later, Aurelia forced herself up from the floor. She was freezing, her fingertips blue and her toes numb. She strode toward the bed, her stomach churning as she crawled onto the mattress, sliding under the sheets and quilt.

It smelled like him. Sickly sweet. She clenched her fists, the fabric of the sheets bunching under her grip. The image of Theo hanging with his hands bound haunted her. Alain would do it to her, she had no doubt. She had no choice but to be obedient. For now.

Tears slid from her eyes, soaking into the down pillows. Her eyelids were heavy, and as soon as she began to warm, she had to fight the pull of sleep. But why stay awake? Why force herself to endure wakefulness when she couldn't stop anything that happened to her?

Aurelia drifted, swimming in shadows, until a jolt lanced through her. The mattress shifted. She'd heard the door again. The sound of footsteps through the room.

The mattress dipped further, followed by the rustle of

sheets. He was there. Lying next to her. Aurelia's body turned to ice, hardening into stone as she sucked air through her teeth. She forced her eyes to remain closed, praying to Soléne that he would not touch her.

"I'm glad to see you've listened," Alain whispered. "It doesn't have to be difficult, this arrangement between the two of us. In fact, it could be pleasant. If you wish." His words were snake-like, slithering through her mind.

His breath warmed the back of her neck. Aurelia forced the whimper that threatened to escape back down her throat.

"Shhh." Alain shifted on the bed. "You are so precious. You do not need to be afraid, I will give you anything you wish."

Don't touch me. Don't touch me. Aurelia's shoulders ached, her hands and legs trembling again.

Alain let out a sigh. "Turn to me. I wish to see your face."

Aurelia shook so hard, the bed creaked. She did not want to turn, but she remembered his fingers on her jaw. The hard glint in his eye. She forced her body to move and rolled beneath the sheets.

"Ah. There you are. So beautiful." Alain propped himself up on his elbow, looming over her. He wore no shirt, his bottom half covered in the bedding. He smiled and brushed a strand of hair from her cheek. "This will get easier. I promise."

He lowered himself to his pillow, still watching her face. And then it was as if her body doubled in weight. A blanket wrapped around her mind, slowing her thoughts to cold honey.

His glamour. He was manipulating her, but she didn't care. For a moment, it felt good not to think. To hide. Even if she still lay in plain sight.

Aurelia closed her eyes, unable to suffer the image of him inches in front of her face for another second. She dropped into the feeling of nothingness. Hoping she would never wake.

———

Aurelia didn't realize she'd slept until her eyes flew open at the touch of a hand on her shoulder. *Alain. Lying in bed.* She jolted, throwing her arm out in alarm and connecting with the side of someone's face.

A strong hand caught her wrist. "Good morning to you, too."

"Let go of me!" She cried out in panic as she registered the face hovering over her. She yanked her arm from Theo, and he released her. Aurelia scrambled back on the bed, turning to face him. "What are you doing here?"

Theo's hair was mussed, his expression drawn. Aurelia scanned the room, her eyes landing on the shutters. There was no light coming between the slats. She noted the candle on the desk in the corner. When had that been lit?

He grunted. "Alain is ready for you."

He may as well have thrown a bucket of ice water in her face. Aurelia began to shiver. She was still in her clothes from sundown with Fiona the night before. Or had it been two nights? She was already losing track of time.

The fabric was beginning to feel stiff after soaking in her sweat and tears. She patted herself down under the covers. Everything seemed to be intact. She would've woken if Alain had . . . bile rose in her throat. She would know. Even with his glamour, she couldn't have slept through him touching her.

Aurelia's voice trembled. "It's not sunrise. He said—"

"It doesn't matter what he said. He's requested your presence."

Aurelia pursed her lips, her eyes beginning to burn. No. She would not cry. Not in front of Theo or any other vampire. She had to find a way through this, and it wasn't going to be by appealing to their nonexistent compassion.

She was a tool to them. Alain wanted her blood. She had to figure out how to use that as leverage. She had to discover the truth of the prophecy.

If she could talk to her parents, maybe she could get some of the answers she sought. Some clue as to what she was supposed to do, what Soléne wanted from her. There was plenty in their prophecies about the arrival of she who was sent to bind, but no instructions on what they were supposed to do once she arrived.

Would the Goddess leave her so defenseless? So alone? There was nothing inside her that felt like even a shred of guidance.

Aurelia threw her legs off the bed and stood, desperate to use the privy. She took one step, and the world tilted sideways. Theo cursed under his breath and was at her side in an instant, propping her up as he had most of the day prior.

"Did you drink anything?" It sounded more like an accusation than a question.

Had she drunk since her first meeting with Alain? A glass of wine, but that was the only thing she'd put in her mouth since arriving here. Aurelia pushed against his chest, reaching instead for the wall. "I'll be out in a moment."

Theo refused to let go. "You're going to topple over and hit your head."

"What does it matter to you?" Aurelia looked up, her eyes cold. "Or will your master punish you if I'm damaged?"

Something flickered behind Theo's eyes, and Aurelia almost felt guilty for saying it. "You need to eat and drink or—"

"Or what?" she snapped, then froze as realization struck. Her parents always had a large meal the night before they went to the temple to give their offerings. Alain told her he wished to keep her strong. Food and water strengthened their blood.

Which meant, if she refused to eat and drink, maybe it

would weaken her further. Either she wouldn't have enough blood or it wouldn't be as potent. Perhaps then he would be willing to negotiate with her?

Aurelia kept this triumph from showing on her face. "Let go of me, Theo. I'm fine. I'll keep my hands on the wall if that will satisfy your concern for my well-being." Part of her wanted to slip. To give herself a cut or a bruise. To waste more of her precious resource and watch him be chastised for his carelessness. But then she thought of Theo hanging from the ropes. Of Theo's back covered in blood.

His blood had been red just like hers.

She glowered at him. He'd followed her, tried to keep her for his own, and now he had the gall to pretend he cared whether she suffered?

Theo's grip relaxed, and she stepped into the small closet, slamming the door in his face. She pulled up the sleeves of her tunic, checking her wrist. No new marks. She felt along her neck, her middle. Nothing felt tender. The skin was unbroken.

Satisfied, Aurelia's pulse calmed as she used the facilities, washed, and opened the door. Theo hadn't moved. Aurelia pressed her back against the wall. "I will go with you. But I will not eat."

Theo nodded, then turned and paced across the room. His arm shot out like lightning, gripped the back of the chair at the desk, and slammed it forward into the end of the bed with a crack.

Aurelia jumped, her eyes widening.

"And what about the others?" Theo's eyes glinted, his mouth twisted.

"What others?"

"You do not believe the prophecy? Still? After seeing what your blood is capable of?" Theo passed her and pushed the shutters open. The sky above was still inky, but there in the distance was lightening blue.

Aurelia stared at him, all thoughts wiped from her mind as she processed his words. He was angry about . . . the prophecy? She expected him to be annoyed that she was fighting Alain, and he was being punished for it. That he was bound to her compliance.

Theo gripped the windowsill and dragged in a long breath, slowly exhaling before shutting the windows and stalking back toward the bed. "I did not ask for this life. And yet, I am bound to it. I have looked forward to the day when she—" He stopped, swallowing hard, and looked up, meeting her eyes. "To the day when *you* would come."

"Is that why you tried to take me?"

Theo's brow pinched. "What?"

"Alain told me what you were after. Why he strung you up."

Theo laughed, stalking closer, his eyes wild. "Seems he earned your trust."

"I don't trust anyone. You, least of all." Aurelia's heart beat long and slow in her chest. The walls of the room seemed to draw closer, squeezing the air until it was so compressed she could barely draw it into her lungs.

Theo's eyes were hard. "Good."

I did not choose this life. His words sank into her like the olive oil her mother used to rub into her skin. No. Of course he didn't. None of the Nosferatu had asked for their curse. Le Sombre was vengeful, full of spite. He was no respecter of persons when he sought company in the shadow. It was why Soléne took pity on the creatures of the dark. Why she imbued guardians with her power, gave them the ability to satisfy a vampire's thirst while escaping death.

Soléne and Le Sombre. Light and darkness. It was because

of their rift that the world was torn in the first place. The words of the prophecy spiraled through her thoughts. If she was sent to bind, to restore . . . wouldn't that be the breaking that needed mending?

Gods. Aurelia blew out a breath. She'd been terrified when she thought her task was between vampires and guardians, but between Le Sombre and Soléne?

"You've seen proof of your power." Theo spoke, and Aurelia blinked. "It seems it is wasted."

Anger rose in her, seeping out of her center and lighting up her extremities. Wasted? What in the Goddess's name was he talking about? "My blood has power. It has nothing to do with me."

Theo scoffed. "That's something to admit." He crossed the room and reached for her arm. When she pulled back, he grabbed it anyway and hauled her toward the door.

"I can walk."

"As you so aptly demonstrated earlier." He opened the door and dragged her into the hall.

Aurelia wanted to weep. She couldn't escape them. If Theo wasn't forcing her to the dining hall, she was cordoned off in Alain's quarters or worse, lying beside him. They were stronger, faster, and they could scent her blood. The fact that any part of her felt glad that it was Theo who woke her instead of Alain filled her with shame. They were all the same. Selfish. Cruel.

"Will another vampire be assigned to me?" Aurelia shivered as they passed the door she'd burst through earlier. Her eyes lingered, her head turning as she waited for any sound from within. There was nothing.

"Unlikely."

Aurelia snapped her eyes forward as the walls began to spin again. "I'd like someone else assigned."

"And why is that? Am I not satisfactory?" His voice held a hint of amusement, and Aurelia's eyes flashed.

"I have complaints."

"Hmm." His voice rumbled in his chest, sending a jolt of heat through her middle. That same low burn from the temple.

Aurelia stiffened, arching to create distance between her shoulder blade and the right side of his chest. She hated his glamour—it affected her more than the others. Even more, she hated him for using it. Theo didn't seem to care or notice, but she didn't want him to be the one touching her or waking her up in the morning.

"How often must you feed?" she asked, keeping her voice light. Perhaps this strange feeling was amplified because her blood still ran in his veins.

"It depends."

"On what?"

Theo turned the corner, leading her down a new hallway and a set of stairs. They weren't going to the same room they'd been in before. "On our activity level."

Aurelia nodded. "And if you're active?"

"Every three sundowns."

Three. This was the second since he'd fed at the temple. After one more, her blood would hopefully be out of his system, and then . . . A pit opened inside her as she remembered holding her arm through the shroud. Theo didn't have her blood in his system when he held her then. When his thumb circled her wrist.

"Watch where you're going," Theo growled, pulling her up as she stumbled on the first step.

Aurelia hated that she clung to him. She was weak. She did need to eat and drink. But if that was the only way to maintain some control over the situation, she would starve.

They entered through a wide set of double doors at the

landing, and Aurelia's knees locked. Alain stood on a dais dressed in a gaudy pleated tunic, low-cut and open over his chest. At his left stood three vampires dressed in black, and on his right?

The vampire Aurelia had seen before she slept. Towering over the guardian and her daughter on their knees.

13

Theo stepped away from her, but kept a hand on her lower back as they walked further into the room. Whether to make sure she didn't run or waver on her feet, she wasn't sure, but she disliked it nonetheless. Tremors had already started up again in her arms and legs, the sight of Alain and the vampire enough to make her feel as if her bones were made of brittle branches.

Alain watched them approach, the corner of his mouth lifting. "You don't trust her? Or you've grown fond of her, Theo. Which is it?"

Theo's hand tightened. "She is weak. You commanded me to keep her well."

The corners of Alain's mouth turned up. "So I did."

Aurelia didn't know a smile could look threatening before meeting him. Now the sight of his curved lips made her want to shrivel. He'd lain beside her. Breathed against her skin.

Alain motioned to bowls and platters set on a sideboard, and Aurelia sucked in a breath. More vampires stood there along with other guardians. She'd been so focused on Alain, she hadn't noticed.

Her heart lifted from the floor of her chest a fraction. With so many people there and armed with the knowledge that vampires only fed every three days, perhaps he wasn't planning a repeat performance.

"Please. Partake." Alain descended the two wide steps of the dais to stand in front of her. This room wasn't as decorated as the first, but the ceiling was still vaulted, the walls smooth and polished, pale as alabaster, and the upholstered chairs of fine make. It looked like a hollowed-out stage for a performance or grand dance, with a platform for musicians.

A finger landed beneath her chin, turning her head, and that sickly sweet scent washed over her. Alain stood so close, his breath washed over her cheek. "Did you not hear what I said?"

Aurelia sucked in a breath, but couldn't fill her lungs with her head tilted at such an unnatural angle. "I'm not hungry."

A slow smile spread across his face. "Not hungry. Hmm. And yet Theo believes you are weak." He dropped his finger, clasping his hands behind his back. He did not retreat. "That leads me to believe that you are refusing my offerings for a purpose." He paced away from her, then paused, looking back at her over his shoulder. "What could that be?"

Aurelia wet her parched lips. "I—"

"Have I not given you everything you could want? A warm bed? Servants to dote on you? Protection? I've seen the accommodations you're used to in the village, and these are far more generous. So tell me. What might your other demands be?"

Was it just her imagination, or did Theo's fingers twitch? They were still on her back, despite Alain's mockery.

Aurelia bit back the snide retort that sat on the tip of her tongue and said, "I do not wish to stay here. I request to be sent to my family."

Alain nodded, his brow furrowing. "I understand. Unfortunately, that isn't an option. Nor will it ever be. You've seen the prophecy. You are to stay here with me until we can bind the light and dark—"

"But I don't understand how I am to do that. My parents are wiser than I. They have knowledge that could be helpful for me—for us," Aurelia amended. Perhaps if he believed her on his side, he'd be more amenable to giving her leave. "If I could at least speak to them—"

Alain was suddenly in front of her again. "Dear one, you don't need to know what you're doing. That is why I'm here. I have lived since the beginning, and while I do not doubt that your parents carry wisdom, they do not understand the curse as I do." He reached out a hand, pushing Theo's away and grasping her around the waist, pulling her against him. "I understand it is difficult to process this drastic change, but it is your destiny."

Aurelia tensed, and her spine felt as if it were about to crack like a twig bent over a knee.

Alain reached up, pushing a loose strand of hair from her face. Aurelia shivered, and the pleased smile that spread over his face made her queasy. "Would you prefer to fill your plate or shall I?" he murmured, his eyes soft and pitying.

The scent of him made her stomach roil, and she turned her head, searching for clean air, working to draw a solid breath. "Thank you, but I'm not hungry at the moment." That time it was very nearly true. She thought if she put anything in her mouth with that rotting scent burned in her nostrils, she would instantly throw it back up.

Alain stiffened, making a low sound in his throat. He stepped back, releasing her. Theo reached out as she stepped back, but Alain snapped his fingers. "Don't touch her." He turned and pointed to Clémentine, who still stood on the dais. "Make her a plate."

Clémentine's lips pursed, but she didn't question. She descended the steps, sweeping her golden hair over her shoulder, and strode to the table, picking up a porcelain plate. She didn't ask what food to place on it, just went down the line, adding one of everything. Pieces of fruit, fresh flatbread, dried nuts, and meat.

Aurelia's mouth began to water, then ache as Clémentine filled a glass with citrus-infused water. Though her throat burned and her hands trembled, she would refuse it.

Alain motioned for Clémentine to set the plate, fork, and glass on a small, oval table between a pair of upholstered chairs. She did so, then moved out of his line of sight. Aurelia swallowed hard, working to keep her gaze from dropping to the decadent spread.

"I do not wish to make you uncomfortable, but I cannot allow you to waste away." Alain exhaled in frustration. "I wish you to be an honored guest here, Aurelia."

Aurelia drew a full breath as he approached. He stopped in front of her, his expression pleading. He'd done this before. And then his hand had connected with her cheek.

"I would like to speak with my parents." This was her only leverage. If Alain didn't want her to be weak, then he would need to give her something.

Alain's lip twitched. "Mmm. I see." He nodded, clasping his hands behind his back. "You'd like to speak with the covenant breakers?"

"They're not—"

"You blame me for this, but had your caretakers been honest, there would have been no need for any upheaval."

Aurelia began searching through time and memory,

rewriting her personal history. What would've happened had her parents told the truth? Would Alain have taken her as a new child? Would he have raised her? Taken her blood before she was of age?

"The wheels in your head are spinning." Alain again reached out a hand, brushing her cheek. "Let me tell you what it would've been like. I would've brought your family here. I would have provided them with everything they could want or need. You would have been a princess. Worshipped. Adored."

"I was happy with the life I led."

Alain blinked, wetting his lips. "I hope you will see in time. I seek only to fulfill that which has been foretold." He released a slow breath. "I must continue with all that prophecy foretells, so I ask again. Will you please join me for a meal?"

Aurelia met his gaze, but did not respond. After a few moments, Alain gave an apologetic smile, then turned and motioned for the vampires still standing at attention on the dais. The three males descended the stairs and strode toward them. Alain turned to face her as they stopped at his side, the four of them forming an impenetrable wall.

"Theo." Alain again snapped his fingers, and Theo instantly gripped her shoulders. She tensed, trying to wrestle away from him as he forced her to the chair.

"Stop fighting," he hissed in her ear.

"I won't."

Theo's knee hit the table as he forced her down to the seat, sending the plate of food and glass of water sprawling with a clatter. Aurelia lifted her head, her eyes burning.

Alain tsked. "Theo, be gentle, please." He nodded at the man on his right. The one they'd caught unawares in his room. The one who called her Alain's pet. "Aurelia, this is Augustus. After partaking of your blood, I was able to walk freely in the sunlight, just like Theo. These three members of my coven travel often on my errand, and it would be convenient for them to leave during daylight hours."

Augustus's eyes glazed as he wet his lips and stalked forward. Aurelia gasped, her eyes widening. Was he—?

"She is weak," Theo barked.

"By choice." Alain shook his head. "I do not wish this to be a burden, but I cannot force her to eat. Yet I am bound by duty—"

"What duty?" Aurelia clawed at Theo's hands, but he adjusted his position. One arm around her waist, holding her to the chair, the other over her arms and chest, forcing her to stay upright. "Don't. I can't—" The words died on her tongue as the vampire knelt in front of her, grasping her calves when she tried to kick. Augustus' eyes wandered over her, and then, grinding his hips against her legs and pinning her further, he snatched one arm and lifted it over her head.

He dragged a lazy finger over the delicate skin on the underside of her arm, slowing when he reached her elbow. "You will understand your place soon enough."

Aurelia bucked, but Theo held firm. Tears of rage filled her eyes as Aurelia fought Augustus's glamour. His presence felt oily and slick, coating her with a film. The vampire lowered his head, his hot tongue tasting her before he bit down. She gasped, her eyes rolling back in her head. She was going to be sick. Her body heaved, and she coughed, but there was nothing in her stomach to expel. She gagged again and again as the vampire drank, her head growing fuzzy as he finished, straightening. Glutted and drunk.

"You." Alain pointed at the vampire next in line.

Aurelia couldn't fight this time. Theo's arms no longer held her back, but held her upright. As the second vampire approached, Aurelia's head rolled. Her body seemed to sink into the chair, falling closer to the floor. She didn't realize her eyes were closed until a hand pressed against her cheek, forcing her head to the side, and she whimpered in surprise.

She barely felt the sting of pain. The rush of nausea. Flashes of heat and cold, her head so heavy it felt like it could crush her spine.

His breath hissed in her ears.

The world closed in around her, and all went dark.

———

A slow pinprick of light broke through the clouds of her consciousness. Aurelia slowly became aware of her body, leaden and raw. Her face was pressed against something. She shook her head, desperate for air, and rolled onto her back, sucking in a lungful.

Her eyes blinked open, her eyelids seeming to scrape against sand. Her vision was blurry, but she could make out a silhouetted figure against what seemed to be a wall of light.

"Where am I?" she murmured.

There was a crack. A shriek. Aurelia pushed herself upright, her eyes wide. She blinked, trying to make sense of what she was seeing.

Alain gripped Vala by the hair, hauling her over the stones and pressing her against the stone pillar. "You're awake? Wonderful."

Aurelia tried to scramble to her feet, but her head swirled, the room rolling around her. Another cry. A broken sob. "Vala?" Her sister. Alain had her sister.

This was a dream, it had to be. How long had she been unconscious? How could he have gotten to her family so quickly?

The scene in front of her sharpened as she planted herself

on all fours. Alain pulled out a knife, toying with the neckline of Vala's tunic.

"Stop!" Aurelia rasped. She searched the room for the others, for Theo. There was no one.

Aurelia shook so hard, her stomach roiled. She gagged, but there was nothing to throw up.

"You will not eat?" Alain growled, slashing the knife through the fabric, exposing Vala's shift. She whimpered, pressing her hands flat against the polished stone.

"Stop!" Aurelia cried out again. She gasped for air, dragging herself forward on hands and knees. How far would Alain go? How many people would he punish? After Vala, would he turn to Nora? This was madness. She couldn't allow this. She wasn't strong enough. "I will eat!"

Alain whipped his head toward her, his hand still twisted in Vala's hair. Aurelia scrambled forward, pulling olives and figs from the floor and shoving them into her mouth. She chewed, nearly choking, her mouth was so dry.

Aurelia pulled out the pits and found the small bowl beside the fallen platter. Next, she bit into a piece of flatbread. Her stomach sighed with relief, and shame twisted around her middle as Vala sank to the floor, covering her face with her hands.

Alain slid the knife back into its holster. He smoothed his tunic before crossing the room toward her. "More," he commanded, and Aurelia obediently took a piece of honeycomb. All of it tasted like ash on her tongue.

Alain snatched a carafe of wine from a side table and poured her a glass. He waited for her to swallow, then handed it to her. "You will eat with me. Every meal. You will not hesitate." Aurelia nodded, taking the goblet with trembling fingers and raising it to her lips. She took a drink, nearly sloshing wine on her chin.

Alain leaned closer. "I'm disappointed, Daughter of Light. I assumed you would care more about your people. About the prophecy." He hovered and as she lowered the goblet, reached up and swiped his thumb over her lower lip. He stared at the drop of blood-red wine on his skin, then lapped it up with his tongue. He exhaled as if the entire encounter had exhausted him.

The door slammed open, and Theo burst in. "Alain. You are needed on the crest." He didn't lower his eyes to look at her. Didn't glance at Vala sobbing on the floor.

Alain's expression hardened. "Can't you see I have matters to attend to?"

Theo's throat bobbed. "It seems they have been attended. I can clean this up."

Alain considered, his eyes dropping to Aurelia, still holding the wine glass. "I will fetch Clémentine to return the girl." He wrinkled his nose. "Prepare Aurelia to attend the baths. I will expect her in my quarters by sunrise."

Theo nodded once, then stood unmoving as Alain swept from the room.

14

"You have less than a minute." Theo stalked forward, helping Aurelia to her feet.

"I don't wish to go to the—"

"To talk with your sister," he growled, helping her to where Vala sat.

Aurelia blinked, looking up at him in surprise. "You aren't taking me now?"

"You heard Alain. He's sending Clémentine. If you wish to speak with her—"

"Yes, alright." Aurelia dropped to her knees, reaching out and pulling her sister close. "Vala. I'm so sorry, Vala. I didn't know—"

Vala wrapped her arms around her, squeezing tight enough, Aurelia could barely breathe. "I didn't know where you were. Mother and Father, they won't talk about it. Mother hasn't come out of her room since you left." Vala's tears soaked her hair.

"I was trying to force him to let me see you all, but I didn't expect—"

"It's not your fault."

"It is my fault!"

They talked over each other, both gasping for breath. Tears wouldn't come to Aurelia's eyes, but her shoulders shook and her head throbbed.

Vala finally pulled back. "You can't stay here. You must come home."

Aurelia's face pinched. "Did Mother tell you—"

"No. But Father did. Aurelia, you were born—"

"Please. Don't say it." She bit the inside of her cheek to keep from dropping into hysterics. "I don't know what to do."

Vala's glistening eyes bored into hers. "The Goddess will help you. I know she will."

Aurelia nearly laughed out loud. The Goddess? The Goddess hadn't offered her a thing. If she had been chosen, why had she never felt her presence? Never understood her calling or discovered her power?

"Alain's finished with play time?"

Aurelia jolted as Clémentine pushed through the door into the room. She glanced between Theo and the two women clasping each other on the floor, raising an eyebrow. "A little family reunion, I see."

Theo motioned for Aurelia to stand. She squeezed Vala's hands and did so.

"Let her come with me." Vala scrambled up from the floor. "Please, let her—"

Clémentine blurred across the room, moving between Aurelia and Vala. "That's quite enough. Theo?"

He took Aurelia's arm and turned her toward the door. He dropped his hand as soon as the door closed behind them, and they walked in silence down the corridor. Everything inside Aurelia felt numb. Hollowed out. Vala had been in Alain's clutches. He'd brought her here, threatened her harm.

Aurelia trembled when they reached the room, her body revolting at the idea of entering Alain's bedchamber once again. She leaned against the door frame. "Where were you? When I woke?"

Theo's jaw tensed. "Alain commanded me to take his place. At a meeting of allies."

"Alain has allies?" She gave him a skeptical look. Theo didn't answer. "So it wasn't you who retrieved my sister?"

Theo shook his head.

"Would you have done it if he asked you?"

Theo scrubbed a hand over his jaw. "I am to prepare you for the baths."

Aurelia stayed put. "You held me down. While they took my blood."

"I was—"

"Following orders. Right." Aurelia watched him. "But you let me talk with her. Why?"

Theo's expression hardened. "There was time."

"You didn't have to do it."

Theo glanced back down the hall. He fidgeted with his tunic. He was nervous. Was he worried someone would overhear them?

Aurelia straightened and stepped into the room. Theo's eyes flared in surprise. She waited a moment, but when he didn't follow, she took a step back. "I don't know how to prepare for the bath."

Theo's lips twitched. He looked once more over his shoulder, then followed her into the room.

"Allowing me to speak with my sister was a kindness," Aurelia hissed the second the door was shut. "Why do you follow his orders? Why do you not—?"

Theo moved so fast that Aurelia stumbled back, her calves hitting the bed. "I don't have a choice," he growled.

"Ha!" Aurelia threw out her hands. "You're one of the most powerful creatures on earth. What is keeping you here?" Theo didn't answer, his face stony. "Go ahead," Aurelia continued. "Keep your face blank and pretend to be noble. Pretend that you have no ownership in this situation. But the truth is that you are too cowardly to leave if you are opposed to—"

"You believe I am opposed?"

She swallowed hard. Had she imagined it? The look of disgust in his eyes when Clémentine removed his bonds in the room off the courtyard? The kindness he'd offered her with Vala? Had there been more?

Aurelia questioned herself. He'd held her down while vampires fed. He'd forced her to the dining room. Back to this bed chamber.

Theo's eyes darted away from her. "Did you wish to be at the temple that day?" He stalked past her into the room, feigning nonchalance, but she wasn't fooled. He was agitated. Ruffled. Raw power seemed to ripple under his skin.

Aurelia kept her eyes trained on his back. "No." It was the truth. Mostly.

"Yet you did not leave. Too *cowardly?*" He turned to face her, his lips curling up.

Aurelia clenched her jaw so hard, she tasted iron. Theo's eyelids flickered, and her stomach dropped. *How long had it been since he'd taken her blood?*

There wasn't any light outside the window. Two sundowns. Tomorrow Theo would have to feed. Would Alain offer her to him? *Had he already?* The scene in the dining room plagued her thoughts. "How many fed?" She hated that she'd passed out. That she had no idea what had happened to her body during those moments.

Theo's nostrils flared. "All four, though the fourth was not satisfied."

"My apologies." Aurelia's throat tightened. "Did you—?" She imagined Theo curled over her, his lips against her skin. The rush in her veins. Would she have stayed asleep during that?

Theo shook his head.

"Alain did not allow you to feed?" Aurelia murmured. The idea of having her body touched and used while she wasn't conscious made her stomach writhe. The fact that Alain had allowed others to taste her blood filled her with dread.

Theo's eyes darkened. "Perhaps I also did not wish to eat." The words rumbled through her.

Aurelia's eyes narrowed. What was he trying to accomplish? Was he seeking some twisted form of trust? Did he seek to undermine Alain? Take her blood for himself as Alain accused?

He followed orders, yes, but she thought of the guardian on her knees. The vampire Theo berated. Was it also Alain's order that vampires were respectful of her kind? She doubted that very much.

Aurelia breathed hard. Perhaps she was a coward. Perhaps they both were. She'd always followed her parent's orders, and Theo obeyed Alain. If he couldn't escape his master, what hope did she have?

"I need to know why." Aurelia gripped the wall, willing her knees to hold. "Why do you not leave when he treats you so? What power does he have that I do not understand?"

A muscle in Theo's jaw flexed and released. "A servant will be here soon. You must undress—"

"Tell me why!" Her throat was so thick, it came out as a strangled cry.

Theo ground his teeth. His eyes dropped, then lifted to the door. "Wait here."

"Theo, I will not bathe unless—"

She gasped as Theo pressed her up against the wall, his body flush with hers. "I may take orders from Alain, but I am not bound to take them from you."

Bound. Had she heard him use that word before? Aurelia forced herself to breathe. To relax. She closed her eyes, listening to his ragged breath in her ear. "He has power over you. Doesn't he? A covenant or oath?"

Theo was still, his chest pressing against hers with each rapid inhale. And then he was an arm's length in front of her, his eyes wild. "Do not threaten me." Aurelia nodded quickly, her cheeks flushed. "You will wait here."

She didn't move—didn't breathe—until Theo left the room, slamming the door behind him.

———

Aurelia was still pressed against the wall when a knock came at the door moments later. She froze, her heart jumping into her throat. Alain didn't knock. Neither did Theo.

It was probably the servant. Someone to take her to the baths. She glanced around, searching for a robe—anything she could wear once she undressed. When she couldn't find anything, she drew a deep breath and pulled the door open.

A woman stood there, her hair short, cropped above her ears. She only rose to Aurelia's shoulders, her features fragile and birdlike.

"She's not going to bite. You can let her in," a male voice muttered, and Aurelia looked up. Theo stood in the shadows, leaning against the wall behind her.

Aurelia moved from the doorway, allowing the woman entrance. When she tried to close the door, Theo pressed his hand against it.

"I must undress—"

"This is not your servant," he snapped, then pushed his way into the room. Aurelia glowered at him and pushed the door closed. Theo turned to the woman. "You must be quick."

She nodded, perching on the bed. Aurelia stayed by the door, not sure what she would do if Alain or anyone else tried to enter. But it wasn't she who would have to answer for this. She could plead ignorance. It was Theo who wasn't sending her to the baths as he should.

"My name is Raya. I am a guardian like yourself." She smiled warmly.

Aurelia held her breath, looking between the two of them. The woman was unrecognizable—she didn't resemble the woman she'd seen in the room or anyone at either of her meetings with Alain. "You live here?"

Raya nodded, and Aurelia searched her face. So many guardians she didn't know. How many were kept here? Was it possible that her parents were truly oblivious? A million questions swirled through her head.

"Did he force you here?" Aurelia glared at Theo.

Raya's eyes widened. Then she threw back her head and laughed. "Oh my." Her hand flew to her chest. "I'm sorry, that took me by surprise." She shot an accusing look at Theo. "Have you been a terror?" She waved him off, muttering to herself. "Must've been, for her to ask a question like that." Raya turned her attention back to Aurelia. "No, I was not forced. Anyway, where was I? I'm a guardian—"

"I got that part." Aurelia stared at her. Had she just acted like Theo was . . . a nuisance?

"Yes, I'm repeating myself. My apologies. I understand you must go to the baths, so I'll make this quick. Theo says you don't believe much about the prophecy—"

"I never said that."

"You don't believe you're a part of it," Theo snapped.

Raya shot him a look. "Hush! You don't speak to a woman like that, Goddess above. How long have you been cursed? Long enough to have learned some manners."

Aurelia's eyes nearly popped out of her head.

Raya placed her hands in her lap. "As I was saying, I believe all of it. I believe no creations on this earth should be damned to live under the power of the shadow. And I believe guardians should be released from their servitude. The prophecy promises both through the goodness and light of Soléne. I believe Soléne has provided a way for light and shadow to be restored. Do not ask me how this is to be accomplished. It is far beyond my understanding."

Aurelia swallowed. At least she wasn't alone in feeling like she was grasping at clouds when she tried to make sense of those words. She remembered how, as children, they used to play during the river's flooding. The water, swelling to the edges of the woods, churned with sticks, stones, and mud, mixing everything into an opaque mess. It was too dangerous to venture into the rush, but the overflowing river always left behind small pools.

She and her sisters would sift through those ponds, searching for creatures—fish, snails, frogs, and tadpoles—that had been swept up and stranded, unable to find their way back.

Aurelia pursed her lips. "You say you do not believe creatures should be cursed by Le Sombre, and yet you are held here. In direct violation of our covenants."

Raya watched her, the corner of her mouth curling. "Justice for one is a delicious distraction, don't you think? I do not place myself above our people. If Soléne sees fit for me to serve here instead of there, it is not for me to decide."

"So you accept your fate?"

Raya's smile grew wider. "Acceptance is a useful tool, yes. It gets me through the harder sunsets. But most sunrises I stand at the ready." Raya hopped off the bed and walked toward Theo. "This man—for he was a man once—felt the sun on his face for the first time in hundreds of years. If that is not the breaking of a curse, I do not know what is."

Theo's eyes flickered. He turned from her, his arms still crossed tightly over his chest.

"But it will not last. My blood will not run through his veins much longer." Aurelia noticed the circles forming under his eyes.

"Do you know this?" Raya turned back to her. "Does anyone? We have a prophecy, but it does not tell us how this breaking will occur—"

Theo held up a hand, his eyes suddenly fixed on the door. Aurelia's stomach plummeted. Alain. If he was approaching, then—

Theo flicked like shadow across the room, pulling the door open and yanking someone inside.

"Damn it, Theo!" A woman shoved him away, her hair chestnut brown, her skin and eyes . . . she wasn't a vampire. Another guardian? Or human? "You made me drop my snack!" She leaned down and picked up a plum from the stone. She dusted it off on her tunic, then took a juicy bite.

Theo's stance was rigid, his mouth a thin line. "I didn't realize you were back already."

Back? Aurelia gaped at her as she chewed. Had she chosen to come here? Willingly? And if so—

"Our time in Nicea was cut short." The woman glanced up as if only just then noticing Theo wasn't alone in the room. "Oh, I do apologize, let me introduce myself." The woman wiped her free hand on her traveling pants and held it out. Aurelia took it. "I'm Helena. And you are?"

"Aurelia."

The moment she spoke her name, Helena's eyes widened. Her eyes dropped, scanning over her, assessing. "Hmm. You're prettier than Florentine let on."

"You've already spoken with him?" Theo asked, his voice low.

Helena scoffed. "Well, of course I have. You were off at the crest."

Aurelia gaped at her. She spoke as if she were in control, as if Theo was lucky to have found her at the door.

Helena nodded once at Raya. "I have to admit, I didn't expect to find you all here together." She raised an eyebrow. "Is this a pleasure thing? Something to take your mind off of—"

"Get out," Theo growled.

Helena looked affronted. "Here I came to keep you company on duty and this is the response I get?"

"Manners," Raya tutted.

Helena tossed her hair over her shoulder. "Well, I won't keep you. Raya, come with me. I believe we have visitors."

Raya nodded gravely and shuffled toward the door, turning to look at Aurelia. "Your body needs a long soak. You will be free from all this in the baths. Don't rush."

Aurelia frowned as she moved to the door. Helena took another bite of plum. "You were correct, Theo. If you were wondering." She gave him a look, then quickly flashed a smile and exited the room.

The door closed. Aurelia and Theo stood alone in the room.

"Who is she?" Aurelia asked.

Theo grunted. "You couldn't tell?"

Aurelia took a guess. "Another guardian? But . . . who is she?" *To you.* Aurelia wasn't brazen enough to add that last part. There was a strange energy there. They had history. But what past could exist between a guardian and a vampire?

A flush crept up her neck as she thought of Helena's words.

A pleasure thing. No. They couldn't possibly. But even as she pushed the thought away, it seemed to grow roots.

Was it impossible? Guardians found physical pleasure despite not reproducing the way humans did. She didn't understand the human process perfectly, but it required a male and a female to create a human child.

Guardians, on the other hand, were gifted children by Soléne herself—guardians who had passed, now finding new life. Like Fiona. Chosen to create new life. Vampires, however, didn't reproduce at all. Did their bodies even . . . have the capability humans and guardians did?

He was a man once.

Aurelia's flush deepened. Physical pleasure was one of the gifts guardians enjoyed. But had that been stripped from vampires as part of their curse?

A ghost of the sensation of Theo's lips on her wrist made her skin prickle.

Then she thought of Alain lying beside her in bed, and an icy shiver ran down her spine. She straightened, suddenly hyper aware of her body. Now that she'd eaten and pangs of hunger weren't wracking her middle, she noticed the itch along her scalp, stickiness on her skin, and irritation where her dirty clothes rubbed.

"Helena works directly with Alain. We do not know her specific assignments, though I have my suspicions." Again, Theo kept his voice low.

"What do you believe he's asked Helena to do?" *And what was he right about?* Blood rushed in her ears. Theo wouldn't answer her, she was sure of it. She hurried into another thought before he could snap a retort. "Did you bring Raya here to convince me? Do you wish me to defy Alain somehow when you refuse?"

Theo appraised her, his eyes narrowing as he frowned. "I doubt I can convince you of anything."

Aurelia stilled. "Probably not."

He took a step closer to her, his eyes drifting to the bed. "You will bathe. And you will not speak of Helena. To anyone." Aurelia nodded her agreement. "Alain desires to build connections with other covens."

"There are other covens close to the village?" Aurelia gaped at him.

"Close is relative," Theo murmured. "I believe Helena is speaking with their guardians."

Other guardians. Aurelia's eyes widened. There were other villages near enough to visit?

She cleared her throat, schooling her expression. Why would guardians have anything to do with vampire relationships? And why would Helena be willing to do anything on Alain's behalf? Was she also bound as Theo was? "She is allowed to come and go?"

Theo's expression clouded over. "Undress. I will summon a servant." He turned abruptly and stalked toward the door. Aurelia couldn't stand it any longer. She reached up and pulled the pin from her hair, letting her locks fall loose over her shoulders and running her fingers over her scalp.

Theo turned and froze, his mouth parting slightly. He snapped it closed, then exited the room.

15

Aurelia stood alone in Alain's bedchamber, the door clicking shut behind Theo. He'd instructed her to undress for her bath, and now she was supposed to simply strip down and stand in her room naked until the servant came to retrieve her?

Her fingers twitched as they hovered over the buttons of her tunic. She couldn't be nude when the woman—or man?—arrived. Aurelia shuddered. She'd find a towel to wrap around herself, but where would she go? Would they allow her into the communal baths or would they bring a basin into Alain's room? She shivered at the thought of being exposed there.

Yet she didn't feel quite as desperate. Theo had brought a guardian to her room. Raya lived here, had lived here for years, and she wasn't balking or crying herself to sleep every night. She was . . . happy. No, happy wasn't the right word. Determined. What had she said? Lying in wait?

That image, of guardians trapped inside these walls, readying weapons, filled her with hope. Were all of them like

Raya? The men and women she'd seen standing along the walls of the dining hall?

And what of the other vampires? Did Alain hold them as he did Theo? He held something over their heads, and she needed to discover what it was. If the bonds of their coven were tenuous, perhaps she stood a chance. However he'd forced their obedience, she could find it. Work to unravel it.

Aurelia flicked open the buttons. She was about to lift the tunic over her head when the door opened, and she spun. A young woman stepped into the room, her expression calm as she closed the door behind her. Another guardian—she guessed that since she had yet to meet a human here—dressed in a simple linen gown, her dark hair pulled back into a tight bun.

Aurelia's hands dropped, pulling her clothing tight. The servant didn't react to her partial state of undress. She held a white robe in her hands, the fabric shimmering in the lamp light. "I'm here to escort you to the baths."

Aurelia's eyes dropped to the robe, her skin prickling.

The woman stepped forward, holding the robe out in front of her. "You'll need to remove all your clothing."

"I understand," Aurelia muttered. She wasn't an imbecile. The woman didn't look away as she pulled the tunic over her head. She dropped the fabric to the floor, then pulled off her trousers and worked on her undergarments, her arms covering as much of herself as she could.

The woman stepped forward and held the robe out in front of her. Aurelia took it, her fingers brushing against the soft fabric. She slid her arms through the sleeves and pulled them tight around her waist, tying the sash.

It felt like butter. Soft and smooth against her skin. The servant nodded her approval, then picked up her dirty clothes and turned toward the door. She opened it, holding it wide for Aurelia.

Aurelia stepped through the door, her pulse quickening as she found Theo standing in the archway. His eyes dropped over her, landing on her bare legs, his nostrils flaring.

He was hungry. That was all. The skin on her wrist prickled, and she had to focus to keep from lifting her hand.

The woman stepped forward and tilted her head toward Theo. "Shall we?"

Aurelia balked. He was coming? *Apparently so.* Theo waited until she passed, then followed behind her. His glamour swirled around her like a mist. She drew in a breath, her chest tightening.

It must be worse when vampires needed to feed, which made sense. They would need more power to lure their victims when they were suffering hunger. So why didn't he leave? Go to the temple?

Aurelia's thoughts swirled, her nudity and Theo's glamour taking her to places she avoided under normal circumstances. Her body flashed hot as the soft fabric brushed against her skin. She hadn't thought much of pleasure. Of taking a lover. She hadn't been of age, and then she'd always thought she'd wait for Caelen.

His face rose in her mind. His hair the color of pine bark. His deep voice. His laugh making her belly flutter.

Had he heard the news? Had her father or Vala and Nora told everyone in the village or was she simply another guardian who had gone missing? *Was this where they'd all ended up?*

Aurelia swallowed, her throat constricting. She'd never spend another night in her hut. Unless she could find a way out of this, she'd never have the chance to build a family of her own. To have an everyday life. Grief rolled through her in waves. She didn't realize how much she wanted it until it was taken from her.

Aurelia clenched her fists, waiting for the swell of emotion to pass. Some moments she was numb, and some she was drowning. Could she not settle somewhere in the middle instead of swinging like a pendulum?

The woman led them down a flight of stairs and through a set of double doors. They opened into a long hallway. She smelled the baths before she saw them. Humidity laced with the tang of oil and salt.

The servant opened another set of doors, but before ushering her through, turned to Theo. "This is where we will part."

Theo's lips twitched. "I was told—"

"Alain commanded me to bathe. I don't need a chaperone." Aurelia stared him down. Theo's eyes darkened. *He didn't take orders from her.*

"Males are not allowed beyond the threshold." The servant gave him an expectant look.

Theo spoke through gritted teeth. "This is an unusual circumstance."

"If you wish to see me naked, you only need ask," Aurelia chided. She didn't know where this brazen side of her was coming from, but his admissions infused her with new power. False or not, she liked watching him squirm. It wasn't her he was afraid of, she knew. It was Alain's claim on her that made him antsy. Still. She enjoyed it a little too much.

Theo's eyes locked on hers. "I will wait here." He turned his attention to the servant. "You'll not leave her side."

The woman nodded, then held the door and watched Aurelia enter. They stepped into a short hallway lined with flickering oil sconces, then passed into a large open room.

Steam curled in the air, and the scent of exotic oils overwhelmed her senses.

She let her eyes roam over the space, unable to quell the awe that washed over her. Intricate tile work lined the walls, and ambient lighting bathed the room in a warm, inviting glow. Various pools dotted the space, each more luxurious than the last, with hand-painted tile and brass workings. The water shimmered, crystal clear, and Aurelia's pulse quickened.

Women moved between the pools, their bodies flushed and glistening. Guardians. All of them. They had to be.

Aurelia breathed a sigh of relief. Nudity was expected at the baths in the village. She clenched her jaw, pushing back her tears at the normalcy of it.

Her gaze landed on a woman with long, dark hair twisted into a knot at the nape of her neck. Her skin was smooth, her muscles toned. Another woman with sun-kissed skin and curves stepped into a pool, her laughter echoing off the walls.

They were enjoying themselves. Just like Raya, they didn't seem to be withdrawn or oppressed. And this . . . it was pure luxury. Opulence. More than the village could offer.

Had these women been fooled? Lulled into complacency with comfort? Flattered by Alain's words and promises?

The servant turned to her, motioning for her to remove her robe. Aurelia's fingers trembled as she untied the knot at her waist and let the fabric fall to the floor. She stepped forward, her breath catching in her throat as the servant led her to a padded mat. She lay down as instructed, her skin prickling against the draft of air whispering over her midsection.

The servant began to work, her hands gentle and firm as she scrubbed Aurelia's skin with a mixture of honey and salt. Aurelia's breath hitched as the rough texture of the scrub rasped against her skin. *Gods, it felt good.*

The woman's hands glided over Aurelia's arms and legs,

and when she flipped to her stomach, worked the muscles of her back and shoulders. She closed her eyes and sank into the sensation of it, the mix of pleasure, bordering on discomfort.

When the servant finished, she poured warm water over her body, washing away the scrub. Aurelia's breath hitched as the water cascaded over her skin, then she bit her lip to keep from sighing as water soaked her hair. The servant massaged her scalp, cleansing her hair with something that smelled of lavender and rosemary.

She was back in the tub behind the house, leaning her head back as her mother scrubbed. Her hands weren't always gentle, but she hummed as she washed. Aurelia's head, neck, and shoulders had sung the rest of the night.

What was she fighting against? Right now, her sisters were likely scrubbing pots or tending to the fire, depending on the time of day. Here, she couldn't keep track.

But this wasn't her choice. Had she been given the choice, would it have made a difference? Would she have ever accepted this, even if she were convinced the prophecy she'd read on Alain's scroll was true?

Regardless, at that moment, it was difficult to be outraged. To be afraid. Even when she tried to reach for it.

When the servant finished, she helped Aurelia to her feet and led her to one of the pools. Aurelia sank into the near-scalding water, her muscles relaxing as she submerged herself.

"Thank you," she murmured, then caught the woman's hand before she turned to clean the mat. "What is your name?"

The servant blinked. "Cambria."

Aurelia released her hand, but not before noticing the symbol on the underside of her arm. *A tribal tattoo.* Guardians didn't mar their skin. She had to be human.

Guardians. Humans. The vampires had built an entire community here without her parents' knowledge.

A weight settled on her chest. *Or they were aware of every-thing.* Her mother had lied about her own birth, so what would keep her from hiding this, too?

That knowledge ached. While she'd disagreed with them on many things growing up, she'd never questioned their integrity.

Cambria cleaned and prepared the area where she'd scrubbed Aurelia, then moved to the side of the pool, preparing a tincture in a glass vial. The other women were still bathing in the other pools. For the moment, she was alone.

"Do you live here inside the walls?" Aurelia asked.

Cambria's brow twitched. "Yes."

"Did you . . . come here by choice?" How much did she know? Was she aware of who she served?

Cambria didn't answer. She poured the contents of the vial into the pool, and the water fizzed, releasing a fragrant, herbal steam. Without a word, she poured more oil into her hands, then rounded the tub and began massaging it into Aurelia's shoulders.

Aurelia leaned forward, pressing into her knees to stay balanced. Cambria moved on to her hair with a brush, combing through the wet strands.

"I've always lived here," Cambria whispered. "Since I was a child."

Aurelia stilled, not wanting to speak too soon and spook her. After a moment, she asked, "Have you ever been beyond the walls?"

Cambria set the brush on the edge of the tub and stood. "There is no need. I am provided with everything I desire here."

"But—"

"Ah, I see you've taken my advice." A woman's voice sounded to their right, and Aurelia turned in surprise. Raya. She was stripped down and wasted no time stepping over the tiled edge of the pool, slipping into the water. "You may leave us." She smiled at Cambria, but the servant stood rigidly.

"I was told not to leave her side."

Raya scoffed. "By whom? Theo? He will get over it." She shooed her off, then let out a long sigh. "This pool is always my favorite. The hottest temperature."

Cambria strode to the side of the room and sat on a bench, her eyes still trained on the two of them. Aurelia lowered her voice. "I didn't realize you'd be here."

"Well, I'd hoped to find you. Now we can speak without an audience." Raya leaned her head back, closing her eyes and resting against the edge of the pool.

Aurelia held back her words until they nearly ripped from her throat. "What am I to do?" she whispered. "If I am she, if I am meant to bind the light and dark, how am I supposed to accomplish it?"

Raya floated a moment more before opening her eyes and sitting straight. "A prophecy is inescapable, my dear. You don't have to accomplish anything."

Aurelia blinked at her. "I don't understand."

Raya cupped her hands, scooping up water and sloshing it up over her face. She wiped her eyes and nose, then swept her hair back from her cheeks. "Soléne will use you as she sees fit. You are a tool in her hands. We all are. Soléne and Le Sombre will be bound once more, and the power necessary is already in your blood."

Aurelia frowned. "But Alain wants to use it. He's already taking it—"

"So it will be for the moment. If Soléne wishes a new path, she will carve it."

"And I do nothing? All of us have to accept this injustice?" Aurelia's chest felt tight enough to burst. The heat from the pool and the frustration burning inside her made her vision swim.

Nothing. Wasn't that what all guardians had done? They had been dutiful, they'd fulfilled their covenants, only to be taken advantage of.

Raya leaned in, her eyes glinting in the dim light. "No, dear one. Never accept. Instead, be ready."

16

Aurelia stepped into the cool air of the hall, steam trailing from her scrubbed body. She clung to the delicate robe Cambria had wrapped around her shoulders. The fabric felt like the brush of a willow blossom, and her skin tinged red and raw beneath it.

Theo appeared from the shadows, and even the sight of him wasn't enough to stop her conversation with Raya from cycling in her thoughts. She was supposed to wait? To do nothing?

Cambria tugged nervously at her tunic, avoiding Theo's gaze as he scanned the two of them.

He grunted. "How long does it take to bathe?"

"There was much to attend to." Cambria nodded curtly, then turned and strode away from them, returning to the baths.

Aurelia fiddled with the tie on her robe, and Theo caught her wrist with two fingers, as if he was picking up waste from the street.

"Theo." She wanted it to come out as an accusation, but it

was breathless. If existing in Alain's manor was a puzzle, within the past few hours, Theo had become the most dangerous piece. He was inconsistent. Volatile. Worse, she didn't trust herself to make the right move.

"What did she say to you?" Theo's eyes were dark, searching.

Aurelia worked to swallow the lump in her throat, twin marks burning on her wrist where Theo held her. They were no longer his. They may have been Alain's or Augustus's. But somehow, they only burned for him. "She washed me. That was all." Raya didn't seem to think Theo was a threat, but she wasn't convinced.

"How was it?" His voice was crisp.

"The water was warmer than I expected." The knitted socks Cambria had given her scuffed against the floor, but she was grateful not to feel cold tile against her feet.

Aurelia followed him under another archway, through another roomful of shadows. The air felt cooler and lighter, and the glow of the sconces receded behind them. Dread pooled in her stomach, and she tried to slow their pace. She didn't want to follow where he was leading. To the bedchamber. To Alain.

Her pulse thudded. Theo was quiet, and she could almost convince herself she'd imagined everything that happened before the baths.

He hadn't admitted anything, but he had brought Raya. Was he truly concerned about the prophecy?

A stone seemed to drop through her middle. Theo cared about his curse. He desired his freedom. That was what this was about.

They reached the end of the corridor, and Aurelia slowed. "Is he in there?"

Theo turned back, his hand in his pocket. "I don't know."

Alain had said sunrise. Aurelia shifted on her feet. "Where is the crest?"

"A meeting place."

"Is it far?"

"Not for us."

Vampires moved quickly. She'd witnessed it. But how far could they travel? It had taken her father half the day to reach the merchant's tents the last time they'd visited. "Do you know the southern spring? Where the tribes often trade?"

Theo nodded. "I do."

"Is the crest farther than that?"

"Yes."

Hope flickered in her chest. Perhaps Alain was tired and he'd return later than expected.

But he would return eventually.

She couldn't do this. She couldn't crawl into his bed night after night and wake to him slipping under the sheets. What if he didn't keep his hands to himself? What if he asked for more than just her blood?

What if he wore her down?

What if she started to believe him?

"Two days." Theo's voice was low.

Aurelia looked up, her eyes burning. "What?"

"I'll answer your questions in two days' time."

Her breathing quickened. "All of them?"

"No."

"Then—"

"I'll answer the ones I can."

Aurelia wet her lips. "I want to choose one." Theo opened his mouth to argue, but she cut him off. "It's two days in his bed. Two days of him—" Her throat caught. Theo's expression darkened. "I want to choose one. You must answer it."

His jaw worked. "I can't promise it."

Aurelia considered this. She wanted to push, but she had nothing to hold over his head. She couldn't leave, and they both knew it, and she wouldn't risk another member of her family being targeted. "I'm not sure I can trust your word anyway."

The corner of Theo's mouth twitched. "Then we have a deal."

Aurelia's eyes flicked past him down the corridor. Two days. It was arbitrary. Why would Theo ask her for such a commitment without any reasoning?

But she didn't know if she could trust him. What could he say that would make her feel at ease? Nothing. What other choice did she have?

She gritted her teeth. "Fine. Two days."

Theo watched her for a moment. She drew a deep breath, then forced herself to continue down the hall.

17

Aurelia woke to silence and the sting of her own body. Every muscle ached, stiff from clenching her muscles and flinching at every sound outside the window. She lay still, listening. Only the hush of wind against the shutters. No footsteps. No low murmur of Alain's voice curling into the corners or a shift on the mattress.

She was alone. The relief struck so deep it left her hollow.

Aurelia pushed herself upright. Her joints crackled, skin tacky with old sweat. The simple linen shift clung to her, twisted and wrinkled from the restless night. Her ribs ached where she'd curled around herself.

Light speared through the gaps in the shutters, pouring stripes of gold across the floor. Dust floated in the beams, lazy and slow. For one aching moment, it was beautiful.

Her throat closed. Grief rose, bitter and sudden. Not simple or clean, but raw, clotted with anger and shame. She missed it. All of it. Her family, her friends, her home. She'd taken for granted the safety she enjoyed there, mistaking the complexities of family life for wrongness. So much of her angst had been conjured in her head.

She dragged in a breath. Two days. That was what Theo had promised. Two days, then he would answer her questions. She'd made it through the night, and now she only had to endure and hope he kept his word.

Aurelia pressed her palm against her sternum. Was she hanging her survival on the oath of a vampire? Could he be trusted any more than Alain? It was a battle of villains, and at that moment, Alain was sitting at the top.

A scraping hunger gnawed at her belly. She swung her legs off the bed. Her toes curled at the chill of the stone. Across the room, a platter waited on the desk.

Bread. Soft cheese. Olives slick with oil. A fig, split open and bleeding like a fresh wound.

Aurelia hesitated. The last time Alain had offered food, it had not been kindness but a noose tightening around her sister's throat until she had no choice but to obey.

Her stomach cramped. What choice did she have? She crossed the room and snatched the bread first, tearing off a hunk with her teeth. It tasted of woodsmoke and salt, rough and dense, but it filled the hollow space inside her. She shoved a sliver of cheese after it, the tang blooming sharp across her tongue.

She ate with disdain, and when the edge dulled, she wiped her mouth on the back of her hand and turned toward the room. She would not waste this hour.

Aurelia moved fast, her fingers searching every seam and crevice of the furniture. She pulled the drawers of the desk open to find ink and scraps of parchment, then moved to the bed and slid her hands along the frame, the underside of the mattress. Only dust and a dry sprig of what might once have been sage.

Interesting, but not at all what she'd hoped for. If Alain held something over Theo and the others, where would he keep it? If not in his chambers, did he have another secret place?

She searched the floor, hunting for a loose tile, but found nothing. She stood and slumped onto the bed, heaving a breath.

A caged bird. That's what she was. She could flutter and flap against the bars as much as she wished, but Alain had sent his message with perfect clarity. He was in control. How long would it take before she stopped searching? Stopped fighting? How long before—

The latch clicked. Aurelia jumped from the bed, heart hammering against her ribs. She smoothed the shift over her hips, forced herself to breathe, to stand still. Normal. Innocent.

Alain swept into the room. His riding coat hung open, dust streaking the hem, and his boots left faint prints across the floor. His eyes found her instantly.

Shadows pooled beneath his eyes and cheekbones, but the moment he saw her, something fever-bright flickered behind his gaze. He smiled, wide and reckless, as if he'd stumbled across a treasure he'd thought lost.

"Aurelia." His voice broke like a young man's. He strode to the desk and removed his coat, then stripped off his shirt. The muscles in his back were roped and lean. Across his skin, carved in ink the color of ash, stretched runes she did not recognize—ancient, knotted patterns that twisted over his shoulders and down his spine.

Aurelia looked away before she could be caught staring. She didn't want him to mistake her curiosity for interest, or worse, desire.

He didn't bother pulling on new clothes and instead rushed across the room. Alain caught her hands in his, gripping them too tightly, his palms rough and cold. "You stayed," he whispered. "You waited for me."

Aurelia frowned, then quickly schooled her expression to indifference. She'd stayed? Waited? He hadn't given her a choice.

Alain released her hands with an abruptness that made her stumble. He bent to unlace his boots, moving with jerky, restless energy.

He spoke as he worked, words tumbling out. "They are ungrateful, you know. All of them. They don't understand what I'm offering, though I haven't exactly told them what power I have at my fingertips. I thought about stepping into the sun, but it isn't time. Not yet." He looked up in wonder. "That will come soon."

Alain straightened, barefoot now, and turned toward the wall. His gaze caught on the ancient fresco—an emperor rendered in ochre and rust, laurel crown slipping over a proud brow. He stared at it for a long moment. His fingers lifted, tracing the bottom right corner where the plaster jutted just slightly from the wall.

A tremor passed through his hand. "Imperator," he murmured. "Chosen by gods. Worshiped by men. And still—" He pressed the corner hard enough to whiten his knuckles. "Still betrayed."

Alain turned to face her and cocked his head. "Your breathing has increased. Your blood rushes in your veins—"

"You frighten me," Aurelia whispered, refusing to let him think any physical reaction on her part to his presence was anything other than terror.

"You sleep in my bed. I doubt my presence comes as a surprise."

Alain crossed toward her, reaching for her hand. When she recoiled, he caught her arm. She froze, ice sliding down her spine. With one pull, Alain could tear the limb from her body.

Aurelia held her breath as Alain's other hand lifted to her waist, gripping her hip and dragging her closer. "My dear, do you not understand this yet? You and I are to be bound. Light and shadow."

She held stiff, unwilling to relax against him. Bound? The word flared through her. There was a reason they fulfilled their service in a sanctified place. Separate. Balanced. "Guardians are meant to be with their own kind."

He chuckled low in his throat. "You have read the prophecy, and yet you do not see. I hold more of Le Sombre's power than any other vampire alive. And you, more of Soléne's light."

A cold sweat broke out on Aurelia's brow. "Guardians offer blood. We live and die as mortals. My life will slip away as every guardian before me. That is why—"

"Are you saying I do not speak truth?"

"I am saying you misunderstand the prophecy."

"I do not misunderstand. Guardians, as you say, live and die as mortals to be reborn. You rely on history to understand your past, but I and the other vampires here in my coven have lived it. It wasn't always like this. Guardians became more wary. They became drunk on their own power—their ability to withhold or give the sustenance we need."

"We do not withhold."

"Do you not? And what if I wished to feed every day?"

"That is not what—"

"Your council has determined, yes, I'm quite aware. But it is you who misunderstands. Guardians and vampires used to live as one. None of this separation or walls between us."

Aurelia shook her head. "That cannot be true. It is too dangerous."

"Dangerous?" Alain scoffed. "It was beautiful. And your

kind wish to strip us of that companionship. But our bonds are powerful. Light and shadow were always meant to be complete. Soléne and Le Sombre bound together once more. Do you not think Soléne would provide a type of these things —a symbol to show us how this must be done? And now her power is here, running through your veins."

Alain released her wrist and trailed his hand up her arm, settling his palm between her neck and shoulder, his fingers splaying across the side of her neck and the vein that pulsed there. "Do not make me take it."

Aurelia's eyes burned, her throat so thick she thought she might choke. "Give it because you wish me to have it." Alain dropped his head, the tip of his nose brushing her cheek. "There is so much you do not know. So much I could show you."

Her muscles tightened until she thought her bones might snap. Alain's lips brushed her jaw, and she let out a whimper.

Alain groaned, his fingers tightening over her skin as Aurelia's thoughts seemed to acquire weight. His glamour, oily and slick, slowed her heart, her breath. "You know what I say is true." Another brush of his lips.

Aurelia fought against the tendrils of power numbing her mind, prodding at the surface of the descending bubble. She would not be controlled. She may not have discovered a path through the walls, but she would not be a slave to her weakness within them.

With a sharp push, Aurelia drove through the film, emerging into fresh air beyond the haze. She gasped, her eyes flying wide. Alain jerked his head back. Was it that simple? Could she break through a glamour with sheer force of will?

Alain's eyes met hers, but before he could speak, something crashed outside the door in the hall. He growled, his grip tightening around Aurelia's waist. Shouts arose, and Alain dropped her, stalking to the door and flinging it open. "What is—" He paused, then lowered his voice.

Aurelia shifted on her feet, wishing she could will him to exit and close the door behind him. Not that she'd have the courage to hold him off.

Alain turned back to her, his face clearing like a storm suddenly stilled. "I have good news. I'd completely forgotten. We are having a feast tomorrow night. A true celebration. In your honor."

Her gut twisted.

"You will be dressed," Alain continued, his tone brooking no argument. "They must see you for what you are. It is not time yet for the others to know you, but my coven will understand the depth of my commitment." He took a step closer, his eyes dragging again to her throat. "The Goddess has chosen us, Aurelia. Both of us. We have been selected to end this battle between light and dark."

Battle. Up until days ago, Aurelia would've laughed at the notion. There was no battle. There were covenants. Service. Agreements honored for centuries. Guardians and vampires bound by duty, by ritual, by survival.

"The Goddess has offered me an olive branch." Alain stepped closer again. "A path to bring the world back to its proper form. You are that gift, Aurelia."

Her mouth was dry. She forced her voice low, soft, deferential. "And if the Goddess wished for balance?"

The question slipped out before she could call it back.

Alain stilled. "Balance," he murmured, as if testing the word on his tongue. "Balance is an illusion. It always has been. If even the gods and goddesses wrestle with one another, what hope do mortals have? No, there must be order."

Aurelia swallowed hard. "Do we not have order in the covenants?"

"You call that order?" Alain cut her off, voice rising with sharp heat. "No, the covenants have weakened us. The guardians chain us in half-lives, feeding scraps to kings."

Aurelia said nothing.

He paced before her, hands moving restlessly at his sides. "You will see it soon enough, When you stand at my side, when they kneel. You will understand."

Aurelia's heart slammed against her ribs. She bowed her head lower, biting the inside of her cheek. *Two days.* "Yes. I see." The words stuck in her throat like burrs.

Alain stepped forward until his feet nearly touched hers. His fingers lifted, tilting her chin up, forcing her to meet his gaze. "You are mine," he said, the words a quiet oath. "Chosen. Bound. There is no other path for either of us."

Aurelia looked into his eyes and did the only thing she could do. She lied with every part of herself. "I understand," she whispered.

Alain sighed. "Good, good." He dropped his hand. "I will have the servants prepare for this evening, but first, you will follow me. Helena is waiting."

18

Alain led her down a narrow stone hall, one hand light against her back. Aurelia forced herself not to cringe. Though the light was bright in the upper rooms, they'd descended to the lower level. Here, the torchlight flickered, catching the golden thread in the tunic Alain provided her.

He stopped before a door bound in black iron, worn smooth around the handle by centuries of use. "Here we are." He opened the door and ushered her inside.

The room beyond was small, suffocating. No windows. Only a single brazier guttering in the corner, casting long, quivering shadows along the rough stone walls. The air smelled of old ash and something faintly metallic.

Helena waited inside, draped in dove-gray linen, her hair coiled tightly at the crown of her head. She lowered her head in a respectful bow as Alain entered. Aurelia hovered just inside the doorway. Alain turned to face her. "I hated seeing them touch you. It made my skin crawl." His gaze softened. "You're mine. It is not for others to mar what belongs to me."

The words slithered around her ribs, cold and clinging. He stepped closer, reaching out to brush a strand of hair from her cheek. His fingers barely grazed her skin, but she flinched all the same.

He smiled, as if mistaking the recoil for shyness. "I've found a better way. More practical. Less . . . messy. I'm sorry it won't be as pleasant for you, but it will spare you far worse."

He kissed her temple, a soft press of lips that sent ice sliding down her spine, then turned and strode from the room, the door clicking shut behind him. The silence left in his wake buzzed in her ears.

Helena straightened. The docile mask slid from her face like shed skin. "Well. I'm impressed."

Aurelia blew out a shaky breath. "With what?"

Helena glanced up. "With you." She crossed to a long, low table and unrolled a bundle of instruments. "You looked for all the world like you didn't want to rip out his heart." Silver glinted in the unsteady firelight. "Which, I'm assuming you do?"

Aurelia held her tongue. Theo had spoken with Helena as if she were a friend, but had that been a ruse?

"Smart. Don't answer that." Helena motioned to the chair in front of her. "You'll want to sit. This will take some time."

Aurelia's limbs felt numb as she did as she was asked. She settled into the chair as Helena selected a thin blade honed to a razor's edge. She didn't bother with ceremony. She took Aurelia's arm, turning it palm-up, her grip firm. "We are down in this goddess-forsaken room so they don't scent you. They can detect our blood from a thousand paces away, did you know this?"

Aurelia shook her head. She'd never considered it. Guardians and vampires lived separately and only came in contact on the dais or through the shroud. She'd never entertained the possibility that guardians would be sought out . . . hunted.

"When a vein is opened . . . " Helena shrugged one shoulder. "Even when they've fed, it drives them mad. Gives us a strange sort of power, does it not?"

Aurelia swallowed hard. The brazier's smoke coiled into her nose, thick and bitter. Helena pressed the blade to the inside of her arm, and Aurelia hissed a breath at the sting. Blood welled up at once, dark and rich. Helena caught it in a vial, tilting it with practiced ease.

The sound was worse than the pain. A soft, rhythmic dripping. The first vial filled slowly, a thick line of red snaking up the glass. Helena corked it, set it aside, and reached for another.

The ache spread up Aurelia's arm as she worked, dull at first, then sharper, a burn that set her teeth on edge. The world narrowed to the scrape of Helena's instruments, the wet sound of blood sliding into glass, the cloying heat of the fire.

Two vials. Three. Four.

Her head grew heavy, listing slightly to one side. The walls seemed to pulse with each slowing beat of her heart. Helena cut again, opening a new line higher on her forearm when the first flow slowed.

The fire blurred at the edges of her vision. Then the cold crept in.

Helena finished the tenth vial before her hands paused. She watched Aurelia for a long moment, then wiped the blood from her arm with a rough cloth and wrapped an herbed bandage around it, knotting it tight. "You need to lie down."

Aurelia didn't argue. Her legs trembled too much to stand upright anyway. She let Helena guide her onto a low pallet tucked against the wall. She sat, leaning back against the stone wall. Helena pressed a cracked clay cup into her hands. "Drink."

The water was tepid and tasted of earth and stone, but Aurelia gulped it down greedily. Helena set a plate beside her—more bread, a wedge of goat cheese, a scattering of dried figs. The first bite made her stomach turn, but she forced it down.

Helena watched her. "I'm a friend, you know." Aurelia swallowed, glancing down at the wrap on her arm. Helena laughed. "A fair point, but you and I both know that we do what we must." She sat in the chair, leaning forward over her knees.

Aurelia took another drink, her heart hammering in her chest as her body refreshed and healed. It wouldn't take long, but she hated this feeling. The heaviness in her head. Or was it more the tightness in her chest? That didn't come from the lack of blood.

She was alone with a guardian. A woman who walked freely among the vampires, who lived with them. But Alain trusted Helena with her blood. Who was she fooling?

Aurelia wiped the back of her hand across her mouth. "How long have you worked for Alain?"

Helena smiled. "A good question, but a better one would be: what do I do for him?" She stood, then reached into the fire with a long iron rod, shifting a log so the flames bloomed higher. "I work with guardians. Other covens. Not your village, he believes that is already well in hand. He wishes to spread his influence."

Aurelia blinked, her body colder than the room warranted.

"Many villages are desperate," Helena continued. "The covens rule without honor. They take too much, bleed their guardians dry. Vampires are possessive. They call it loyalty, but it looks more like ownership. Alain desires to align them. Bring order."

There was that word again. So many questions warred in Aurelia's head that she couldn't form only one of them into speech. The idea sounded good. It sounded *right*. But when Aurelia closed her eyes, all she saw was Alain's smile—sharp and hollow—and the wounds he left on everyone he touched.

"I want him dead." Helena dropped the fire poker, and the flames hissed, spitting against the stone hearth.

Aurelia jumped. "You—"

"I don't believe in an order where guardians have no power. I don't believe in a goddess who sends her lambs to the slaughter."

Helena tilted her head slightly, studying her. Not pressing. Observing.

Aurelia picked at the hem of her tunic pooled over her thighs, gathering courage like water through cupped hands. What if Helena was truly loyal? What if this was another trap, another net cast wide and patient? But . . . if she wasn't leaving this place, she had to trust someone.

Aurelia sat up straighter as the dizziness faded, her pulse finding a steadier rhythm. The cloth bandage itched against her skin, the ache of the blood loss lingering, but the worst of the faintness ebbed.

Say nothing. Say everything. The truth clawed at the back of her throat, but fear nailed her tongue down. She opened her mouth—closed it. Then finally, she whispered, "Do you know a way?"

A slow smile spread over Helena's lips. "I'm working on it."

The words dropped into Aurelia like a stone through ice. Vampires were immortal. While guardians died and were reborn, vampires could not be released from their curse. At least, that was the truth she'd always known.

Helena moved back to her instruments. "You're not alone. When Theo answers you . . . I'll be there. As will others."

Aurelia didn't move. Didn't dare blink. How did she know about her questions? About Theo's promise? For a breath, hope flared—bright and treacherous.

Helena gathered another set of vials and cleaned the small blade with a dash of alcohol. Her face slipped back into its neutral mask. "Until then, let's not give him any reason to question our loyalty, shall we?"

———

Aurelia slept. That time when she woke, she wasn't in Alain's bed. Not in his chamber. The room was pitch black.

"Good. I thought I was going to have to wake you." A chair scraped over stone, and the flicker of a candle made Aurelia blink. The light moved closer, and she was able to make out Helena's face. "I told Alain you needed to rest under my care. You've been here all night."

Aurelia pushed up from the floor and felt for her wrist. The bandages were gone, the skin unmarred. *All night.* She hadn't returned to Alain's chambers. Her heart leaped with relief. "Thank you."

Helena smiled, set the candle on the table, and helped her up from the pallet. The door creaked open behind them.

Cambria entered, head bowed, a folded robe of deep indigo cradled in her arms. When another, larger figure followed, Aurelia instinctively stepped back.

Helena scoffed. "Theo, I told you—"

"You kept her all night." Theo's body filled the doorway, his expression dark.

"I wasn't bleeding her all night if that's your concern." Helena put a hand on her hip.

"You shouldn't have done it at all."

She threw out a hand. "Please, instruct me. How is it that you disobey your commands?" She waited, but when he didn't respond, Helena nodded once. "That's what I thought."

Theo turned, and his gaze locked with Aurelia's.

Helena let out a puff of air. "Satisfied?"

A muscle in Theo's jaw clenched, then he swept from the room. Cambria waited a moment, then approached Aurelia quietly and handed her the robe. "Come. There is much to do."

19

Aurelia followed Cambria from the room and down a series of maze-like corridors until they somehow arrived back at the baths. This time, the bath chamber was steamed with perfumed water with the scent of crushed rose and mint curling thick in the air. Cambria and two other women, both human, stripped her, guiding her into the first pool.

They scrubbed her skin with rough cloths, scouring away every trace of blood, sweat, and fear. Her arms trembled under their hands, the fresh skin on her forearm tingling as they worked around it.

When they finished, they led her to a carved bench where platters waited—fresh bread still warm from the ovens, honey dripping from combs, plump grapes, roasted meat seasoned with wild herbs. Every meal was accompanied by guilt. At that moment, her family was home gathering, stoking the fire, preparing, and roasting. Then they would serve and clean, preparing for the next meal in the evening. And here she was. Being scrubbed, dressed, and served like she was a queen.

Aurelia ate mechanically, letting the food fill the hollow place inside her until she could think without shaking. They combed her hair next, drying it with thick linen before oiling the strands until they gleamed like river-slick stone. They braided tiny wildflowers through the plaits—white and gold, petals so fragile they trembled with each breath.

Her skin was oiled and perfumed, her nails shaped and polished until they caught the candlelight. When they were finished, they dressed her in a gown of deep blue, embroidered with a pattern of sunbursts at the hem and cuffs. The fabric clung to her like water.

Cambria guided her back to her chamber and turned her to the polished bronze mirror. Aurelia stared. The girl reflected back at her did not look like the one who had huddled in Alain's bed, knotting herself smaller with each breath.

It was her eyes. Past the gleaming skin, the shimmering fabric. They were dull and sharp all at once. The acute panic of a soul drowning.

Aurelia's fingers drifted up, touching the plaited flowers. They were bent and folded, trapped until they wilted. She would not meet the same fate. Raya was satisfied to wait, but she was not. This was her second day. Tomorrow she would have her answers, and Helena promised she'd be present. *I want him dead.*

Aurelia's resolve hardened.

"You look lovely." Cambria floated behind her.

"I look like a fraud."

Cambria let out a small laugh, then schooled her expression. She hesitated a moment, then said, "Are you who they say you are?"

Aurelia let out a slow breath. "I don't know." What did she know? She'd seen the proof Alain offered, the power in her blood. But she hadn't seen or felt anything for herself.

Cambria glanced toward the door. "It's time. Alain would like you to be ready when the others arrive."

"The feast."

Cambria nodded.

"Who will attend?"

The servant shrugged. "All of them."

———

The feast hall unfolded before her like a vision half-remembered from a dream. Not one of her dreams, though. Her imagination never could've conjured something so grand. The ceiling soared so high it vanished into darkness, strung with banners stitched in crimson and gold. Massive candelabras hung like stars, their hundreds of flames bathing the room in molten light. Smoke from the wall sconces curled along the vaulted arches, gilding the carved stone with moving shadows.

Black marble veined in white gleamed under their feet. Tables stretched the length of the room, decorated with platters of roasted boar, heaps of figs and dates, wheels of cheese cracked open to reveal their soft hearts. The smell was intoxicating.

Vampires and guardians mingled without walls between them. It rattled her more than the grandeur. The guardians stood proud in ceremonial whites and deep greens. They laughed, filled their plates, and stood shoulder to shoulder with vampires as if they were kin. Aurelia could not make sense of it.

Vampires didn't eat this food, and yet they provided it in excess. They seemed to enjoy the show of it. They carried themselves with puffed-out chests and straight shoulders, not ashamed in the least of who they were.

Alain met her at the door dressed in a midnight robe and

linked his arm with hers. "You are perfection," he murmured, pulling her into the room. He held himself like a king. Not at all like the apologetic creature on the dais at the ceremony. Had it all been for show?

He guided her through the throng, and heads turned as they passed. Whispers rippled through the hall. She caught the gleam of jealousy in their too-bright eyes. Saw the tight lines at the corners of their mouths as Alain paraded her past them.

The skin between her shoulder blades prickled. That didn't feel like loyalty. Like pride. Were they all like Theo? Did Alain keep them here by coercion? She thought of Helena, how she visited other villages and found unrest. Were covens the same? Did any of them live in the peace that was promised?

Alain smiled, all teeth. Aurelia gathered her courage like a skirt around her ankles. If she looked curious, intrigued—if she flattered him—would he let his guard down? She cleared her throat. "Are they all as powerful as you?"

Alain's chest swelled slightly, his stride lengthening. "No, they are not. The first vampires—those made in the beginning —were strong, but many lacked discipline. They couldn't restrain themselves from changing others, and with every creation, they fractured their strength. Split it between themselves and the humans they turned."

Aurelia frowned. "You didn't?"

He shook his head. "I withstood the temptation and have been favored for my discipline."

They passed a tall, hawk-nosed vampire in deep red, who offered a tight nod. Alain ignored him.

"What about Augustus?" Aurelia asked.

Alain snorted. "Weak. Laps up my scraps like a dog."

Scraps. Was that what she was, then? Aurelia spotted Clémentine across the hall, her lips a brilliant ruby red.

"And her?" Aurelia pressed.

Alain barely glanced at her. "Weaker still because she believes she has my favor."

Aurelia wet her lips, heart hammering. She chose her next words carefully. "And Theo?"

The shift in Alain was immediate. He stiffened, the smile flickering for the briefest instant. "Theo is the weakest of them all."

Aurelia kept her face smooth, forcing herself to draw a slow, deep breath. Alain could hear her heartbeat and trace her pulse. She couldn't let him notice the shift.

Alain's grip tightened on her arm. "I found him whimpering on the ground like a wounded animal. He would've died within the day had I not taken pity on him."

Pity. She doubted the word meant the same thing to him as it did to her. Aurelia dared one more question. "Can vampires die?"

Alain's head snapped around to look at her fully, irritation twisting his features. "No. We are immortal." He loosened his hand, smoothing the tension away with a pat to her wrist that made her skin crawl. "You're distracting me. Come."

Aurelia nodded, her mind racing. Vampires could not die, and yet Alain had admitted that Theo was near death when he found him. Theo must have been human. But if Alain hadn't turned him . . . who had?

Alain tugged her through the crush of bodies. They stopped before a gathering of vampires along the far wall who quickly parted for him to make introductions. Their names went in one ear and out the other. Aurelia searched the crowd for—she stilled, surprised at the word that flickered through her thoughts.

Friends.

Her ribs cinched. It was too strong for what Helena and Theo were to her. Even Raya and Cambria. It was dangerous to allow that trust to build when she still knew so little. But she'd already opened the door with Helena. If she was aligned with the others, was there any point in holding back?

"Don't move." A low voice floated over her right shoulder. She knew it instantly. Her stomach dropped through her middle, and the skin on her wrist began to burn. *Theo.* "Smile at his stories, but keep listening."

Aurelia kept her gaze forward, plastering a small smile on her lips as she tilted her head, pretending to listen. Where was he? They were against the wall. There was nothing behind her besides stone and—

"Curtains," Theo murmured. "If you don't take a breath, you're going to pass out."

Aurelia dragged air into her lungs. Alain's eyes flicked to hers. She blushed, which only seemed to delight him. He continued his story, and she blew out a shaky breath, hoping he was distracted enough to ignore her.

"Alain is leaving at dawn," Theo continued. "He will try to take you with him." The floor seemed to tilt beneath her feet. Theo's voice threaded closer. "You must find a way to stay behind."

Panic rose, fast and hot. *Find a way?* Theo had been the one encouraging her to stop fighting Alain, and now he was asking her to manipulate him? She wasn't able to defy his request for a meal. She very much doubted she'd have any leverage where this was concerned.

Aurelia wanted to turn, to ask for more information, but the space behind her again felt cold. Empty. She stared blankly at Alain's profile as he laughed, spinning the end of his story to raucous applause. He slid his hand over her waist.

The feast blurred around her as Alain steered her on to another group, then another. She couldn't mention the journey, and she couldn't ask to stay once he did. If she made it apparent she wanted to be there without him, he'd cling to her more tightly. She needed an excuse he couldn't argue away.

Aurelia considered, running through possibilities and casting them all aside. Then, as she glanced down at a sprig of rosemary on a guardian's plate, the idea bloomed. Hellebore. *She could be sick.*

It wouldn't be difficult. He was well aware she'd been drained of blood over the past day, and now he offered her rich food and wine. She only needed to tip herself further over the edge.

Aurelia waited, biding her time. Smiling and nodding. When Alain's attention snagged on another group of admirers, Aurelia slipped a step to the side, finally catching sight of Helena. She wasn't far, but Aurelia couldn't leave Alain's side without attracting unwanted attention. Instead, she kept her eyes on Helena, willing her to glance over.

It felt like half the evening passed before she finally lifted her head and caught Aurelia's gaze. With a slight tilt of her head, Aurelia invited her to move. Helena was wise. She moved to another guardian, stopping for a moment of conversation before moving to the next, all the while circling closer to where Aurelia stood with Alain.

When she finally appeared near their circle, she feigned surprise and approached them both with her arms outstretched. Aurelia waited until Helena leaned in to embrace her, then whispered, "Hellebore," in her ear.

Helena pulled back, her face still smoothed into a pleasant smile. "And which do you prefer, the herbed or fruited cheese?"

20

Aurelia clutched the rough edge of the stone basin, her body heaving, torn apart from the inside out. The hellebore she'd swallowed, bitter and gritty, burned its way back up, violent and unrelenting. Her stomach convulsed again, a sharp tearing sensation, and bile splattered into the basin.

Sweat slicked her skin. Cold one moment, searing the next. Her trousers clung to her thighs, heavy with the damp. She gasped for breath, each inhale dragging the taste of vomit and sour wine deeper into her lungs.

Her head dropped, the coolness of the stone a brief mercy. The door slammed open so hard it rebounded off the wall. Alain stormed in, his face a thunderhead—silver hair wild, eyes fever-bright with rage. "What have you done?"

Aurelia couldn't lift her head. Another wave tore through her, wringing her dry, leaving her mouth and chin slick with spit.

Alain paced, his hands fisting and unfisting at his sides. "We were meant to leave by dawn!"

Helena burst through the door, skirts swirling, her face set hard. "What did you *do* to her?" she snapped, dropping to her knees and gathering Aurelia's hair at her neck.

Alain growled, "Her body is weak. I've done nothing but provide the best care."

Helena ignored him. She pressed a hand to Aurelia's forehead. "You'll have to delay. I've seen this before. It won't pass for at least a day, and she won't be fit for travel."

"Impossible." Alain slammed a hand against the wooden door.

Helena tossed him a sharp look. "You'll kill her if you force her to travel. Is that worth whatever timeline you're trying to keep?"

Aurelia sagged against Helena's side, barely able to keep her eyes open. Her skin burned, her heart fluttering.

Alain crouched, his mouth twisting. He leaned closer, sniffing—then recoiled, disgust flashing across his features. "I can't make out her scent."

"She's ill." Helena held out a hand, exasperated. "Just because you've never experienced it doesn't make it less real."

He stood, stepping back as if worried he could catch it. "If you leave her side—"

"I won't. Assign Theo—"

"Not Theo," Aurelia gasped, a flash of an idea sparking. She peered up at Alain with watery eyes. "You said he was weak."

Alain's brow twitched. "You were listening."

She nodded, her skin slick with sweat. "I always listen."

Alain's lips parted. "I assure you, Theo will do as I ask." He crouched, but didn't reach for her. "It is precisely because of his weakness that he's useful to us."

Us. That word sent her into another fit. Alain straightened, backing through the door. "Keep her comfortable. I will be back as soon as I can."

Helena nodded. He turned on his heel and stormed out, the door slamming hard enough to rattle the walls. Aurelia wanted to feel relief, but she was in too much pain. It felt as if her organs were being flipped inside out with a fork.

But she'd done it. With Helena's help, she'd accomplished what Theo asked.

Helena blew out a breath and put an arm around her shoulders. "You've impressed me twice now. That's difficult to do."

Aurelia let herself lean into the touch for a moment. Just long enough to remember she was still breathing. "Thank you."

"For which part? There's quite a lot to thank me for."

Aurelia laughed, then inhaled sharply at the stabbing pain in her stomach.

"Where did you come up with that tactic?" Helena reached for a small cloth and dipped it into the cool water of the wash-basin. "Telling him you don't wish Theo to be on watch. You put him on a pedestal while also setting his teeth on edge."

Aurelia nodded once, and the motion made her woozy. "I thought if he saw I took his word—" She curled into herself as another cramp tore through her midsection.

"Shh. You don't need to speak." Helena pressed the damp cloth to the back of her neck. "Just endure."

Aurelia suffered through the worst of it, and when her body was so exhausted she barely noticed the cramping, she drifted into sleep on a small, burning ember of triumph. She had won this battle. A small thing. A single stone tossed into the river.

But it had changed the current. She had power here. Not much, but some. That was enough to give her hope.

Aurelia slept like the dead and awoke to pounding in her head and the murmur of voices. Her lips were dry and cracked, her throat raw, but her stomach seemed to have settled. She opened her eyes, searching for the sources of the noise, and found Helena lounging in the chair near the hearth, boot propped on the low table, sipping from a chipped clay cup.

Across from her sprawled a man Aurelia did not know—fair-haired, fine-boned, with a kind of careless beauty. His tunic was unbuttoned halfway down his chest, his arm slung over the back of a chair that hadn't been there before.

Next to him . . . Aurelia's breath snagged. Theo leaned against the far wall, his arms crossed. He looked different in the casual sprawl of conversation, his face relaxed into something dangerously close to a smile. It softened the sharp lines of his mouth, carved faint grooves at the corners of his eyes.

"You're an idiot, Florent." Helena kicked her boot against the table leg for emphasis.

"It worked, didn't it?" Florent replied, flashing a grin so disarming that Aurelia almost forgot she still felt sick. "The old man never even knew it was me who switched the wines."

"You got caught."

"I *almost* got away with it," Florent corrected, holding up a finger. "There's a difference."

Aurelia pulled the blanket higher over her chest. Her body sank into the mattress, finally at peace after the hellebore passed. Empty, drained, but lighter.

Alain was gone. For how long, she had no idea, but Helena, Theo, and their friend didn't seem to be concerned. They spoke like old friends, ribbing each other, speaking plainly. It reminded her of sitting around the fire at home, and that sent a pang deep through her chest.

Theo's eyes flicked up to meet hers. A flash of something passed between them, quick and hot. What was that look? Frustration? Disapproval? She looked away first. Her cheeks burned.

"You're awake." Helena set down her cup and leaned forward. "How are you feeling?"

It took a little effort, but she pushed herself up to sitting. She didn't want to think about how she looked. With how weak her limbs felt, she was certainly a sight to behold.

Aurelia wet her parched lips. "Like I swallowed hot coals."

The man called Florent snorted. "She's tougher than you thought, eh, Theo?"

Theo glowered at him. "I didn't say—"

"Please, continue talking about her like she isn't sitting there in front of you." Helena gave Aurelia an apologetic glance. "They've lived long enough to forget their manners."

"He never had any," Theo muttered.

Florent rounded Helena's chair and walked toward the bed. "Aurelia, I don't believe we've been introduced, I'm—"

Theo pushed off the wall in a blur, stopping in front of him and barring his way. Florent scoffed. "What the hell, Theo?"

"She's heard your name." His voice was a low growl. Aurelia held her breath. What was he doing? Had he brought Florent into Alain's chamber without trusting him fully?

Florent stepped back, his jaw flexing. "Do you think I'm like the others? Seriously?"

"Like the others?" Aurelia clutched the sheets. What "others" was he referring to? And why would Theo assume they'd want to get closer to her?

Helena blew out a breath in exasperation. "It doesn't matter. I tied the wards as Alain requested, and as soon as we leave, only Theo, myself, and Alain will be free to enter.

Aurelia gaped at her. "You warded this room? You know how?" That revelation momentarily eclipsed the fact that there were only three people allowed to enter the chamber, and Theo was one of them.

Helena raised an eyebrow. "Why else do you think Alain keeps me so close?"

Tying wards. Was it possible? Aurelia had read old accounts and stories, but they were nothing more than fables in her head. Some said their ancestors' knowledge had been forbidden. Some said it had simply been forgotten. Most believed it was a fanciful tale spun to build camaraderie.

Helena leaned over her knees. "Not everything useful comes with a parade and a scroll," she said. "Some things survive quietly."

Aurelia dropped her gaze, heart hammering. If Helena could tie wards—If she could still shape the old magic—then she was dangerous in ways Alain probably barely understood.

Or maybe he understood perfectly.

Florent scrubbed his jaw. "I'm surprised he allowed you to use any of the old magic."

Theo grunted. "For once, his paranoia worked in our favor."

Aurelia looked between the three of them. With every phrase they uttered, it felt as if she'd need a week to catch up on the history that lay behind it. They were immortal. They'd probably already lived a hundred of her lifetimes.

"Alain believes himself a divine ruler," Florent nudged the edge of the chair with his boot. "Chosen by whatever gods are left to drag the covens into a new age of prosperity."

Helena scoffed. "Like Caesar. Dreaming of an empire while the ground rots beneath their feet."

Aurelia rubbed a thumb over the muscles pinching between her brows. "I don't understand. Do all of you wish to exact your revenge?"

Theo shook his head while the other two nodded.

"I want him for myself, but these two don't agree with my methods," Helena said.

Theo dragged a hand through his hair. He leaned against the wall, head bowed and brow lowered. His lashes brushed his cheeks as he wrestled with whatever he was about to say next. It broke something small and secret in her chest.

He didn't choose this. He was once a boy. A man. He once loved and lived. Now he was frozen in time, forced into servitude just as she was.

Theo finally spoke. "What will it solve? Fighting Alain will only leave a gaping hole to be filled by another leader just like him. The only way out of this is through the prophecy." He lifted his eyes to hers. "Alain doesn't want unity. He wants *dominion.*"

Helena leaned back in her chair, gaze heavy. "No vampire can rule. Not for long. Power and control are built into your very nature. Sooner or later, conquest consumes everything else."

Theo turned from Florent, his posture still imposing. "I'm not talking about ruling. Alain is wrong about many things, but he isn't wrong about this. Aurelia holds the power spoken of in prophecy, and we only need to unlock it."

Aurelia straightened, her throat burning and tight. "If you wish to use me as a tool, you and Alain are no different."

Theo bristled, his eyes dark as they wandered over her form beneath the sheets before landing on her face. "Alain and I are opposite creatures."

"Then prove it," she pleaded. "I've asked to visit with my family—"

"I allowed you to speak with—"

"Allowed?" Aurelia's jaw tightened. "I am not your pet, just as I'm not Alain's. You say you only act on his orders, and I did as you asked. I found a way to stay back while he traveled, and for what? To bow to a new master?"

Helena laughed out loud, standing from the chair. Aurelia

swallowed the lump in her throat. She hadn't meant it to be rude, but it was the truth.

Theo's nostrils flared. "I only wish to discover what the Goddess intends."

"Perhaps the Goddess intends for her to act for herself." Helena's mouth quirked into a smile.

Something warm and solid flared to life inside Aurelia. Act. That was what she needed to do. She couldn't sit in this room day after day, hoping for someone to save her. As much as she loved her family, they wouldn't get two paces inside the walls before being thrown out. The vampires here were too afraid of Alain to form any kind of resistance, and—

Aurelia froze. Theo had promised her answers, and while they'd explained some, her curiosity still itched at the back of her head. What did Alain have on Theo? Just as she opened her mouth to remind him of their agreement, Helena spoke up.

"I don't disagree, I only think you're being too passive. We can't understand the prophecy without seeing both parts. Alain doesn't keep copies of the guardians' scrolls. Your Bearers of the Balance have them, I presume?"

Aurelia nodded, her throat thickening. "Yes. My parents."

Helena gave Theo a meaningful look. "Then it's time we paid them a visit."

21

There wasn't time for Aurelia to ask any more questions before they dressed and left the manor house. They walked quickly, keeping to the woods since it was daylight. She and Helena pushed into the longhouse before anyone in the village could notice two strangers standing at her parents' door. Aurelia wore a thick cloak the color of midnight. She'd kept the hood pulled low over her face, hopeful that even if they were spotted, nobody would guess who she was. It was late, well past the dying of the fire, but they couldn't be too careful.

As they stumbled into the entryway, the first thing she noticed was that the sword was missing from above the mantle.

Aurelia again felt the strangeness of life swirling around her without the ability to catch it or make it stop. She remembered how this was supposed to look. Noticed when things were out of place.

Her father stormed out, a beam in his hand, just as he had when she returned with Fiona. Tears pricked her eyes. It was too familiar, too close to her heart, and if she was going to survive behind the walls, she couldn't let any part of her soften.

"Aurelia?" Her father lowered his hand, his chest heaving.

She didn't know the day or time, didn't remember how long it had been since she'd last stood in this place. All of it came rushing back as she bolted forward, throwing her arms around her father.

"You're here. You're here." He dropped the wooden post in his hands with a hollow clatter, repeating the words into the crown of her head. Tears streamed down her cheeks as her mother joined them, then her sisters and brother, and then behind them—

"Fiona?" Aurelia pulled back as her friend ran to her, her arms flinging tight around Aurelia's neck. She crushed her close, trembling with the effort not to weep aloud. "What are you doing here?"

"You're safe," Fiona choked out, pulling back to cup Aurelia's face. "We thought—" She broke off, swallowing hard.

"I'm safe," Aurelia whispered, finally noticing that all of them wore their day-to-day clothing. Her brow furrowed, but before she could ask what was going on, her mother herded them toward the table, already pulling down dried bread, a half wheel of cheese, anything she had on hand. Her voice wavered with frantic kindness. "Sit, eat—let me make something—"

Helena stepped between them. "I'm sorry, but there's no time."

Her mother stilled, then nodded once and stepped back from the shelves.

Aurelia drew a deep breath. "This is Helena. She's—well, she's a guardian. Not from here—"

"I come from Northern Nice, but I've lived behind the

coven walls for nearly six seasonrings," Helena interjected. Fiona and Aurelia's siblings couldn't hide their surprise, but Aurelia's parents' expressions didn't change.

Aurelia's frown deepened. This information hadn't taken them off guard. Helena had just announced that she lived with the vampires behind the walls, and it had earned zero reaction from her parents, the Bearers of the Balance.

"You know of this," Aurelia whispered.

Her father's lips pursed. "We have heard of such things."

Aurelia's chest tightened. "When we spoke of guardians leaving, disappearing without a trace, did you not think to mention it?" The grief and betrayal she'd felt in the courtyard broke wide open again. How had they buried these secrets? She didn't want to blame them—didn't want to be angry—but resentment grew in her like rising leavened bread.

Her mother shifted uncomfortably. "Why are you here, Aurelia?"

She didn't answer the question. Words built up on Aurelia's tongue until she could no longer hold them back. "Was everything you told me a lie? You hid the day of my birth, truths about our relationship with the coven. What else did you keep from us?"

Helena stepped forward and put a hand on her shoulder. She didn't need to say anything. This was not the time to seek her personal answers—they needed information on the prophecy.

When she spoke again, her voice was low and calm. "We would like to see the prophecy. There are no guardian records available behind the walls."

Her mother swallowed hard. "Did he show you their words?"

Aurelia didn't need any clarification. She understood

exactly what her mother was asking. Alain. The vampire prophecy. She nodded.

Her father crossed to the stone chest near the hearth and lifted the lid. He pulled out the wrapped bundle she'd been so familiar with as a child and set it gently on the table, then unwrapped the linen layers.

Inside lay the scroll. The parchment was thick, crackled with age. Her father took his time spreading it open. Even though they'd read it hundreds of times, everyone leaned closer. The ink was faded but still legible, the script careful and precise. Aurelia scrolled, searching for the paragraph she wanted, and began to read.

Until the Day of Light, guardians will wait. They will serve. They will protect. And when she who is sent to bind appears, they will follow.

Aurelia stared at the words, feeling their shape twist and stretch inside her chest. Follow. But where? To what end?

Her mind stumbled over it, hunting for firm ground. They were meant to follow her, but how could she lead when she had no direction? She looked up, meeting her father's gaze across the table.

His mouth was tight, his hands clenched into fists against the wood. "We were meant to wait. To protect until she came."

"And now she's here," Fiona whispered, reaching over to squeeze Aurelia's hand.

Aurelia shook her head, a lump forming in her throat. Weight seemed to drop on her shoulders, pressing her into the floor until she made an impression. She fixated on the scroll, and continued to read, willing something to jump from the text that she hadn't seen before—something that would spark understanding.

In the time of eternal twilight, Solène and Le Sombre existed in perfect harmony as one being, a union of light and dark, maintaining the delicate balance of the world created for humanity. Together, they ruled over all, a peaceful force that mirrored the beauty of dawn and dusk where their realms of light and shadow met.

Blood rushed in her ears. A rift between god and goddess. She who was sent to bind.

The gods, pleased with this balance, watched with pride. But as ages passed, even the gods grew weary of endless harmony. They teased and prodded. They planted seeds of discontent. Until the unity of Solène and Le Sombre fractured. Torn into two opposing forces— light yearning for dominion, shadow aching for life.

Le Sombre, in his grief, birthed the dark companions— vampires—cursed to thirst for what they could never truly possess. Solène pleaded for peace, but without her, Le Sombre could not see beyond his own sorrow.

The words wrapped around Aurelia like smoke. Heavy. Bitter.

There was nothing. No instructions, no clarifications. "What am I supposed to do?" she whispered. "You believe I am the one to heal, but—"

"I'm sorry." Her mother whispered. "I never wished for this burden to be yours, and I hoped by keeping it from you, you'd discover the Goddess on your own. That you would find under-standing, be drawn to your path." She gestured to the scroll. "I've studied every word. Pondered. Prayed. It speaks with confidence, Aurelia. There is no doubt in these lines."

The room fell silent. Aurelia's throat worked as she warred with the grief and frustration inside her. Why would a goddess give a prophecy if nobody knew how to interpret it? How were her parents the Bearers of the Balance and yet had no more understanding than she did?

Helena spoke up. "Maybe the action doesn't matter. Maybe the Goddess only expects us to act. Her power runs in your veins. Gods and goddesses do not wait for instruction."

Aurelia pondered this. Let it spread out in her mind like slow molasses. Raya had encouraged her to wait, to be ready. Now, Helena believed she should act. "Can we make a copy of this? Just this section?" She pointed at the lines of text.

Her mother nodded, then went in search of an empty scroll.

Aurelia turned to Fiona, her mind searching for any distraction from the impossible problem in front of her. "Why are you here at my home?"

Fiona gave her a small smile. "Come with me a moment?"

Aurelia nodded. How did Fiona always see her when she was about to crumble? She glanced at her parents for approval. When her father nodded, she followed Fiona into the room that had been hers for one night.

Aurelia ran her fingers over the smooth wood of the bed frame. Her father carved this for her, and she'd never once used it.

Fiona blew out a breath. "You don't have to do this. We could run. I'd go with you. Anywhere."

Aurelia smiled and reached for Fiona's hands. For a moment, she latched onto the idea. Running through the woods toward the tribes in the valley. Wandering through their fires, this time not only staying to the outskirts but finding a place with them.

She saw Alain's anger. His cruelty sweeping through the village, the guardians suffering for no reason because it wouldn't take long for him to find her. "I could just as much run from this as you can from the life in your belly."

Fiona squeezed her hands. They were no longer young girls who could pretend. Neither said what hung between them— the life they'd imagined, the summers by the river, the whispered futures. Aurelia pulled in a shaky breath. "How are you feeling?"

Fiona laughed softly. "Like someone replaced my body with a stranger's." She sat on the edge of the bed. "I'm scared. For both of us."

Aurelia settled beside her. "I don't understand any of this. I don't know how to fix it. I don't know what the prophecy wants from me."

Fiona bumped her shoulder against Aurelia's, a crooked smile tilting her mouth as she dropped a hand on her belly. "I don't know how to do this either. I wake up every day feeling like I'm drowning. But my body knows what to do, even when my mind doesn't." She dropped her eyes. "Maybe the power you seek is already inside of you. Growing without your knowledge." Her brow furrowed. "Maybe you don't have to understand it. Maybe it already knows what to do."

Tears stung Aurelia's eyes, and she didn't bother blinking them back. She wrapped her arms around Fiona, burying her face in her friend's shoulder. They clung to each other—not as the girls they had been, but as the fractured, unsteady women they didn't yet know how to be.

When they pulled apart, Aurelia stood, straightened her tunic, and squared her shoulders. They'd been gone long enough. While she didn't believe Alain would return that night, he had eyes and ears behind the walls. They'd already risked too much by entering the village.

Fiona stood and threaded their arms together as they walked back to the hall. "You aren't alone. We'll do everything we can to prepare. To be ready."

A chill traveled down Aurelia's spine. *Ready for what?* They re-entered the room, and Aurelia took a moment to speak with each member of her family. They were safe. She would do whatever it took to keep it that way.

"I want to help you," Aurelia whispered as she and Helena snuck from the house. She believed in Raya's words and Fiona's. They gave her strength. Hope. But the idea of sitting back and waiting for her power to manifest felt even more unbearable after seeing her family again face to face.

"Good." Helena strode beside her, steady, silent.

Aurelia didn't know what "help" meant. Helena had hinted at plans she was working on, but she hadn't shared the specifics. Would it be possible for Aurelia to do anything with Alain keeping her under lock and key?

They moved quickly beneath the cover of the trees, the sun filtering through new leaves in broken shards. Birds chirped from high branches, indifferent to the danger of their passage. Aurelia kept close to Helena's side, her heart a steady thrum in her chest.

They ducked under a twisted alder. "Why does he stay here? What does Alain have over him?" It was the question she planned to ask him, but now she likely wouldn't get a chance.

Helena didn't answer at first. They wound through a thin stretch of underbrush, sap catching on Aurelia's sleeve. When they reached the edge of the trees, Helena finally stopped, one hand braced against a lichen-covered trunk.

Helena paused. "Have you asked him?"

Aurelia shook her head. "No. I was waiting for the right moment."

"There's never a right moment with Theo."

Aurelia didn't know what to say to that. Did she mean he never answered questions about himself? Or was she referring to the way they'd disagreed in Alain's quarters earlier?

Helena looked ahead, voice barely more than a breath. "It was after a battle. Long before Alain found him. Theo was still human. Leading a patrol of warriors home, some injured, some dying. They made it to the edge of his village. He thought they were safe."

Aurelia's throat tightened.

"They entered their village to silence. No cries, no sound at all. Smoke and blood and . . . " Helena trailed off. "He was attacked before he could reach home. Bitten."

"By Alain?"

Helena let out a caustic laugh. "No. Not by Alain. His power remains intact."

Aurelia frowned. "And Theo?" Her stomach turned at the memory of the body in the woods. Which fate would she choose? Death or an eternal curse?

"Theo has not changed any human," Helena snapped.

"Then he's as powerful as Alain. So why does Theo allow himself to be ordered around? To be punished?"

Helena sighed, peering into the clearing between the trees and the walls of the coven. "Theo must not know if I tell you this."

Aurelia's pulse pounded in her ears. "I can keep a secret."

Helena worried her lower lip. "Alain took a vial of his venom. Tricked him into giving it before he was fully lucid. If Theo ever turns against him, Alain will use it against him. It's always been the leash. Not only for Theo."

They stood there in silence for a moment, Aurelia reeling.

The past blur of sunrises and sunsets clicked into place. *Alain could use his venom.* Choose to turn a human with it, strip his power.

Helena called her forward toward the walls. She held her breath as they rounded the bend toward the lower courtyard, aiming for the postern door where the kitchen servants came and went unseen.

The sun was high enough that the pathways were mostly clear behind the walls. But as they neared the covered walkway, a figure stepped from the arch into their path.

Augustus.

22

Aurelia pulled her hood further over her head just as Helena snatched up her wrist and held it tight. It was light out, and she was wearing a full cloak. Surely Augustus would think that odd.

Augustus's eyes narrowed when he caught sight of Helena. "What are you doing, skulking about?"

"Always the poet." Helena flashed a smile. "I could ask you the same thing."

Augustus glanced down at her hand circling Aurelia's wrist. "Who's this?"

"How the hell should I know? Alain asked me to retrieve her." Helena's hand tensed, and Aurelia's blood ran cold. They could not be discovered. If she were found outside of Alain's quarters, he would be notified the second he returned.

Augustus peered closer and lifted a hand, but Helena slapped it away. He hissed. "How dare you touch me?"

Helena stood her ground as he postured. "You know what will happen to you if you harm me."

His nostrils flared. The faintest wrinkle creased Augustus's brow, and he drew back slightly, as if repelled by some sour scent. His mouth curled in distaste. "Your human needs to bathe."

Aurelia's heart stuttered. Human?

Helena arched a brow, cool and unimpressed. "I'll make note of it."

Augustus studied her. Aurelia kept her gaze fixed on the ground, her breath shallow and slow. At last, he clicked his tongue against his teeth and stalked past them.

Helena waited a moment, then continued on her path. She didn't rush and didn't look back. Aurelia matched her pace, the kitchen door just ahead, the stone steps worn smooth by years of quiet comings and goings.

Helena pulled it open and ushered Aurelia inside. They hurried through the low halls, footsteps light and quick. But the closer they came to Alain's quarters, the tighter Aurelia's chest pulled.

He wasn't there. She reminded herself that the room would be empty, that she would be alone. Still, her breath shortened, and her palms began to sweat. By the time they reached the shadowed archway near Alain's door, Aurelia's heart battered her ribs hard enough to bruise.

A flicker of movement slid from the shadows, and Aurelia sucked in a breath, stalling behind Helena.

"Theo." Helena's hand flew to her chest. "Are you trying to give me a fit?"

Theo stepped out from the shadow as if he'd always been part of it, tall and rough-edged, his hair mussed. Something akin to relief cracked through Aurelia's fear, and it troubled her. She shouldn't be glad to see him. To see any of them.

But now that she knew a piece of his story, she couldn't look at him the same. He was trapped, just as she was.

Helena's shoulders relaxed. "Ran into Augustus. He caught a whiff of her and almost gagged."

Theo's mouth twitched. "Must be the hellebore. I can't scent her either." He glanced over. "Did he ask questions?"

Helena shrugged. "I told him Alain sent me. He slithered off."

Theo's gaze pinned Aurelia to the wall. "Did you find what you were looking for?"

Aurelia pressed her palms against the rough stone. What was she looking for? She banished thoughts of Alain extracting venom from Theo's fangs and instead searched for memories of the morning. Her family. The prophecy.

"No." Aurelia shook her head, hoping to hide the flush in her cheeks. Theo and Florent hadn't wanted her and Helena to leave the walls. They told them both there wouldn't be any new information from the guardians, and as much as she hated to admit it, they'd been right.

Aurelia fingered the copied scroll in the pocket of her cloak. "That's incorrect. I did find what I was looking for." Theo's eyes narrowed a fraction. Aurelia didn't balk. "I needed to see the prophecy again. To ask my questions. To know I wasn't missing something."

Theo wet his lips. "So you're right where you started."

She shook her head. She still didn't know what her next step was, but now she knew who had to take it.

It was hers.

She couldn't rely on her family or the Guardian Council or even the words of the prophecy. Her blood held power. She was born on the day of light. Though she felt like a wooden boat untied from its mooring, she was the only one who could plunge the paddle into the depths and attempt to steer.

Theo grunted. "You're hungry."

Aurelia blinked, then glanced down to find that her hand

had crept up without thinking, resting on her stomach. Heat flared under Aurelia's skin, sharp with embarrassment.

Helena exhaled. "As riveting as this conversation is, I need to return to my quarters." She jerked her chin toward Alain's door. "We'll talk later?"

Aurelia nodded as her body stiffened. Her feet refused to move.

"I'll take care of it." Theo strode forward, his stance wide and imposing. "We'll take a late meal in the study."

"Alain did say you were useful to us."

Theo's jaw twitched. "What an effusive compliment."

Helena gave Aurelia one long look—something almost like approval flashing across her features. "Don't leave her alone, Theo. If you must go, retrieve me."

He nodded, then she turned on her heel and disappeared down the corridor. Theo didn't speak. He only motioned for her to turn and then strode past her, expecting her to follow.

Aurelia pulled her cloak around her, now worried that if anyone saw her face and didn't smell her guardian blood, they'd have a more pressing problem on their hands. She lowered her chin and inhaled deeply. She couldn't smell anything out of the ordinary, but then again, she'd never understood what vampires scented in the first place.

The hall was quiet as she fell into step beside Theo, the echo of their footsteps folding into the hush of morning. Light slanted long through the windows, and the servants were likely busy preparing for supper.

"Did others go with Alain?"

Theo nodded his head, but didn't give her a specific answer. Augustus wasn't one of his companions, and she wondered who he kept close. Clémentine? She seemed to always be at his side.

Neither of them spoke as they climbed the narrow stairs.

When they reached the small study tucked behind the east wing—one of the many rooms Aurelia had never entered—Theo opened the door and let her pass first.

There was a small table and chairs in front of a set of shelves, flanked by three arching windows. Theo motioned for her to sit, then stalked out of the room.

Aurelia's heart quickened. What if someone found her here? Why would Theo leave her alone when he'd been so cautious before?

Then she remembered the way Augustus had recoiled. Hellebore. Not likely that anyone else had discovered this side effect since a guardian would never ingest it willingly. Aurelia shuddered, the ghost of a cramp passing through her stomach.

It had been worth it.

She leaned toward the glass. The window's curved frame and mottled glass fragmented her reflection, but she could still piece her portrait together. She was paler than usual, and her eyes looked rather gaunt.

There was no reason to keep staring. She leaned back in her chair and crossed her arms, glancing at the door. How long would it take for Theo to return?

She never knew what to expect when she saw him. Only that she couldn't deny she anticipated those moments. It was the strangest thing. Her body relaxed when he was near, even if he never said a word. There was a steadiness. A comfort to his presence in a room. He made silence feel like something she wanted to crawl inside.

She was lost in thought when the door opened and Theo crossed the threshold holding a tray with a carafe of both water and wine, a basket of still-warm bread, sliced pear, and a wedge of soft cheese. The second Theo set it on the table, Aurelia dove in.

Theo stepped back and stood near the window. "It was smart. To make yourself sick."

"Hm. I might've said stupid." She layered the pear and cheese on the bread and took a bite; the sweet and tangy flavors melded over her tongue. Theo's gaze slid toward her, and she looked away. Had he just paid her a compliment? "Why did you not want me to go with him?"

Theo frowned. "It wasn't a personal preference. We needed time."

Aurelia took another bite. "What did you expect we'd accomplish?"

He shifted his weight, slipping a hand in the pocket of his pants. "It doesn't matter. Helena had other ideas."

It did matter. Aurelia could barely restrain herself from asking why he wanted her to stay. Did he feel any sort of compassion for her? For her circumstance? He'd been harsh, but he'd also shown her small kindnesses.

What kind of man had he been underneath his curse? Away from Alain and the chains that held him here?

What would he have asked of her in Alain's absence? Helena had suggested they visit her family against Theo and Florent's wishes. Though he'd argued, he hadn't stopped them. Why had he been waiting for them upon their return?

She felt for the scroll in her cloak pocket. "Have you seen it? The guardian prophecy?"

Theo shook his head, and she pulled it out, setting it on the table. "It's only a copy."

Theo unfurled the scroll and scanned the text. When he was finished, he allowed the parchment to curl back into itself. He returned to the window, looking out across the grounds. "You haven't asked your question."

Aurelia stilled. The air in the room seemed to be sucked out through the cracks around the door. "Were you planning to answer?"

A muscle in Theo's jaw flexed. "Is that your question?"

Aurelia's cheeks flushed. "No, I—" She clamped her mouth closed. "I haven't decided."

Theo turned his head. "You seemed certain after the baths."

The heat in her cheeks deepened. She had been certain. She wanted to ask what leverage Alain had, but Helena had answered that for her. Now she struggled to come up with a question that seemed as imperative, or carried as much weight.

"She told you," Theo snapped.

Aurelia's lips parted. She cleared her throat. "Told me what?"

"You're a terrible liar." Theo turned his back, prowling toward the bookshelf. He pulled a book free, and the spine cracked as he allowed it to fall open in his hands.

Aurelia set down the last hunk of bread, searching for some way to explain herself. She was a terrible liar, but she didn't want to betray Helena's trust. "It was necessary for me to know what power Alain has. Helena believes we must—"

Theo slammed the book closed and whirled to face her. "Alain's power has nothing to do with the prophecy. It has nothing to do with you. Helena is a guardian. She doesn't understand this." He motioned at himself. "She is filled with plots and ideals, but the only way to break this curse is by fulfilling the prophecy."

"How?" Aurelia stood and pointed to the scroll still sitting on the table. "What instructions did you find there? Or in your prophecy?"

Theo's nostrils flared. "The Goddess expects—"

"Do not tell me what the Goddess expects. I have spent

years studying and praying, working to know of the Goddess, and my head and heart remain empty. If she will not speak to the guardians, she will not speak to a vampire."

Theo's eyes darkened. He turned and slipped the book back into place on the shelf, then moved in a blur to stand opposite her. Aurelia jolted.

"Are you finished?" He pressed his hands into the table, staring at the food still on her plate.

She set her jaw. She wouldn't let him intimidate her just because she'd said something he didn't like. "Yes."

Theo stepped back and motioned to the door. Aurelia stepped clear of her chair and moved toward it, lifting her hood. They walked in silence down the stairs and then through the corridor that led to Alain's chambers.

Her chest tightened with every step. The thought of opening the door and stepping inside made her want to heave up the food she'd just eaten. The smell of the room, the feel of the sheets. All of it made her insides squirm.

She stopped at the end of the hall, staring at the shadows flicking over the door from the lit sconces on the wall. "I don't want to go in. Even if he's not there."

Theo looked at her for a long moment. Not with impatience. Not with pity.

"Don't say it," she whispered. "Don't say that I have no choice. That I have to stop fighting him. That I'm weak because I can't find my power—"

"I never said you were weak."

She scoffed. "You may as well have." Aurelia folded her arms around herself to keep her hands from trembling. She stared at the door for a long moment, then turned to Theo. "I have my question."

Theo waited for her to continue.

Aurelia's heart seemed to lift into her throat. "Can I stay

somewhere else?" Exhaustion rolled over her in a wave. She hadn't truly slept since she'd arrived. It had been fitful, interrupted. Her body ached, and after being in her room that morning, all she wanted was to curl up in a safe place. To truly rest.

She watched Theo's face, her eyes pleading.

"Helena warded this room. It's the safest place for you."

Aurelia shook her head. "I don't feel safe." She held herself tighter. "Please."

Theo's lips twitched, then he exhaled in a rush. "Follow me."

23

Theo led her up the same narrow stairwell they'd climbed to reach the study. They passed that door and walked further down the hall, then descended three steps to a small landing. Theo pushed open the heavy door and moved to the side to let her in.

The room was small, tucked beneath the sloping curve of the outer wall. The ceiling bowed low with timber beams, rough-hewn and dark with age. Only a single window slit the far wall, just wide enough to let in a shaft of light.

The bed was plain, narrow, with a coarse blanket thrown over it. A battered chest sat at its foot. A simple chair. A desk littered with a few sheets of parchment, a dagger, a stub of a candle. No rugs. No silks. No mirrors.

It was nothing like Alain's.

Aurelia exhaled with relief and drifted deeper into the room, her boots brushing against the stone floor. She ran her fingers along the coarse weave of the blanket and touched the edge of the chair. She brushed against the simple tunics hanging from a hook on the wall—no embroidery, no silver clasps. Just rough linen.

There was nothing personal. Nothing claiming space beyond necessity.

Except—

On the desk, half-shadowed by the failing light, sat a metal ring. Aurelia picked it up carefully, turning it between her fingers. It wasn't jewelry, not exactly. Too thick. Too plain. Like a torc, but the style was different—older, heavier, with faint, swirling carvings worn almost smooth with time.

She startled when Theo's hand brushed hers. He took the ring from her, running his thumb over the edge before setting it back on the desk.

Her stomach plummeted. It was his. All of this—she was standing in his room, touching his things. "I'm sorry. I thought—"

"You can rest here." Theo stepped back, motioning to the bed.

Aurelia turned. This was where he slept. She glanced out the window, the sun bathing the gardens in gold. "Shouldn't you be sleeping?"

Theo shrugged. "I sleep when I can. I don't need as much as you."

Aurelia glanced back at the bed. It called to her, and she couldn't resist a second longer. She walked forward and sat on the mattress, then took off her boots and folded herself beneath the blanket.

Theo didn't seem to notice her. He walked to the armoire and opened it, then stripped off the plain, dark tunic he'd been wearing. Aurelia's breath caught. His body was a work of art. Like it had been sculpted. Every muscle perfectly in place, his proportions excessively masculine.

Scrolls of black lines and symbols rose from the waistband

of his trousers, snaking across his back and side. As she peered, trying to determine their meaning, she realized Theo had stopped moving and glanced up. His eyes were on her.

"Sorry, I—sorry." She stumbled over her words, forcing her gaze to the ceiling.

Theo didn't say a word. Movement in peripheral vision told her he was re-dressing, but she refused to allow herself to watch even though she desperately wanted to.

"You've never seen them before?" Theo's voice was low.

"Seen what?" It was stupid to play innocent—he'd seen her gawking—but she couldn't help herself. When he didn't respond, she swallowed her pride and turned her head. "What are they?"

Theo was fully dressed, standing in front of the armoire. "None of us know with certainty. They appear on our skin."

"All at once?"

He shook his head. "Over time."

Aurelia propped herself up on her arm. "What prompts it?"

"Some seem to be connected to . . . certain events. Others . . ." He pursed his lips as if he'd said too much.

"Are there any you're sure are linked to something?" Her curiosity itched like the oil of a stinging thistle. She wanted to know. She wanted to see.

Theo strode forward, his hand playing with the hem of his clean tunic. Heat dropped in Aurelia's middle like steaming cider.

He stopped in front of her and lifted the fabric, revealing a swirl along his side. "This."

Her fingers twitched. She wanted to reach out and run them over his skin. "What is it?" The symbol was circular with two lines spearing either end.

"That is up for interpretation."

Aurelia looked up, her mouth dry. "When did it appear?"

He wet his lips and drew a breath. "On the Day of Light."

The breath pulled from her lungs, and blood rushed in her ears. "Did it appear for all of you?"

Theo let the fabric fall, his eyes locked on hers. "No."

Aurelia forced a breath as Theo took a step back. He stalked back to the desk. Aurelia tried to watch, to see what he was doing, but his actions were blocked by his frame.

It was quite a long moment, and Aurelia's eyelids began to droop. What did it mean that a symbol had appeared on Theo's skin the same day she was born? Did it have anything to do with her or was it a mark from the goddess? Could vampires be chosen as she was? What would he be chosen for?

Aurelia struggled against the weight in her head drawing her toward sleep. She had so many questions. "Have you ever tried to find the vial Alain keeps?" she asked with a yawn.

When he spoke, Theo's voice seemed closer than she expected. *When had she closed her eyes?*

Something on the bed moved. A blanket? It didn't frighten her. Not in the least.

"Yes."

———

The first thing she registered was warmth. Not the biting heat of fever or fire, but a soft, golden light spreading across her skin like honey. Her limbs were heavy with rest, the blankets cocooned around her waist. No ache in her throat. No tremble in her hands. For once, her body was at peace. Completely, utterly still.

Then she registered pressure. A hand lay on her shoulder, but it didn't frighten her. She stirred, a sound catching in her throat. The hand tightened, pulling her up from the depths of sleep.

Aurelia's eyes blinked open. The room was dim, late afternoon light pooling on the floor like spilled milk. She looked up and found him. Theo stood beside the bed, one hand on her, the other braced on the carved bedpost. His expression was tense, his jaw tight, his eyes scanning the door as if he were expecting it to open.

She was in his room. Lying in his bed. "I—" she started and faltered. How long had she been sleeping?

Theo didn't look at her. "You need to get up." She sat slowly, the blanket falling to her hips. Her skin tingled where his hand had been. "Alain is here."

Theo pulled her cloak from the nearby chair and tossed it toward her. *When had she taken that off?* "Hurry." His voice frayed at the edges.

She stood quickly, wrapping the cloak around her shoulders, her feet cool against the stone floor. She pulled on her boots and followed him toward the door. Theo touched the small of her back to guide her through. The pressure of his hand was brief—seconds, maybe less—but her stomach flipped.

She felt like she'd slept for days. Her body was loose, no longer wound so tight she thought it might snap. She hadn't dreamed or tossed and turned. It was blissful.

"Too slow." Theo pulled her against his chest, scooping her legs off the floor and running to the stairs. Could she call it running? She clung to his neck as he descended to the bottom level and tore down the hall.

She sucked in a breath as he set her down in front of the door. "Get inside. Now."

She swallowed hard, her heart racing. Theo glanced down, and she realized her hands were still linked around his neck. She dropped them and gripped the door handle. "Thank you."

Theo nodded and then turned to press himself against the

stone wall. As if he'd been standing watch the entire time. He straightened his back, lifted his head, and stared down the vacant hall. She'd never seen anything quite so lonely.

Aurelia stepped in and closed the door behind her. She stood for a moment in the quiet and let out a long, slow breath as tension coiled again through her muscles. The room felt too still, too neat. She hung her cloak on the hook behind the door, dropped her boots at the foot of the bed, and mussed the coverlet, adjusting the blanket she hadn't disturbed. It had to look like she'd slept here. That she'd stayed.

She pulled the brush from the vanity and ran it through her hair, untangling what she could. Her eyes lifted to the mirror, catching the flush still in her cheeks. She no longer looked gaunt and pale.

Something had shifted in her since she'd left with Helena that morning. Whether it was reading the prophecy or—

Her eyes flew wide. The prophecy. Had she picked it up? The last she'd seen of it, it was sitting on the table in the study.

Aurelia bolted for the cloak and rummaged in the pocket. Nothing. Her heart slammed against her ribs. If anyone found that—if a servant read the words or worse, threw it out with the trash—

A voice rang out in the hall. Bright, exalted, filling the halls with triumph like a returning emperor. Aurelia ran to the window and sat in the chair, pretending to admire the gardens. Alain would hear her heart racing, would note the pulse in her neck. She closed her eyes and drew a breath, held it, then released. She repeated this three times before the door swung open behind her.

Alain entered in a rush of cool air and trailing velvet. His silver hair was damp from the mist, eyes lit with some private glee. He looked at her like a prize he'd come to collect.

"Aurelia." He came forward, hands outstretched, voice rich with false warmth. "You've been waiting for me."

It felt as if she were in a constant time loop. He'd said that before.

Bile rose in her throat, but she stood from the chair. Helena's words ran through her head, lowering her hackles. She was not alone in this, not anymore. "I didn't know when you'd return."

He smiled and touched her cheek. She didn't flinch. Not anymore. That was part of the game.

"I found it." His fingers traced her jaw. "What I set aside all those years ago. Kept safe. For this moment." His thumb pressed beneath her chin, lifting her gaze to his. "For you."

Something coiled in her stomach. "I'm glad you are pleased." *You're a terrible liar.*

He leaned closer, his breath brushing her ear. "You don't know how long I've waited. How long I've planned." His hand slid down her arm, wrapping around her wrist. "We're nearly there. All that's left is you."

Vampires are possessive. They call it loyalty, but it looks more like ownership.

"Come to me," Alain murmured. He reached behind her and pulled the curtains closed. "This is a special occasion, is it not?" He pulled her to him, his face now cloaked in shadow, and pressed his fingers into the small of her back.

How different it felt from Theo's. She longed to cry out, to catch his attention in the hall. To go with him back up the stairs and curl up in his blankets.

"I want you to give it to me," Alain whispered. Aurelia froze. Was he going to do this every time he returned? "Your blood. Not because I take it. Because you offer it."

Her throat tightened. She stared at the ceiling, willing her soul to separate from her body. Could she hope for another distraction in the hall?

"Do you believe in the prophecy, Aurelia? Do you believe you are light?"

Her breath came in ragged gasps. She nodded once, and Alain smiled against her cheek. He pulled back to look at her, then lifted a hand to move her hair, baring her throat. "Ask me to take it."

Aurelia trembled, the lump in her throat so thick, she could barely breathe. "Will you take my blood?"

Alain's eyes flared. "Beg me."

"Please. Take it. I want you to have it."

He nearly purred, "Good girl." He dipped his head, and his fangs slid into her neck with terrifying grace. No struggle. No violence. Just a sickening intimacy, the slow pull of her blood leaving her, warmth draining from her limbs.

Her body swayed, traitorously pliant. Her head dropped back as his glamour washed over her. Just when she thought she was going to be sick, Alain pulled back. He kissed the bite once, softly.

"Two weeks," he whispered. "At the blood moon. We will fulfill the prophecy, and you will be bound to me."

Her head was fuzzy, the words barely landing before slipping away. Bound? The blood moon? What was he talking about?

A knock sounded at the door, and hope bloomed in her chest. Theo. Had he heard something? Felt it?

Alain brushed his lips over her cheek and walked back to open it.

Not Theo.

Of course it wasn't him. What was wrong with her? She was hoping for another vampire to rescue her? She was going insane. Latching onto any small kindness.

Helena peered over Alain's shoulder. When she saw the expression on Aurelia's face, her expression hardened.

"I asked you to take her after we shared a meal." Alain's voice was stern.

Helena kept her eyes on Aurelia. "I have a matter to attend to. It must be now."

Alain's grip tightened on the door, but he eventually stepped back and motioned for Aurelia to join Helena. "You weren't here when I arrived."

"Theo was standing watch." Helena turned, scanning the hall.

"I dismissed him." Alain smiled. "Make sure she's back as soon as possible."

"Of course." Helena waited for Aurelia, then started off down the corridor. Neither of them spoke. The halls were bustling now, vampires waking up for the evening. They passed without fanfare, descending to the quiet, forgotten room near the cellars. Aurelia's legs trembled with each step.

Inside, the brazier burned, casting them in amber. Helena shut the door behind them and bolted it.

She turned. "Did he hurt you?"

Aurelia tried to answer. But all that came was a sob. The first nearly cracked her ribs. The second folded her in half. The third tore through her like ripping fabric.

She didn't know when Helena moved, but suddenly she was there, steady hands guiding her to the bench, gripping her shoulders. "Breathe," she whispered. Aurelia shook her head, unable to speak. "I'm going to gut him."

"No," Aurelia gasped. "Not yet. I can still—"

"Still what?" Helena's voice was sharp now. She pulled a knife from her belt.

Aurelia looked at her, their faces inches apart, her breath coming in shallow, uneven pulls. "I let him. I told him to feed. If this is going to work, he needs to think of me as loyal."

Helena's jaw tightened. She sat back slowly, the knife resting between them.

"As long as he holds half the coven in his grip, we have no recourse. You said he holds their venom. He must keep it somewhere."

Helena shook her head. "They've searched. All of them. He's probably buried it or left it in another part of the world."

Aurelia considered this. "No. I don't think so." She dragged in a deep breath. "Think of how he treats me. He wants me near him at all times. He wants me watched. And the others, Theo, Florent—he keeps them close. He's like a dragon, surrounding himself with the treasures he's collected."

Helena chewed on her lip. "But he left to find something. An item he needed."

Aurelia deflated. That was true. He'd been gone for over an entire day, which meant he must've traveled far at the speeds vampires were capable of. "I don't know. Maybe that theory doesn't hold."

Helena rose and rolled up her sleeves. She reached for a clean set of instruments. "It's worth looking. You have more access to him than any of us have."

Aurelia shivered at that thought, then offered her arm. There was no mark left from their first session. Helena held her gently, turning her hand palm-up, then picked up the blade. "I will not take much. Just enough to keep him satisfied."

The kiss of metal split skin. Aurelia hissed softly as the blood welled, then fell—slow, rhythmic drips—into the waiting vial.

Aurelia swallowed, focusing on anything but the slow ache building in her arm. "I will search for it."

"It's dangerous, Aurelia."

"I know." Danger had frightened her a few days ago, but now it seemed inevitable. She was already in danger every second of her life there in the manor house. "Whatever Alain's plans are, in two weeks' time, he needs me alive."

"Death is not what I'm concerned with," Helena murmured.

Aurelia swallowed hard. "Can we convince him I must be healthy? Strong? He already believes I must be cared for."

"I will do my best. Alain also believes you are to submit to him. I'm not sure he'll see the exclusivity of either prerogative." Helena removed the vial and pressed a bandage to the wound, then re-sterilized the blade with a cloth soaked in spirits. The smell stung Aurelia's nose. "If we find the venom, we break his hold on Theo, Florent, Clémentine, and the others."

"Clémentine?"

Helena nodded. Her mouth tightened as she fit the stopper into the second vial. "But it won't be enough to take his leash." She twisted the vial between her fingers. "The prophecy demands the curse be broken. Entirely."

"I don't know how the Goddess intends to heal her rift with Le Sombre."

Helena drew a long breath. "I believe the work of Le Sombre must be undone. Vampires were born from shadow. They don't belong here. They never did. The prophecy states that the light must submit, but don't you believe the guardians have submitted long enough? How long must we wait? How long must we serve when vampires do not treat us as equals?" The fire threw shadows across Helena's face, highlighting the lines of fury etched in her brow.

Aurelia chose her next words carefully. "But if the prophecy speaks of binding light and dark—"

"Think of it." Helena held up the knife. "Binding only

begins after the threat is broken. You don't bind your hand to a blade while it's still cutting you."

Aurelia's mind flitted back to evenings in the kitchen with her mother. The smell of onions and crushed herbs. She'd been small, barely tall enough to see into the clay bowl, when her mother showed her how to blend the oil of a pressed olive with sharp vinegar. "They don't want to hold each other, not without help." She'd added a spoonful of ground mustard seed, then stirred, slow and steady, until the liquid thickened, golden and smooth.

Aurelia had only thought of flavor then. But now, the memory struck deeper. Light and dark couldn't bind on their own. Something had to make them hold. "What of our covenants?" she asked.

Helena scoffed. "The vampires broke theirs first. We no longer live as the Goddess intended. She will inflict her consequences."

Aurelia bit her lip. She didn't speak the thought rising inside her. Theo didn't choose this. He had lost everything, been turned without consent, and chained ever since. What of vampires like him? Who hadn't abused the covenant? Who had suffered and were suffering with no hope of death?

Helena leaned forward, tilting the vial, watching the blood swirl. "There's power in this. Not just for them. It can't be only for them." Aurelia stared at her blood, hypnotic and dark. Helena's voice was low. "Your blood is the key, I'm sure of it. It awakens something in them. There has to be more."

Aurelia said nothing. Doubt licked at her spine like cold fingers. But she nodded, agreed, then silently made herself a vow. Find the venom. Free the ones chained by it. Strip Alain of everything he'd stolen. And when the time came, decide for herself what the prophecy truly meant.

If she found an answer, Helena would stand by her side. She was sure of it.

24

The days passed in soft-footed silence. Aurelia woke, dressed, and smiled when expected. She kissed Alain's cheek when he leaned close. She laughed at the right moments during meals, asked about coven politics, and feigned interest in his speeches.

It was exhausting. But necessary.

Alain was growing skittish. Not suspicious, not yet—but something near it. His touch lingered longer than it used to, as though checking the seams of her mask for cracks. She gave him none. She played the part flawlessly. But it meant she had to move more carefully. No stolen moments. No risky glances.

And no Theo.

She hadn't seen him since Alain's return. Not in the corridors, not at meals, not even in the periphery of Alain's ever-present entourage. It was like he'd vanished from the house entirely.

The absence carved itself deeper with every hour.

At least she had Helena, and together they were tireless. They searched three new wings—mostly unused storage rooms, rotting scroll vaults, a half-collapsed wine cellar. The dust was so thick in places it made her eyes swell. Aurelia kept waiting for a flicker of something. A sealed drawer, a hidden room. But there was nothing.

"We're looking for a shadow in a house full of them," Helena muttered as they left the southern wing. Her braid was loose, her jaw tight with frustration. Aurelia could say nothing to buoy her up.

All she could do was watch.

She mapped the rooms Alain frequented, cataloged his routine, his habits, the small drawers he used, the clothing he chose. She went through each item in his armoire and waited for a moment to search the clothes he wore. But Alain never changed into a robe when he bathed, and she was too frightened to get close to him when they were alone.

On days when Helena did not come to collect her for blood letting, they devised ways to communicate. Slivers of wax sealed in the hem of Aurelia's shawl. Knots tied into the fringe of Helena's tunic—two meant "meet at the window after second meal," three meant "not safe." They passed messages in discarded parchment. Scratched quick symbols into the soot at the edges of the fireplace. Every movement had meaning. Every glance was a risk.

Each time Aurelia passed the narrow stairwell at the end of the hall from Alain's quarters, she paused. During the hours she spent in her room alone, she calculated distances and rooms she knew in the castle. One in particular.

Theo's room was one floor up, south-facing. He had to be almost exactly above her.

After nearly a week, her worry made her bold. That night, as she sat across from Alain at the supper table, she stirred her stew until the broth turned cloudy. She'd gotten used to him watching her. To the pleased look in his eyes as she took what he offered.

"Is everything alright with the coven?" she asked.

Alain looked amused. "Of course. Have I given you any reason to doubt?"

She gave him her most pious look. "It seems many of those you rely on have been missing. I haven't seen Clémentine in days. Nor Augustus or . . . Theo."

The air seemed to drop in temperature.

Alain stiffened in his chair. He turned his head slowly, his eyes narrowed to slits. "Have you not?"

She shrugged lightly, feigning carelessness. "It seemed odd. They're all typically at your side."

His smile thinned. "Clémentine passed us in the hall yesterday, and Augustus came to the door not two days past."

Aurelia blinked. "How careless of me. I must've forgotten."

Alain watched her, his fingers steepled in front of him on the table. "Theo has asked for other assignments that take him beyond the walls."

She nodded and dropped her gaze back to her bowl, heart thudding. "Well. I hope that hasn't been inconvenient for you."

Alain clicked his tongue. "Not in the least."

———

Two days later, Helena unrolled her instruments in the basement cellar. "I spoke with them."

Aurelia blinked, trying to make sense of her admission. "You spoke with whom?"

"Theo. And Florent." Helena wiped the crook of her arm with a soaked cloth. "I had to. We're not getting anywhere like this."

Aurelia's eyes widened. They'd agreed not to say anything

since it was such a sensitive subject. That and they didn't want to get their hopes up. "And?"

Helena scoffed. "You know Theo."

The blade hovered, clean and sharp. Aurelia turned her face away as Helena made the incision. She was getting used to the sting, but she still didn't like to watch.

"I thought it might be good to know how it might be stored. I wondered if either of them had seen the vials—"

"And?"

"They haven't. It seems the collection process is quite painful." Helena fit the glass vial beneath the wound.

"You don't say."

Helena shot her a look.

Aurelia's mind spun. Alain must keep it in something strong. Sealed.

Without warning, an image flashed in her mind. A talisman, the one her father had worn around his neck. A metal ring tied to a leather cord. He never took it off.

"What if he keeps it on him?" she asked aloud, staring at the dripping blood.

Helena didn't respond right away. When she did, her voice was low. "That would be inconvenient."

"I know." The thought of searching Alain, touching his body, and feeling through his clothes, turned her stomach. Would it even be possible without Alain catching on?

Aurelia's head was beginning to fog. Helena adjusted the vial. "It's certainly one place we haven't searched. I doubt Theo and Florent have tried. They've never had access to him the way you do."

He did lie with her in bed. Sometimes he slept. Had she ever seen him change or drop his used clothes on the floor?

"I'll find a way to search him." Aurelia's lips drew into a thin line.

Helena paused, glancing up. "He touches you more now."

Aurelia looked away. "Yes." Neither of them said what it cost.

Helena sat back on her heels and reached for another vial, capping the full one and sliding it into the wooden case beside her. "If you find the venom—if we destroy it—he'll know. Maybe not right away, but soon."

"And then?"

Helena hesitated, as if weighing the next words. "Then we'll see what he really is. When he has nothing left to control."

Aurelia nodded. She could already imagine it. The unraveling. The rage. The way Alain would lash out the moment his illusions of power dissolved. Perhaps she already knew what he was beneath the layers of power he'd created for himself.

"But we need to go further," Helena added. "You know that, don't you?"

Aurelia's brow furrowed. "Further?"

Helena didn't meet her gaze. She pressed a bandage to the wound, then cleaned the scalpel with care. "Alain is the worst of them. But he's not the only one."

The fire crackled in the brazier. Aurelia's breath felt tight in her chest. She didn't like hearing this. Knowing that other guardians were suffering.

Helena stood, walking to the small shelf near the corner where the blood vials were kept. "They meet with him. Claim civility. But underneath? They're still bound to the curse. Still ruled by it. Just because they've polished their cages doesn't mean they aren't monsters."

Aurelia shifted on the cot, her body heavy with blood loss, but her thoughts sharper now. "So many of them didn't choose this."

"They didn't." Helena turned, her expression cool. "But

does that make them safe? What happens when they hunger and the rules slip? You've seen it—how close to the edge even Theo lives."

Aurelia flinched, and Helena softened her tone. "I'm not condemning. He's different. But he's not *free* of it. None of them are. Not really."

Aurelia stared at the floor, her heart heavy. "So what are you saying?"

Helena took a long breath. "I'm saying . . . we can't be distracted. We have to look at this situation logically. Be willing to sacrifice if necessary."

The words hung between them. Aurelia's fingers curled into the thin blanket. She opened her mouth to clarify what sacrifices she was referring to when the door slammed against the wall.

Theo stormed in. He barely glanced at Aurelia, then went straight for Helena. "You let her go looking for it?" His voice was a low snarl.

Helena didn't back down. "It was her idea."

"I wonder where she got it." Theo's eyes cut to Aurelia then —sharp and furious—and she felt it like a gust of heat under her skin. He glanced down at the bandage on her arm. His nostrils flared, and his eyes dilated.

He could smell it. Her still oozing blood.

Theo's throat worked. "You're using her. She's bleeding herself dry, playing games with Alain, risking everything, and you're acting like she's one of your little test subjects."

"She's not *mine*," Helena hissed, stepping closer. "She's the prophecy's. Or have you forgotten?"

"I remember every damn line. Do you? When the earth sighs with shadow—"

"Don't quote it to me." Helena gave him a look of disgust.

"You must need to hear it because you still won't hear the

meaning," he growled. "She's meant to bind, not be your huntress."

"And what would you rather we do? Bow? Wait? Let Alain drain her dry and parade her to the covens like some gifted bride? Is that your version of the prophecy?"

Theo looked like he wanted to rip something from the air and hurl it into the fire. His jaw flexed. "I would rather she live."

"And I would rather she—"

"That's enough," Aurelia snapped. She pushed off the cot and planted her hands on her hips. Both of them turned toward her. "You speak of me like I'm not standing here. You're just as bad as Alain."

Theo bristled, and Helena pursed her lips.

Aurelia drew a breath and continued. "You're right that we don't yet understand how the prophecy will be fulfilled, but this is not your burden." She locked eyes with Theo. "This plan was set in motion because I believe no one deserves to be shackled. If I don't act, how can the Goddess work through me?"

Theo's mouth twisted like he swallowed something bitter. "She can't act through you if Alain slits your throat." His voice snapped across the room. Regret flashed in his expression before his jaw clenched and he turned to stare at the wall.

Aurelia wet her lips. "I don't believe he will. He needs me. He's drunk on the idea of this power, and he believes I'll give it to him. I'm the only person safe from his wrath."

Theo's hands had clenched at his sides, so tight his knuckles blanched. "You don't know that."

She searched his face, but he wouldn't look at her. And that —more than his words—made something twist in her chest. Did he think her weak? Was he concerned for her or for what she could do for him?

"Do we know anything?" The words weren't meant for him. They were just an exhale of the doubt she couldn't kill.

She didn't know enough. Helena was so sure, so convinced that her path was the right one, but Aurelia felt like chaff blowing in the wind. Though Helena hadn't stated it explicitly, Aurelia thought she understood her meaning. She didn't trust the vampires. Didn't believe they were all worthy of saving.

What did she believe?

She thought of the scroll she'd left on the table. "Did you pick up the prophecy? I left the scroll in the study—"

"I have it."

Aurelia nodded. Good. That was good. Her skin itched with frustration. What was she missing?

Theo dropped his eyes, then scrubbed a hand over his jaw. "I don't like it."

"You don't have to like it." Helena turned back to the table, wrapping the knife back in the cloth. "You should be used to that by now."

———

The meat on Aurelia's plate bled into the fig preserve, staining the edge of the silver. Aurelia pushed it around gently, chewing slowly enough to keep from choking. Her body wanted to revolt at the scent of blood-warmed wine, but she smiled as Alain spoke, fingers curled loosely around her goblet.

It had taken her three days to set this up. After pondering in her room after her conversation with Theo and Helena, she made another decision. A small plan she put into action on her own. While she'd studied the guardian prophecy, she'd only read the vampire's version once. She hadn't spent any time dissecting the words. She needed to get her hands on it, but more than that, she needed to talk with someone who had studied as she had.

She laughed at a joke she didn't hear, nodded at the elder vampire across from her with practiced grace, then turned slightly, letting her shoulder brush Alain's.

"Something's been troubling me." Her voice was soft, low enough for just the two of them.

Alain tilted his head. His fingers stopped drumming on the table.

She let the pause stretch—just long enough to bait his curiosity. "The prophecy."

"Which one?" he asked, though his smile already curled in satisfaction.

"There are two, aren't there?" she murmured. "The guardian one I know. But the vampire one you showed me, I would like to learn more about it. You've only shown it to me once."

Alain's posture straightened. Across the table, Augustus stilled.

"There are reasons for that," Alain said, and there was a quiet thrill in his voice. "The meaning has always been reserved for those closest to the line."

Aurelia lifted her gaze. "I want to understand what it means—*all* of it."

Alain's eyes gleamed. "A scholar, then?"

She offered a faint smile. "Not exactly. But I believe there is more at work than what I've been taught. And if I'm to play my part, I need to see the whole board."

Augustus made a derisive sound. Alain ignored it. "The text is older than most of the covens combined. It's been interpreted a hundred different ways. And misinterpreted a hundred more."

"What language was it written in originally?" she asked.

Alain hesitated. Then, with a dismissive wave of his hand, he said, "A dead dialect. Almost no one reads it. It's been transcribed, decoded, and annotated for generations."

"If it's so obscure," she pressed, "how do you know it's accurate?"

Alain stiffened just slightly. "Because I've studied it longer than anyone still walking this earth." He plucked a grape from her plate. "You don't need to worry about accuracy, my dear. Worry about alignment. Timing."

He rolled the grape between his fingers, then crushed it, dropping it on the table.

Aurelia swallowed. This was proving more difficult than she'd anticipated. Of everyone in the coven, only Theo had studied like she had. Pored over symbols and scraps of old verses in the hours no one else was watching. She needed time with him.

Her pulse quickened. Purely to study. Not because she found herself looking for him anytime she left Alain's quarters.

Alain leaned in. "The prophecy culminates in convergence. Shadow and light bound in one vessel. The blood moon marks the hour. Everything in motion bends toward it."

"Why the blood moon?" she asked.

Alain smiled, pleased to be focused back on something he was passionate about. "Because it is the only celestial event when light is swallowed by shadow yet neither vanishes. Both remain—straining, circling, layered atop one another." The words had rhythm. She wondered how many times he'd rehearsed them.

"But even then," he went on, "the eclipse ends. Light reasserts itself. The world tips again."

Aurelia nodded slowly, but her mind was far ahead of his monologue. She tilted her head just enough to let her hair fall slightly across her cheek. "Then I think I ought to learn it.

Don't you?" She dropped her eyes to her plate. "I believe there is power there, something I haven't learned to access."

Alain turned toward her fully now, the gleam of candlelight glinting off his rings. "Power?"

She nodded, tugging on the hook she'd just laid. "I don't know if I can find it on my own. Is there anyone who has studied? Who could teach me?"

Alain stiffened, and she quickly continued.

"I know you know more than anyone," she added. "But I doubt you have time to spend in the library when you're so busy. So needed. I only want to be prepared, the strongest I can be. Not fumbling in the dark."

He didn't speak for a moment. Then he leaned back in his chair, exhaling in a rush. "Augustus will begin your training tomorrow."

Aurelia inclined her head, willing her heart to stay steady.

Augustus frowned. "Wouldn't Theo be—"

"Theo can attend," Alain snapped. "But he will not be alone with her."

Aurelia forced herself to keep breathing evenly. "If that's what you think is best."

Alain leaned closer. "I want you powerful, Aurelia. I want the coven to *tremble* when they see what we've become."

Her skin crawled at the gleam in his eyes, but inside she clung to a newfound confidence. She could play this game and play it well. They would tremble. Of that she was becoming more certain by the day.

25

The library smelled of aged parchment and old wood. Aurelia trailed her fingers along the edge of the table as she entered, noting the tall iron sconces and the thick velvet drapes pulled half-closed against the midday light.

The library was colder than she expected. The windows, tall and narrow, let in dull gray light. It was raining today, not that she would be able to enjoy the weather had it been sunny and mild.

Aurelia stood before the center table, its surface cleared save for a single spread scroll and a few others piled near Theo's elbow. He stood, coat half-unfastened, sleeves rolled to his forearms.

Augustus paced near the hearth, arms crossed, every line of his posture coiled with disdainful control. "Sit. We have limited time."

Aurelia moved to the end of the bench closest to the table's corner. Theo glanced up. He didn't speak, but when he leaned over to adjust the scroll, his knuckles brushed against the edge of her sleeve. Barely a breath. It sent a flash of heat through her. *Had he done that on purpose?*

"This was transcribed from the Eastern covens," Augustus said. "They preserved the oldest oral traditions, though some accounts were overly sentimental."

Theo's mouth twitched, though he said nothing.

Augustus cleared his throat as he leaned over and began to recite. Wonderful. She was going to receive an oratorio.

"When the earth sighs with shadow,

She shall rise, born of light eternal, marked by dawn that never sets.

Her blood shall flow as the river binds the forest and the mountain,

Uniting what was severed—

Light and darkness bound as one,

Blood to blood in death,

Blood to lips in life.

To seal the light, the darkness must know itself;

To seal the dark, the light must submit."

Despite the caustic reading, the words settled into her like an impression on soft clay.

Theo's hand moved across the page to gesture to a line of symbols beneath the verse. His voice was quiet. Controlled. "The early covens believed the blood moon marked the threshold. The moment where submission and knowledge—light and dark—could no longer be kept apart."

Aurelia nodded. "You believe they are equal forces?"

Augustus answered before Theo could speak. "No, of course not. How could they be? If even a god and goddess couldn't stand in balance, how could we achieve this as the cursed?"

Aurelia's hands clenched in her lap. "You believe one must—"

"Submit." Augustus tapped the last line. "Obviously."

Theo spoke carefully. "There are alternate interpretations."

Augustus turned toward him, one brow arched. "You mean the diluted readings. From guardian scribes who wept over harmony as they gave their blood freely?"

"They believed balance was the goal." Theo fixed his eyes on the scroll. "Not conquest."

"Balance is weakness," Augustus replied. "Dominance sustains us. Harmony sedates."

Aurelia exhaled through her nose as Theo's fingers brushed another glyph. His hand was large, masculine, and she knew exactly what his hand felt like against her skin.

Theo pursed his lips. "Some accounts say 'submit' meant surrender of fear. Others—"

"Speak carefully," Augustus warned.

The silence that followed was so thick it pressed against her lungs. Aurelia cleared her throat. "If the prophecy is about union—true union—then maybe both sides are changed. Not simply overtaken."

Theo glanced at her, just once, his expression unreadable.

Augustus looked at her the way one might study a tool. "You're already changed. The blood moon will complete that process. Until then, your task is obedience."

Theo's jaw flexed.

Aurelia folded her hands, outwardly calm. Inside, something flared.

She let her gaze drift down to the symbols on the parchment, then to Theo's hand still braced near the corner. His fingers rested an inch from hers.

Her heart leapt into her throat as she pretended to lean in to get a closer look. Her hand slipped against his. She waited for him to pull back, but he didn't.

Aurelia inhaled slowly, trying not to shake. She didn't

know what it meant, what she was trying to say, but she knew it meant *something*.

Augustus sighed in annoyance. "Reread the words. That will give you enough to think about for today."

She nodded once and took her time, the words blurring before her. Theo's finger moved slowly against hers. Aurelia let the touch flow through her until the heat was unbearable. She stepped back from the table, spine straight. "Thank you." She nodded at both men, then turned and strode from the room.

———

The library was quieter in the mornings. Aurelia arrived each day early, hoping Theo might already be there. He never was. So, she stood by the window, watching the sky bleed from rose to gold.

When they began the lesson, it was all ritual: the laying out of texts, Augustus reciting translated verses like prayers.

But when Theo spoke. His voice was low, pitched for her alone. "Her blood shall flow as the river binds the forest and the mountain." He traced the ancient script with one long finger. "It's not just metaphor. Rivers erode. They change the land they pass through."

Aurelia shivered. "And the forest?"

"It's shelter. Shade. Refuge."

"And the mountain?"

"Endurance," he said. "But only until it breaks."

She swallowed, her throat dry.

One afternoon, when Augustus left to retrieve a scroll from the archives, Theo stepped closer. His arm brushed hers. "Are you getting what you wanted?" he murmured, his eyes trained on a display of navigational instruments.

"Almost."

Theo didn't step back. The silence pressed between them like a held breath, not broken until the creak of a door sent them apart like sparks snapped from a flame.

———

On the fourth day, Alain kept her late. Augustus sat in the corner, silently brooding. Theo was at the center table, sleeves rolled again, fingers stained with ink. His hair was messier than usual, and the sight of it made her stomach swoop.

She sat, and he handed her a parchment with a word from the original text highlighted in red. *Sangere.*

"Does it mean blood?" she asked.

"Yes. But not just blood. *Offering. Oath.*"

Their fingers brushed as she passed it back. A shock of energy shot up her arm, and she let out a puff of air.

Theo's eyes flicked up, his lips parting. Aurelia buried her head in the next scroll.

Later, when Augustus droned on about ancient vampire hierarchies, Theo whispered, "You have ink on your cheek."

Aurelia froze. He reached up and with his thumb, brushed beneath her cheekbone. His touch was light. A single stroke.

She couldn't breathe for ten full seconds.

That night she lay in bed wracked with guilt. She was supposed to be studying, learning, and she was. But she couldn't get Theo out of her head. He, a vampire who believed in the prophecy. Who had a mark on his skin from the day Soléne promised them. The day meant to usher in the end of the curse.

All of it made Alain's attention bearable knowing she had the hope of seeing Theo each morning. That he'd teach her something new, listen to her ideas, touch her without expectation.

Logically, she understood that he was just as dangerous as Alain. But reasoning held no power the second she stepped inside that room.

Helena accompanied her to the library the next morning, and they were nearly to the door when Alain stepped into their path.

Aurelia froze. His eyes were too bright. His smile too smooth.

"There you are." His gaze swept her from head to toe. "You've been hiding in books all week. I was beginning to think Theo had stolen your attention."

Aurelia forced a polite smile. "Only what was necessary for study."

"Necessary," Alain echoed, then reached out and brushed a finger against her cheek. "Well. Tonight, you will have no need to study." Her stomach clenched. "We're holding a ball to celebrate the convergence. The moon is close now, and all of us need to turn our thoughts heavenward."

Helena's posture shifted, tension drawn like a bowstring. "Should she not conserve her energy?"

Alain turned toward her with that same teeth-baring smile. "Oh, Helena. I thought you believed in forging power through joy." His gaze snapped back to Aurelia. "You'll look beautiful. I've already arranged it."

Her skin crawled, but she nodded. "Of course."

He stepped closer, and something in his presence *shifted*. She'd grown used to his hands, to the chill of his closeness, but this was worse. There was a wildness behind his eyes, a barely leashed fervor. "I want them all to see what I've built," he murmured. "What I've claimed."

Aurelia didn't breathe until he walked past them, footsteps vanishing down the stone hall. Helena was already opening the door.

That morning's scroll was thin and delicate, tucked between a folio of lineage texts Theo had set aside.

Aurelia unrolled it gently, running her fingers across the faded ink. "This symbol." She tapped the edge of a spiral entwined with flame. "It repeats here. And here."

Theo leaned in beside her, his arm brushing hers. "Old covenant markings. That particular one is rarely translated properly."

She looked up. "Then what does it mean?"

"It represented a bond." He glanced up. A silent message. *Had he heard about the ball?*

Aurelia went still. "Hmm."

"Not feeding. Not subjugation." He glanced toward Augustus, planted in the chair, then lowered his voice. "Chosen. Between vampire and guardian. A kind of union no longer practiced."

Aurelia blinked. "But it was once allowed?"

Theo nodded. "Before the bloodlines fractured."

Her mind jumped to the memory in her mother's kitchen— the oil and vinegar refusing to bind until the mustard seed was added. A third element. An agent of cohesion.

"Something had to hold it together," she murmured.

"What?"

"Nothing," she said. "Just . . . I was taught that binding opposite forces required a third element. Something that made the union possible."

Aurelia's thoughts spun. It was obvious why Theo was telling her this, but what could she do with it? Alain spoke of a bond, planned for it. But that wasn't one she was choosing. It was a bond she needed to stop.

Augustus rose and stalked toward them. "These are myths. Whispers from a time when the covens were weak. Romantic nonsense that has nothing to do with the prophecy."

Theo didn't flinch. "The prophecy speaks of binding light and dark."

"You weren't alive when those pacts were made. None of us were," Augustus snapped.

Auralia considered this. "Was anyone? Someone here in the coven?" Guardians were reborn, but vampires . . . hadn't Alain said something about being there in the beginning? "Was Alain alive then?"

The silence grew sharp. Theo's eyes darkened, and Augustus looked at her like she'd pressed her thumb into a wound.

Then the knock came. The door creaked open, and Cambria stepped inside, face flushed. "My lady. It's time."

Aurelia sucked in a breath. Had they already passed through the afternoon?

Cambria lowered her eyes. "The feast begins soon. We need to prepare you for the ball."

Aurelia stood slowly, pausing at Theo's voice.

"When a vampire bonds, it is for eternity."

She glanced up. "Guardians are not immortal."

He nodded once. "Their bonds are."

Aurelia's pulse quickened. Everything over the past week snapped into focus. There were only a few days left before the blood moon. Alain planned to bond her.

Shame filled her gut. All week, she'd been skipping to the library, waiting for glances and touches when she should've been focused on Alain. She was still no closer to finding the venom he held. She understood more of the prophecy, but she still didn't know how she could use it to her advantage.

An entire week wasted.

Aurelia gave a small smile, then followed Cambria from the room. No more distractions. She needed to complete her task. And it had to be tonight.

26

The great hall shimmered like a dream. The torches had been replaced with hundreds of hanging brass lanterns suspended in rings from the vaulted ceiling. Rosewater burned in the sconces. Light caught the marble like wine spilled across stone. Strings of onyx and pearl hung between the columns, and red velvet ran from the doors to the dais, pooling like a river of living silk.

Aurelia stood at the threshold in a gown of deep crimson and gold that flared over her hips. Tiny stones had been sewn at the seams of her skirt, and they glinted when she moved. Her hair was pulled back with a golden band, exposing her neck.

She looked like a queen. *Or a sacrifice.* Her mind flew back to the goat being carried through the clearing.

Beside her, Helena stood tall in gray silk and steel-threaded embroidery, her hair pulled into a braid like a rope meant for war. They hadn't spoken since seeing Alain that afternoon.

The hall was full. Guardians stood at the edge of the room, watched by vampires in embroidered coats and layered robes.

Tension coiled between the two groups like a bow drawn too far.

If it was supposed to be a celebration, Aurelia didn't feel it.

Alain found her within seconds of her arrival. "You're breathtaking," he murmured, and when he took her hand, he turned it to press a kiss against her palm, as if sealing a contract. "Let them *see* you, Let them know exactly who will stand at my side when the moon begins to rise."

She plastered on a smile, but as she turned, her eyes caught movement across the crowd.

Theo.

He stood in black, no ornament, no crest. His hair was smooth, a soft wave at his collar, and his face—gods, his face—

Aurelia's breath caught. His eyes were already on her. Every touch in the library layered through her, filling her with ache.

Alain led her forward through the coven, and Aurelia tried to keep her feet moving. Theo didn't look away. Not until Alain's arm looped around her waist and he forced her to turn. Even then, she felt his gaze like a thread between them, stretched, fraying.

She traipsed along on Alain's arm, allowing him to present her to the coven. Eventually, she stood near the edge of the dancers, head tilted in polite conversation with a guardian elder. But her eyes once again searched for him.

She turned and found him at the edge of the floor, closer now. A group of vampires passed between them, and when they were gone, so was he.

Later, she moved at a brush against her elbow. "You should drink something," he murmured. "You've gone pale."

Aurelia stared straight ahead. Alain was still talking. When he finished, she asked for a drink. After a few more hours, the air in the hall had thickened with frivolity and music. The dancers looser now, the laughter louder. Wine flowed for the humans and guardians, and the sour scent mingled with candle smoke and herbs.

Alain's arm still coiled around her waist like a leash. His lips had already found her cheek, her temple, the hollow of her throat.

She swallowed her disgust, knowing this was the moment she'd been waiting for. Now. While everyone watched. He wouldn't dare accuse her here.

She turned to face him, forcing the words past the tightness in her throat. "You said you wanted them to see," she murmured, voice smooth. "Then let them."

His smile spread slow and hungry. He leaned in, and his lips brushed the side of her neck—slow, possessive. His mouth was wet, and she repressed a shudder.

Focus.

Aurelia reached for him, letting one hand trail to his shoulder. Her other hand slipped lower, tracing down the line of his coat. Her fingers worked slowly, methodically, as he pressed her tighter against him.

"Mm," he whispered. "You're learning."

Her skin crawled beneath his breath. She slid her hand around his waist, fingers curling beneath the hem of his jacket. Nothing. Just the heat of his body.

He kissed below her ear, and she sucked in a breath, then forced herself to lean in, to press her body into his as if she wanted him closer, when every instinct screamed to shove him off. Her fingers moved to his outer thigh, sweeping down and then up—slow, careful.

He grunted.

Nothing.

She pressed her palm briefly along the curve of his ribs,

hoping for a hidden seam, a stitched pocket, anything. Still nothing.

Her breath grew tight. She shifted her hand to the inside of his coat—

Please, just something. A shape. A ridge. But there was only smooth lining. No bulge. No vial. No strap. No fastening.

She moved her hand around his back, then gasped as his hand clamped down on her wrist. Hard. Pain shot through her arm, sharp and immediate, and her head snapped back.

"What are you doing?" Alain's voice was low. Menacing.

Her breath caught. She looked up at him, widened her eyes, softened her lips. "Was I not doing it right?"

His eyes searched hers. His grip tightened once more. A warning. And then he let go.

Aurelia turned slightly, casually, as if stretching her neck— just enough to catch sight of Theo across the ballroom. His eyes were dark. His shoulders curled.

Alain leaned close again, his voice sharp as frost. "Touch me like that again, and I'll mark you where they can't see."

Aurelia's smile froze, her lips trembling. Alain took her hand and laughed, then pulled her to the dais.

He raised his voice, motioning for the musicians to halt their playing. "This is the one chosen by the gods. The one foretold. Born of light eternal. She will bring unity. She will release us from our curse!"

A cheer rose up from the crowd.

Alain waited for the noise to die down, then scanned the crowd. "Tonight, she chooses who will share in that promise." He held up her arm, trailing his finger over her veins. "You've heard of the gift of her blood. Tonight is a celebration, and it wouldn't be complete without a gift." His eyes darkened as he stared out at the vampires he called his friends. "You've scented her, have you not?"

Heads nodded, and her stomach roiled.

Alain lowered her arm, turning to face her. "Darling Aurelia, who here is worthy of the blood that runs through your veins?"

Aurelia's heart thundered. Was this her punishment? He would remind her that he held power over her?

She turned and spotted Theo, standing near the back now. The weight of every gaze in the hall pressed against her like stone.

Theo.

His name rang in her head, but she didn't dare say it. "I offer it to you, Alain." She lifted her voice, annunciating every syllable. The words scalded her tongue.

Alain turned toward her, his smile triumphant. The crowd stirred—some nodding, some whispering their disappointment.

He took her hand and lifted it with reverence, but he didn't feed. Instead, he turned back to the crowd, his voice like a bell tolling in shadow. "You've heard her pronouncement. She offers her blood to me and me alone."

His smile sharpened. "And I, in my generosity, will share it."

Aurelia blinked. *What?* There was a long pause—deliberate, theatrical. Then he swept his hand outward.

"Let it be known that I choose who drinks from her veins. *I decide* how power is passed. Not the Goddess. Not the prophecy. Me."

The hall hushed. Alain pointed, slow and cruel, toward a young vampire near the front. "You, Evrard."

The boy's eyes widened.

"And you." Alain pointed to the back with relish, "Theo."

The crowd inhaled in unison. Aurelia's heart sprinted. "Alain—"

He held up a hand, silencing her. "Please. Come forward. Kneel."

Theo did not move. Not at first. Then, with every eye watching, he crossed the marble floor. Evrard joined him, the young vampire's hands clenched nervously at his sides.

They knelt together before them. Alain waited for their heads to bow, then stepped between them, one hand on each shoulder. "Tonight, I remind you all who holds the gift. Who bestows it." He gestured grandly to the crowd. "These two have been granted an honor. Evrard, new to the fold. And Theo." Alain chuckled. "Theo who has already tasted her once. Without permission."

Gasps. A hiss of amusement. Aurelia's stomach twisted.

Alain turned to the assembly. "He found her in the woods. Knew what she was. And instead of bringing her to me, he tried to take her for himself."

Theo's head remained lowered, jaw clenched. He said nothing.

Alain's words slammed into her chest. *Found her in the woods?*

Bonfires. Celebration in the valley. Nosferatu.

It was him. The voice in the trees. The arms pinning her to the tree. He'd told her to go and not speak of it and she hadn't listened.

Alain's voice sharpened. "He paid the price. But tonight . . . I forgive."

He lifted Aurelia's hands and offered them. "Rise." Theo and Evrard stood. "Drink," Alain commanded.

Theo rose beside Evrard, silent, eyes dull as iron. Evrard stepped forward at once, bowing his head.

Theo didn't move. Not one inch.

Alain's smile twisted. "You hesitate? Are you too proud to accept a gift from your master?"

Theo's eyes locked on Aurelia, and she saw the war in him. He didn't want to do it. It was obvious in the way his jaw flexed, the rage simmering in his eyes. He didn't want to touch her—not like this. Not in front of Alain. Not by command.

Her throat tightened as she stared at him, silently begging him. Alain would punish him, and she'd seen what that looked like.

For a beat, he remained still. Then—slowly—he moved. He joined Evrard, taking the opposite side of her.

The hall seemed to disappear. Her blood thundered in her ears as they stood together, and Theo reached for her. He didn't seize her wrist. He took her hand in his, warm and gentle, as if he feared she might shatter.

His thumb brushed the inside of her wrist where he'd fed the first time. That moment rushed back with such clarity, she swayed. The feel of the shroud, the sound of his voice.

Her pulse jumped. Theo didn't look at anyone else. Only her.

And then he bent. His mouth found her skin with exquisite care. One soft brush, then his fangs sank in, slow and reluctant.

And then—

Heat.

Aurelia gasped softly. The sensation was instant. Spreading. A flame blooming beneath her skin. It was pressure, pleasure, some terrible, perfect alchemy that left her trembling.

Her knees buckled, and Theo caught her elbow, steadying her as he had the first time. She worked to breathe, fighting against the wave rolling through her. It was exactly as she remembered. No, better. But this time there was something new, a swelling inside her, growing and reaching out until—

Theo's mouth tore from her skin, his arm flying back. Alain's boot collided with Theo's ribs, and Theo dropped sideways, ripped from her wrist.

Aurelia stumbled, her blood pooling.

"You filthy coward!" Alain roared.

Theo hit the ground hard, the stone cracking beneath his shoulder. A grunt tore from his chest, and he rolled to his side, dragging in a breath. One hand splayed against the floor, blood smeared on his lips. He pushed himself up, teeth clenched tight.

"Hold him," Alain snapped.

Two vampires surged forward. Augustus and another Aurelia didn't recognize. They didn't hesitate.

Augustus struck first, a boot to Theo's side, then another in the same place Alain had struck. Theo curled, breath knocked from his lungs. He didn't cry out. Didn't fight back. Just absorbed it, every blow, every crack of bone against flesh. Blood spattered against the marble.

The second vampire dragged him upright by the collar and slammed a fist into his face.

Aurelia's knees locked as the sound of the hit echoed through the hall. Theo's head snapped sideways, blood streaming from his temple. He spat onto the floor and met Alain's gaze without flinching.

Alain's face was red with fury. He turned toward the crowd, one hand clenched at his chest, the other pointing. "You all saw it. He hunted her. He stalked her before she ever came here. He tried to steal her blood. Her power. Her birthright."

Gasps rippled through the coven. Aurelia's chest seized as the other vampire released Theo and stepped back.

Alain's eyes glowed, mad and radiant. "He followed her from the moment he sensed it. And now—he dares touch what's mine."

Theo coughed, blood wetting his chin. Augustus kicked him in the back of his knee, dropping him back to the stone.

Aurelia clapped a hand over her mouth. She couldn't

breathe past the surge of heat in her throat. None of what Alain said was true, but Theo didn't defend himself. Not once.

Alain turned to Aurelia, breathing hard. "But I forgive you. You couldn't have known." She stood frozen, blood running slowly down her arm. "I'll fix it," Alain murmured. "I'll make it right. You're confused now, but I'll remind you who you belong to."

He grabbed her by the waist and hauled her away from the dais. She stumbled beside him, her body still humming. His hand slid along her hip, and she pulled back.

Alain pressed harder against her, whispering thick against her neck. "Augustus told me how he filled your head with lies. It's not your fault."

He pushed through the doors and spun, shoving her into the wall. His hand landed on her throat, squeezing until she gasped. "I'll teach you how it feels," he whispered. "To be claimed."

His lips found hers—rough, searching.

She tried to pull back. *Theo.* She needed to help him. She needed to make sure he was okay. "Please don't—"

"Shhh," he growled and kissed her harder. His hand slid up her thigh, grasping, bruising her skin.

"Alain!" Helena's voice cut through the corridor like a blade.

He turned, eyes wild. "Leave us."

She didn't stop. "A vampire. One of ours. He's sick."

Alain stared at her, blinking. "That's impossible."

Helena stepped forward. "He's coughing blood. Burning up. I've never seen anything like it in your kind. Guardians, humans, yes, but—"

Alain dropped Aurelia, his chest heaving. "Get up," he barked when he saw her sinking to the floor. She forced herself to stand. "Follow me."

She did as she was told. Helena walked with them, not saying a word. Staring straight ahead. They reached his door, and he threw it open. "I'll come back for you."

He waited for her to step over the threshold, then slammed the door shut and locked it.

As easy as returning a toy to its box.

Aurelia stood frozen, panting. Her blood still hadn't cooled. She wiped her wrist, but the skin still tingled where Theo's mouth had touched it. Where something inside of her had opened.

Alain had seen it.

She pressed her hands to her face. Tried to breathe and failed. She staggered to the window, flung it open, and stared out into the night.

Theo was hurt. Bleeding. Her heart hammered in her chest, the tightness around her lungs unbearable.

Aurelia looked up. Theo's room. It was just one floor up. Barely south.

He was bleeding again because of her.

Aurelia didn't think. She climbed onto the sill. Wind whipped her gown as she leapt into the dark.

27

The wind clawed at Aurelia's gown as she perched on the stone sill above her window. The manor loomed above her—cold, ancient, unforgiving. She didn't look down.

Her fingers found the old chisel marks in the stone, weather-worn grooves from generations past. Her slippers were useless; she kicked them off, bare toes gripping the cold ledge.

She reached. Pulled. The dress snagged. She cursed under her breath, tugging at the hem until it pulled free.

The wind howled, but this wasn't new. She remembered climbing the old pine behind her family's house, fingers sticky with resin, bark scraping her knees. Her father's voice calling her down, half-laughing, half-panicked.

Now she climbed like she had then. Fast, precise, without fear. Her palms burned. Her legs ached. She slipped once, but caught herself. When she reached the sill of Theo's window, her chest heaved, sweat dampening the back of her neck.

She braced herself over the edge, but she didn't have to.

Hands seized her, pulling her inside. The momentum knocked her back against the stone wall, hard.

"What in the name of Solène are you doing?" Theo's voice was a hiss, low and furious, right against her mouth.

He caged her with his body—one arm braced beside her head, the other trembling from the effort. His hair hung wild around his face, and his eyes—

Gods, his eyes. They blazed. His scent was that of sweat and blood. His chest pressed to hers, and she felt each labored breath.

He was hurt. Wheezing. "You climbed the damn wall?" he growled, voice rasping against her jaw. "Do you want to die?"

"I had to see you," she said, breathless.

He cursed under his breath and pulled back half an inch—just enough to scan her face. His pupils were blown wide, his expression a war between fury and disbelief. "Are you insane? If Alain—"

She lifted a hand and touched his side. Her fingers came away slick with blood.

"Stop. I'm already healing."

She didn't listen. Her hand lifted to his jaw, her thumb grazing the cut on his cheekbone, the swelling around his eye. "But you feel it. The pain."

His lips twitched. "Yes." That one word held no bravado. No shield. His eyes roamed over her face, her neck. "Did he—" Theo's voice broke. "Did Alain hurt you?"

She looked up. Met his gaze fully. "No," she whispered. "He tried. But Helena found us."

He inhaled sharply, nostrils flaring. "He touched you."

She didn't answer. She didn't need to. He'd seen how she'd been ripped from the hall. His body shook with restraint, the arm beside her head flexing.

Aurelia lifted her other hand to his shoulder. "I'm fine."

He didn't move. Didn't blink. Then he exhaled, slow and ragged. He lowered his head to step back, but Aurelia caught his arm.

His gaze dropped to where she held him. The muscles beneath her fingers were taut.

This was a risk. She knew it, and she took it anyway. Words filled her mouth, but she bit them back. She stared at his mouth.

"I didn't want to," he whispered. "Not like that. Not with him watching."

Her breath caught. "I know."

They stood there in the silence, the candle flickering from the desk. Then, finally, Theo moved.

He stepped into her space, holding his breath. One of his hands found her jaw, thumb brushing along her cheek.

He dropped his forehead to hers. "Tell me to stop," he murmured.

She didn't.

He waited a long moment, then turned his head and kissed her. Slow. Soft. Just the heat of breath and the tremble of flesh against flesh.

His hand drifted to her waist, and she wrapped her hand around his. He moved like he was learning her. Reading her for the first time.

The kiss deepened, but only by degrees. No hunger. No hurry. Just *gravity*.

Her skin hummed beneath his fingers, alive in places she hadn't known could feel. His touch didn't demand. It *invited*. And somehow, that was worse. Because she wanted it. She'd wanted it since the moment he touched her in the temple.

Guardians didn't set eyes on vampires for a reason. She shouldn't give in to this, shouldn't explore this curiosity, this pull.

And yet—

Theo's lips pressed again to hers, this time with more certainty, and her bones melted like wax around a flame. Her mouth parted, and the sound that escaped her throat was all instinct.

Her hand drifted up his chest, fingers dragging across the fabric of his shirt, feeling the muscle straining underneath. He was holding back. She could sense it.

That was what undid her. Not the kiss. Not his strength. But the way he kissed her like he was afraid this would be the only time.

His mouth broke from hers just long enough for her to breathe in, dizzy and stunned, before he kissed her again. This time deeper, slower, lips parting as his thumb swept along her cheekbone like he was memorizing the shape of her.

She had never wanted anything more. That swelling heat crashed through her, dragging her out to sea. This wasn't just about desire—it was about undoing. About unraveling every-thing she thought she knew about vampires and light and shadow.

He was supposed to be part of the threat. So why did it feel like *he* was the only thing that had ever made her feel safe?

He pulled back just enough to rest his forehead against hers again. His breath ragged. His voice barely there. "Aurelia," he whispered like a warning.

She swallowed. Her fingers still wrapped in the fabric over his chest. "I won't bond with Alain."

Theo pressed into the wall behind her, trying to catch his breath. "I can't—"

"No, I don't expect you to stop it. I'm still working with Helena, but . . ." She paused, considering her next words. "After studying this week, I wonder if Alain might be right."

Theo's expression changed instantly. Tension snapped through him. His hand dropped from her waist.

She held on, willing him not to back away from her. "I wonder if a bond is necessary."

"No." He shook his head, straightening.

She frowned. "Why not?"

He stepped away from her, pacing to the window, and she cringed at the loss of him. "It won't work."

Her frown deepened. "That's not what the prophecy says. You studied it just as I did."

He didn't turn back, didn't answer.

Pressure built behind Aurelia's eyes. "Do you feel this?" She strode forward, grabbing his hand and pressing it to her heart. "Am I the only one—"

"You're not." His throat worked. "You're not the only one."

She threaded her fingers with his. "She who was sent to bind," she whispered.

Theo's head bowed. "It's not right, Aurelia. I can't—"

"Why not?" Her voice trembled.

"Because I'm not the solution you want," he hissed. "Because I'm already losing control."

She leaned in. "You think you're the only one?"

He jerked his hand away. "You don't understand what I'm saying—"

"No, *you* don't understand!" Her words were low and sharp. "Everything I thought I knew is changing. The world isn't what I thought, I am not what I thought. The world we've built between vampires and guardians isn't what was intended. What if healing this curse means embracing pieces of ourselves that—"

"I don't want to embrace any piece of myself." Theo's chest heaved. "This is not who I am. I'm trapped in this body sick with lust, with hunger."

"You didn't choose it."

"It doesn't matter!" He glanced at the door and lowered his voice. "I am cursed. I am darkness, I—"

"Stop," she snapped, standing in front of him and forcing him to meet her eyes. "The Goddess found you worthy of a gift. Who are you to say otherwise?"

He shook his head, an ache pooling behind his eyes. "Aurelia—" His shoulders rose, then dropped with a breath. "You don't know what you're asking."

"I know exactly what I'm asking."

His head snapped toward her, eyes glowing faintly in the low light. And then he was on her. Mouth crashing into hers, hands threading through her hair, dragging her back against him with a growl that vibrated down her spine. "I would break you."

"You won't." She gasped, her knees buckling from the force of it, and he caught her easily, pulling her flush to his chest. His kiss was rough, hungry. All the fury he couldn't speak poured into the shape of her mouth.

"My kind only wants. Takes. They hollow you out."

"You're a terrible liar." She swept her tongue into his mouth and felt his blood boil. She'd never done this, never even imagined it, and yet with him, she couldn't stop her mind from spinning forward at full speed. She wanted everything from him. Every touch, every word. She wanted him to sink his fangs into her, to take, to want.

"Please, Theo. I know what I'm asking."

He tasted like heat and desperation, like every broken piece of him had sharpened, sinking into her and growing roots.

She moaned against his mouth as his hand slid to her lower back, dragging her hard against him. He could *crush* her if he wanted to, but she didn't hold back, didn't hesitate to melt into his arms.

He tore his mouth from hers. "I'm selfish. Dangerous."

She grabbed the front of his shirt, pulling him down again, her mouth skimming his jaw. "You're wrong."

He kissed her again, harder. "I see myself in him. In Alain. In the way he watches you, like he possesses you. And the worst part? I was jealous. I wanted to be the one on the dais. The one claiming you as mine."

He dragged his lips down the side of her throat, baring his teeth and tasting her. "I'm not safe, Aurelia. Not from what I was made to be."

She sucked in a breath, arching against him. "Maybe I don't want safe. Maybe that's not who I was meant to be."

Theo's eyes bore into hers. "Vampires don't love."

She bit his lip. "Not true. Alain loves plenty."

Theo made a sound in his throat, and she smiled against his mouth. "He loves his parties. His platters. And he *loves* that terrible painting—"

She stopped, froze, as ice slid down her spine.

Theo tensed. "What is it?"

Her heart pounded. "The painting," she breathed. "He *loves* it. More than anything. He looks at it, touches it every time he enters the room."

Theo watched her. Waited.

"What if it's not just a painting?" she whispered. "What if that's where he's keeping it?"

Theo's eyes darkened, then he grabbed her and pulled her toward the window.

CHAPTER 28

The fresco loomed above them, two meters tall, spanning almost the full width of the wall. Painted directly onto the stone, its pigments had faded over the years, but the image still carried an aura of reverence. A figure stood at its center, hands outstretched, shadowed by a great wing unfurled behind him.

Alain's favorite emperor.

Theo lifted the candle closer, and Aurelia stared at the lower edge, fingers twitching at her sides. "He touches this corner. Every time."

Theo crouched, studying the bottom right quadrant. "There's no seam."

"There has to be something," she murmured. "A pressure point. A trigger."

She ran her fingers along the cold stone—across the feet of the painted emperor, along the line of a shadowy wolf curled around the hem of the figure's cloak.

Theo pressed both palms flat and tried shifting the panel. Nothing.

Aurelia traced the stone, letting her fingers memorize every rise and fall in texture. Then she felt it—a *dip*. Barely perceptible. Worn smooth from habit. Right beneath the painted claw of the wolf.

"He presses here," she breathed.

Theo joined her, pressing the spot with his thumb. "Does it move?"

She shook her head. "No. But maybe . . ."

Her palm hovered beside it, trying different combinations of pressure.

Theo added his hand, and they pressed together. There was a soft *click*. Theo stepped back as the stone near the center of the fresco gave way—a whisper of movement. The paint didn't split. The wall didn't slide. But something else did.

"Push here," Aurelia said, pointing to the side of the stone. They pressed again, and the whole lower quadrant of the wall eased inward, revealing a small space. Inside the hollow, resting on a cradle of iron hooks, sat a box.

Theo reached in and lifted it out. It was carved of dark wood, so smooth it almost gleamed despite the shadows. The sides were covered in intricate carvings. Vines, talons, twisting beasts, a sun devouring its own rays.

Aurelia held her breath. There was no clasp. No hinge. No keyhole.

Theo turned it slowly in his hands. "No seams. It's one solid piece."

She tried running her fingers along the carvings. Theo tried pressing at the corners. Nothing shifted. No catch. No movement. Aurelia dragged her fingernail down one edge. Tried pressing her thumb into the carved spiral of a serpent.

Still nothing.

Then Theo froze. He sniffed the air, eyes narrowing. "He's coming," he hissed. Aurelia's pulse snapped.

They moved fast. Theo slipped the box back into the hollow while Aurelia pushed at the stone panel. It didn't catch at first. She shoved harder, and it gave—clicking into place just as Alain's steps echoed beyond the door.

Theo crossed the room in a blur, climbing onto the ledge of the window, still holding the candle.

He paused. Their eyes met. Then he slipped into the night. Aurelia lunged for the bed, pulled the coverlet over her, and turned on her side, willing her breath to slow.

Alain entered moments later. Aurelia moved, pretending the sound had disturbed her sleep. She braced herself, but he didn't speak.

There was the shuffling of clothes. The drop of boots. Then the mattress dipped. She held her breath. A moment passed.

Then Alain curled against her back. His arm hovered for a moment, then dropped, settling loosely over her hip. He pressed his forehead to her shoulder.

And began to weep. It started as a hiccup in his breath,

then he shook and whimpered. His arm around her contracted, not possessive, but desperate. As if she were the last thing anchoring him to himself.

Aurelia's mind raced. Was it guilt? Rage? Grief?

She thought of the vampire Helena had spoken of—the one coughing blood, burning with a sickness no one had seen before. Vampires did not get sick. It was an impossibility. A myth.

Alain's tears soaked through the fabric of her dress, hot against her back. She wondered if he noticed that she hadn't changed. That she smelled of wind and rain, of Theo. Though he was just as much to blame for that.

She kept her body still, her breathing deep. Minutes passed. Longer. And somehow, with Alain's breath trembling against her shoulder and her thoughts twisting into threads she couldn't hold, Aurelia drifted until sleep finally pulled her under.

28

The fresco loomed above them, two meters tall, spanning almost the full width of the wall. Painted directly onto the stone, its pigments had faded over the years, but the image still carried an aura of reverence. A figure stood at its center, hands outstretched, shadowed by a great wing unfurled behind him.

Alain's favorite emperor.

Theo lifted the candle closer, and Aurelia stared at the lower edge, fingers twitching at her sides. "He touches this corner. Every time."

Theo crouched, studying the bottom right quadrant. "There's no seam."

"There has to be something," she murmured. "A pressure point. A trigger."

She ran her fingers along the cold stone—across the feet of the painted emperor, along the line of a shadowy wolf curled around the hem of the figure's cloak.

Theo pressed both palms flat and tried shifting the panel. Nothing.

Aurelia traced the stone, letting her fingers memorize every rise and fall in texture. Then she felt it—a *dip*. Barely perceptible. Worn smooth from habit. Right beneath the painted claw of the wolf.

"He presses here," she breathed.

Theo joined her, pressing the spot with his thumb. "Does it move?"

She shook her head. "No. But maybe . . ."

Her palm hovered beside it, trying different combinations of pressure.

Theo added his hand, and they pressed together. There was a soft *click*. Theo stepped back as the stone near the center of the fresco gave way—a whisper of movement. The paint didn't split. The wall didn't slide. But something else did.

"Push here," Aurelia said, pointing to the side of the stone. They pressed again, and the whole lower quadrant of the wall eased inward, revealing a small space. Inside the hollow, resting on a cradle of iron hooks, sat a box.

Theo reached in and lifted it out. It was carved of dark wood, so smooth it almost gleamed despite the shadows. The sides were covered in intricate carvings. Vines, talons, twisting beasts, a sun devouring its own rays.

Aurelia held her breath. There was no clasp. No hinge. No keyhole.

Theo turned it slowly in his hands. "No seams. It's one solid piece."

She tried running her fingers along the carvings. Theo tried pressing at the corners. Nothing shifted. No catch. No movement. Aurelia dragged her fingernail down one edge. Tried pressing her thumb into the carved spiral of a serpent.

Still nothing.

Then Theo froze. He sniffed the air, eyes narrowing. "He's coming," he hissed. Aurelia's pulse snapped.

They moved fast. Theo slipped the box back into the hollow while Aurelia pushed at the stone panel. It didn't catch at first. She shoved harder, and it gave—clicking into place just as Alain's steps echoed beyond the door.

Theo crossed the room in a blur, climbing onto the ledge of the window, still holding the candle.

He paused. Their eyes met. Then he slipped into the night. Aurelia lunged for the bed, pulled the coverlet over her, and turned on her side, willing her breath to slow.

Alain entered moments later. Aurelia moved, pretending the sound had disturbed her sleep. She braced herself, but he didn't speak.

There was the shuffling of clothes. The drop of boots. Then the mattress dipped. She held her breath. A moment passed.

Then Alain curled against her back. His arm hovered for a moment, then dropped, settling loosely over her hip. He pressed his forehead to her shoulder.

And began to weep. It started as a hiccup in his breath, then he shook and whimpered. His arm around her contracted, not possessive, but desperate. As if she were the last thing anchoring him to himself.

Aurelia's mind raced. Was it guilt? Rage? Grief?

She thought of the vampire Helena had spoken of—the one coughing blood, burning with a sickness no one had seen before. Vampires did not get sick. It was an impossibility. A myth.

Alain's tears soaked through the fabric of her dress, hot against her back. She wondered if he noticed that she hadn't changed. That she smelled of wind and rain, of Theo. Though he was just as much to blame for that.

She kept her body still, her breathing deep. Minutes passed. Longer. And somehow, with Alain's breath trembling against her shoulder and her thoughts twisting into threads she couldn't hold, Aurelia drifted until sleep finally pulled her under.

29

The world was washed in gold. Aurelia stood barefoot in a field of wheat that shimmered with light from no sun. The stalks bent away from her as she passed, whispering in the wind. Her plain dress clung to her like a second skin, weightless and white—until she looked down and saw blood blooming across the hem like ink dropped in water. She touched it and found it was still warm.

In the distance, the sky fractured. Half of it was brilliance—warm, pulsing, radiant. The other half was void—pitch black, scattered with stars that pulsed like distant heartbeats. The two halves spiraled toward each other, never touching.

Above her, a woman stood tall, veiled in light, her hair flowing like flame. Aurelia tried to speak, but her lips were sewn shut with golden thread.

Glass vials rested in the soil at her feet, each filled with darkness. One pulsed faintly, a symbol on its side. A crescent wrapped in a circle.

Aurelia reached down, and when her fingers touched the glass, a second vial lit up with the same symbol. She reached for it, but when her fingers held both, the vials disappeared and she fell, tumbling backward through water, then fire, then nothing at all.

She landed in a temple with no doors. A fresco spread across every wall. Aurelia walked to it, pressed her palm against the center.

It came in fragments, at first. A shoreline of glass where blood lapped at the edges. The sky stretched above it in endless twilight—not sun, not night, only the breathless pause in between.

Aurelia stood at the edge of that red river. Light swirled beneath the surface, currents glimmering like starlight scattered in wine.

A girl knelt beside a fire, her hands cupped around a flame that did not burn. A woman with silver streaks in her hair, holding a blade carved with runes Aurelia did not yet know. A child with her same eyes, cradled in the arms of someone faceless, crying out a name.

Across the river stood a figure cloaked in light, skin aglow like the inside of a pearl. Soléne. She did not speak. Behind her, the shadows moved and a second figure stepped forward. Le Sombre. The light dimmed around him but did not vanish. Instead, it bent, joined, became something brighter where they touched.

And between them stood all of *her*. All of them.

The current swept above the banks of the river, sweeping against her ankles, her calves, pulling until she slipped—

Aurelia woke, gasping. She bolted upright in bed, her lungs burning, hands clenched in the bedsheets. Her skin was slick with sweat.

Light streamed in through the window. Her head throbbed. Her arms felt weak. She rose on shaky legs and splashed water onto her face from the wash basin, then scanned the room.

Alain was gone. She didn't know when he left or when he'd be back, but she couldn't waste this moment.

Aurelia went to the fresco. She pressed the same worn spot beneath the wolf's claw. Then the side of the panel. The wall clicked open.

There it was. She hadn't dreamed it. The carved wooden box sat there just as it had the night before.

She lifted it out, cradled it in her hands. This time, she looked closer. There. Hidden among the vines and sigils etched into the surface—one symbol repeated: a crescent inside a circle.

She held her breath, recognizing it from her dream. She placed her thumb in its center. Nothing.

But—

Aurelia pressed the first, then felt for the second. Two vials, both with the same symbol. There was a soft click. The lid opened, and she nearly dropped it.

Inside, nestled in silk, sat at least ten vials of swirling liquid. Each sealed, each labeled in script. She stared, not able to believe it. This was it. The venom Alain had collected. She reached for the vials, scanning for anything recognizable. The script was old and strange, but she saw the letter "T" and pulled that vial out.

The door creaked behind her, and she nearly dropped it as her head snapped up. She froze, her body stiff with fear. The handle turned, and Aurelia still held the box.

30

Helena stared at her holding the box, then at the open wall behind her. "What have you got there?"

Aurelia released a ragged breath. "I found it."

Helena stepped in, shutting the door behind her. Her eyes landed on the box in Aurelia's hands. "You opened it."

Aurelia didn't speak, just held it out. Helena crossed the room in two strides and took the box gently. Reverently. She ran her fingers over the carved lid, then looked inside.

Her eyes widened as she saw the vials. She counted, then counted again.

"Is something wrong?"

Helena exhaled, and her shoulders sagged. She pulled Aurelia into a sudden, fierce embrace. "How could anything be wrong? You found it."

Aurelia's eyes burned. They pulled apart, breathless.

Helena tucked the vials inside the folds of her cloak. "I'll destroy them tonight. Quietly. When he's gone from the house."

Aurelia nodded, chest heaving with relief. She closed the

lid on the box and replaced it, then closed the stone compartment and swept away the sediments that had dropped on the floor.

"He has no hold over the others." Helena beamed at her. Then her eyes widened as she pulled a small folded parchment from her sleeve. "I almost forgot. I came here to give you this. From Raya."

She placed it in Aurelia's palm and crossed to the wardrobe. Aurelia unfolded the note, her fingers tingling. The ink was delicate.

I have reading for you. Meet in the baths."

Aurelia read it twice, then folded it back, searching for a pocket. She didn't have one since she was still in her dress. She needed to change, though, if she was going to the baths . . .

"Did Alain sleep here last night?" Helena inspected the bed.

Aurelia nodded. "I pretended to sleep, and he came to bed. Didn't touch me. Only wept."

Aurelia waited for a smile, some sort of victory cheer, but it didn't come. Instead, Helena pursed her lips. "One of ours is dead."

Aurelia blinked. "Dead?"

"Gone. This morning. His body was wasted. His blood burned black."

"That's not possible," Aurelia whispered.

"It wasn't," Helena said. "Until now."

They sat in silence.

"How could it happen?" Aurelia asked. "You said vampires don't—"

"They don't. I've seen them torn apart. Lit on fire. Drowned. But this . . . " She shook her head. "I don't know what this is."

———

Alain did not return that day. By midafternoon, Aurelia had stopped glancing at the door. She'd considered going through the window again, but couldn't bring herself to risk it. It was stupid what she'd done the night prior. Stupid, and yet she didn't regret one second of it.

She lay on the bed, remembering how it felt to be held by Theo. Touched. Kissed. She couldn't get it out of her head, and the second Cambria entered with a tray of bread, fresh cheese, and figs, Aurelia stood, still in her dress. "I'd like to go to the baths."

Cambria blinked, surprised. Then left the tray and vanished without another word. Aurelia needed the distraction, and she needed to see what Raya had procured for her.

Thankfully, minutes later, Cambria returned with Clémentine and a neatly folded robe.

Clémentine smirked. "Permission granted." Aurelia's pulse quickened. "Hmm, I seem to put her on edge." She winked at Cambria. "That or she's attracted to me."

Aurelia reached for the robe. She hadn't talked with Clémentine since that first night. She'd seen her with Alain and the others, but now she would be at the baths with her? She groaned internally. Would she be able to look at the scrolls?

When she was dressed in her robe, Clémentine and Cambria walked with her through the winding halls and into the baths. No other guardians were present.

"I didn't know vampires could come here." Aurelia played with the edges of her robe.

Clémentine dropped hers, and Aurelia froze mid-step. The robe slipped from Clémentine's shoulders like water, pooling at her ankles. She stepped out of it without hesitation, revealing skin that caught the low light like polished bronze.

Every inch of her was smooth and flawless, curves sculpted like the old gods had taken their time. Aurelia tried not to stare. She slipped out of her own robe more slowly, tucking her arms close as she stepped into the pool. The steam curled around her like smoke, but she felt utterly exposed.

Clémentine had settled at the edge, feet dangling in the water. Her hair, damp at the tips, clung to her collarbones. She didn't wrap a towel around herself. Didn't cross her arms. She stretched, languid and feline, utterly at ease in her body.

Aurelia sank into the water and let her breath go, trying not to notice the way she instinctively curled her legs in or the flicker of comparison clawing through her ribs.

"You heard?" Clémentine asked, finally.

Aurelia nodded. "About the vampire?"

Clémentine didn't answer at first. She slid into the pool, her entrance soundless, graceful. Water lapped at her waist as she moved closer.

"They said it started in his throat. That he choked, then his blood turned thick. Coagulated. His veins cracked. Like dried clay."

Aurelia shivered despite the warmth of the pool. "Has it ever happened before?"

"Not that I've heard. But you know how the stories go." She leaned her elbows on the ledge, tilting her head. "Some say it was poison. Something slipped into his blood."

"Poisoned how?"

Clémentine shrugged. "I don't have to feed for another day at least, so I won't worry about it until then."

The sound of footsteps echoed just beyond the arched threshold. Aurelia turned her head to see Raya enter. She scanned the pool and froze when she saw Clémentine.

She stopped dead. Her entire posture sharpened, chin lifting, and in the same breath, she turned as if to walk out again.

"Oh, don't do that." Clémentine stood, rising from the pool like a siren from a fable, water sliding down the curves of her bare body. "You don't have to be afraid of me. Helena told me everything."

Raya's lips parted.

"I know you're searching for the venom Alain stole." Clémentine smiled as if it were a shared secret. "You're going to free us."

Aurelia blinked, heart skipping. She hadn't expected that. Raya's gaze flicked to Aurelia's, uncertain. But she said nothing —just stepped farther into the room and laid a bundle of cloth-wrapped scrolls on a low table beside one of the stone benches.

"I brought what you asked for." Raya's voice was clipped. Controlled.

"Thank you," Aurelia murmured, rising from the bath. She accepted the drying cloth Cambria handed her and wrapped it tightly around herself.

She crossed to the scrolls and, after drying her hands, unwound the ties. The parchment was yellowed, the edges curled. Some were smudged with the fingerprints of long-dead scribes. Others had delicate inkwork that shimmered faintly when the light hit it just so.

She sat on the bench, knees tucked beneath her, and began to read.

Clémentine followed, still bare as the day she was born, and settled on the chair beside her, one knee draped casually over the other.

Aurelia tried to ignore her as her eyes swept the first scroll —an older text on covenants, the language more symbolic than literal. It described early rites between light and dark, rituals of joining. One passage referenced an ancient practice: "To unite the opposing forces, a blood-bound circle must be sealed with an artifact of choice, tempered by both desire and surrender."

It was translated like the others Theo had shown, but it corroborated what he said. Her pulse kicked. She reached for another.

Clémentine leaned over, reading upside down. "That one's boring. You want the one with the seal at the top."

Aurelia's eyes narrowed, but she turned it over. Bonding. A single word at the top. Her breath caught.

This one was clearer. More structured. It mentioned that the earliest blood bonds required sacred objects—rings, torcs, or pendants—items worn close to the skin, imbued with the intention of mutual binding. No mention of worth, just a personal choice.

She traced the word *choice* with the tip of her finger.

"You won't be the first." Clémentine dropped back in the chair.

Aurelia's head jerked up. "What?"

Clémentine didn't seem to notice the weight of what she'd said. "Alain has bonded many guardians. He collects them, doesn't he? Like chalices and coats. It's all about what he can control." She reached lazily for a dried fig from a dish left beside the chair. "Though I think he finally found what he was looking for all along."

Aurelia could barely hear over the rushing in her ears. "You said Helena told you—about the venom."

Clémentine nodded. "And I told her about the ring."

Aurelia froze. "The ring?"

"Mm." She chewed thoughtfully. "Alain was showing it to Augustus after his trip. It looked old. Important. I didn't get a good look, but it must've been what he went to retrieve. He was grinning like he'd just dug up a god's front tooth."

Aurelia stared at her. Here she was, poring over scrolls, chasing dusty scraps of meaning, while Clémentine had been watching it all unfold.

She'd told Helena. Aurelia's heart sped until she remembered what had happened since the last sunrise. A vampire sick and then dead. Helena had been gone since the ball. She hadn't been available to give either of them updates.

Aurelia spun to Raya, sitting as far from Clémentine as possible. "Raya, is it possible for you to send a message?" She nodded and stood. "I need to speak to Theo immediately."

31

Aurelia sat on the edge of the stone basin, one hand trailing through the warm water, the other clenched in her lap. Her robe clung damply to the backs of her knees. Every sound seemed magnified—the drip of condensation on tile, the slow swish of Clémentine pacing a few steps behind her.

Clémentine had been humming at first. Nervously. But now she was quiet. Aurelia stared at the water, willing Raya to return.

When the heavy wooden door creaked open again, Aurelia spun and saw her.

Raya, and behind her, shadowed by the torchlight, Theo.

Aurelia's breath caught. Her pulse stumbled. He looked normal again. Not wounded, not worn. Beautiful. Healed.

Cambria stood at Raya's shoulder, red in the face, appalled. "You can't bring him in here."

Raya motioned around. "There's nobody here." She ignored Cambria's further protestations and motioned for Aurelia to follow her.

The private chamber of the bath was warm and dim, lit only by a few high sconces. Aurelia stood just beyond the threshold beside the small pool as Theo entered, followed closely by Clémentine, still completely nude.

Theo turned back and didn't seem to notice. "You're not coming in."

"I have permission," Clémentine shot back. "Alain asked me—"

"I don't care what Alain said. He doesn't know I'm here, and Aurelia can only leave through that one door. Wait on the other side of it."

Clémentine's cheeks flushed. "I know just as well as you do—"

"You of all people should understand the need for alone time."

Clémentine blinked, then her eyes widened. "Oh. OH." She stumbled backward, grinning. Her eyes flicked between the two of them. "Forbidden. Ooh, Alain will have you tortured for this."

"Well aware." Theo nodded once, then turned to face Aurelia as the door clicked closed behind him.

Aurelia stood in stunned silence.

Theo's throat worked. "Sorry. Had to get rid of her." The space between them crackled. He stepped forward to meet her at the edge of the bath. "You asked for me."

Aurelia nodded, unsure where to begin. She pulled her robe tighter around her, suddenly feeling exposed. Should she mention the ring? Go back to the prophecy? She opted for that. "I had a dream. I can't properly describe the feeling, but I believe what you said about the prophecy. That it's been misread, though maybe not in the way you thought." She paused, searching for a way to explain. "The submission described doesn't refer to domination or 'power over.' I believe it's about surrendering. To each other."

Theo's jaw twitched. "You're talking about the bonds of old." Aurelia nodded. "There's a reason they were revoked. That kind of bond . . . it's not safe."

"No. It's not." She took a breath. "But what if it's what the Goddess intended?" The prophecy was full of paradoxes and contradictory conditions. This was the only way they made sense.

Theo's gaze flicked to hers. "A bond like that is physical, it opens you up to one another. To feel what the other feels. Being affected by it. It's not just an awareness."

"I understand."

"I don't think you do." Theo's jaw tensed. "The battle I fight—I wouldn't wish it on my worst enemy. I wouldn't wish it on you."

Aurelia's breath quickened. "I know you wouldn't. But that's where our reasoning goes wrong. We expect a bond to serve us, but a bond must be a sacrifice. How else could two opposites meld completely? There must be something that bridges the gap. *To seal the light, the darkness must know itself; To seal the dark, the light must submit.* Both sacrifices of the pieces we desire to cling to."

The air grew heavier as Theo pondered. He nodded. "United in something outside of ourselves. A common goal."

Aurelia lifted her hand to his chest. "Equal. Vulnerable. Leaving our weakness in another's hands." His heart beat beneath her palm. "You are dangerous in your own way, but I —" She sucked in a breath. "I will not live like you do. I will age. Die."

Theo's expression clouded. "Vampires seem to be no longer immune."

Aurelia nodded, worrying her lower lip. Would Theo be

reborn if he died? Or would he be gone forever? She couldn't think about that now. "I would join you in fighting the pull of the shadow. You would join me in grief. In sickness. In death."

Theo didn't argue this time. He reached for her, curling into her until their foreheads touched. She whispered the words she remembered from the scroll—ancient, half-lost, a fragment of a rite. *"Blood to blood in death, blood to lips in life."*

Theo's eyes closed. "I followed you from the temple, not because I wanted your blood. I followed you because . . . it was the first time since I'd been turned that I felt anything at all." He pressed his lips to her cheek. "I couldn't go back to not feeling, and I can't go back now. I'll give you whatever you ask."

Aurelia held him, feeling his chest rise and fall against hers through the thin fabric of her robe. That was all she needed to hear.

She lowered her hand and reached into her pocket, her fingers curling around smooth glass. Aurelia stepped back and held it between them. When she extended her hand and the glass caught the light, when Theo saw his name etched into the curve of the vial, his entire body locked.

He didn't speak, didn't move. His eyes darkened with something vast and desperate. His throat worked. The water in the pool whispered against the tile, hushing their breath.

Theo trembled as he took the vial from her, then dropped to his knees. His head bowed as he clutched the vial to his chest. As though for the first time in a century, he felt the shape of his own soul.

His breath came hard and shallow, the slope of his shoulders shaking. Aurelia moved before she could think. She reached out and touched his face.

Theo gripped her hips, pressing his cheek into the soft curve of her stomach. "Anything. Everything. Whatever you ask." His chest rose like something caged inside him had cracked open and was trying to crawl free.

She ran her fingers through his hair as he struggled, tears spilling over onto her cheeks. He arched like he was starving for her hands. He reached for her, pulling her down to him, sitting her in his lap. His hands slid up her back, circling her neck. His mouth came to her shoulder, the inside of her wrist, and a tremor rolled through his entire frame.

His whole body was a prayer. Not to the gods or goddesses. To her.

He let out a shuddering breath when her lips finally brushed his, and when he kissed her, every wound, every wall, every silence sealed up, filled to the brim.

He kissed her like he wanted to die doing that and nothing else. When he finally pulled back, his voice was wrecked and hoarse, a single breath against her throat. "I'm yours, Aurelia. Body and soul. Please let me make you mine."

32

Aurelia stood beneath the ancient stone where the red moon hung like a suspended wound through the opening in the domed ceiling. It painted the marble, the faces, the shrouds—everything tinged in dusky rose.

She'd been here once before, when the sky was clear and bright, and the temple felt divine. The columns had soared like sacred trees, each one carved to resemble twisting branches reaching toward the gods. Light had filtered through the open dome in golden shafts, dust floating like blessings. The shrouds then had seemed soft, holy, even, white fabric encircling the heart of the room like the arms of ancestors.

But now?

Now the columns clawed upward like blackened roots. Every detail carved in stone felt alive in the firelight, watching. The shrouds didn't float gently now. They hung limp and heavy, their translucence turned opaque by the blood-stained glow above. They loomed like veils for the dead.

Alain's voice rolled through the temple, measured and

grand. He stood at the head of the circle like an elder. He spoke of covenants. Of balance restored. Of her blood, freely given, as the bridge between light and shadow.

But Aurelia wasn't listening to his words. She watched his hands. Waiting for the ring.

Theo was poised. Ready to take it. They had poured his venom out together, and Alain could no longer strip Theo of his power.

Aurelia caught his eye from where she stood beside Alain, and then something scraped over stone. A tremor ran through the floor. From behind the altar came the echo of footfalls. Fast. Sure. Then a cry, and the guardians flooded in.

They surged from the hidden corridor like a tide, cloaked in muted leathers and old bronze. Her people. The ones who lit candles in windows and carved prayers into the doorframes of their homes. The ones who stood between the light and the dark and asked for nothing in return.

For one breathless second, pride swelled so violently in her chest she thought it might break her ribs. *They came.* But that pride twisted almost instantly into dread.

Not now. Not like this.

At their front was her father. His cloak caught in the torchlight, and in his hands—

Aurelia gasped. The sword. The one that had hung above their hearth since she was a child. The one missing from its place the day she returned. He held it now with both hands, runes glowing faintly along the blade's core.

He raised it with purpose, and her heart seized. *No. Not this way.*

"No!" Aurelia shouted, stepping forward before her mind could catch up. Her voice cracked through the temple like a whip. "Stop!"

Alain crouched, ready to strike. Augustus lunged, fangs

bared—and she saw the moment it would all go wrong. *They'll die. My father will die.*

She threw herself into the heart of it all, between her father's blade and Alain's outstretched arm. "Stand down!" The force of her cry echoed through the temple. Everything stilled.

Her father's eyes found hers—wild and terrified. "Aurelia, what—"

"This is the loyalty your covenants inspire?" Alain's lips curled, sharp with satisfaction.

Aurelia turned on him. Fury licked at her throat. "I choose this." She spoke loud enough for every voice in the chamber to fall silent. "Not because you asked, but because the gods require it of me."

Her voice didn't shake. Her spine didn't bend. Let them all see.

She stepped back into the circle, into the blood-drenched moonlight—and it cut across her face, splitting her shadow in two. *Light and dark. Both. Always both.* "I will finish the ceremony."

Gasps rippled through the crowd, but she didn't flinch. Her father held her gaze for a long moment. Then, slowly, achingly, he lowered the sword. One by one, the other guardians followed, stepping into place like a wall around her.

She turned toward Alain. He watched her like a man savoring a victory he believed already his.

And then he reached into his robe. The ring glinted in the light. Silver. Veined with something dark.

He held it aloft, and a gasp sounded in the crowd. One of the vampires staggered, clutching their throat.

Another dropped to their knees.

Blood pooled from their noses, their ears. Black. Viscous. Wrong.

A moment later, another collapsed, convulsing.

The ring trembled in Alain's hand, and for the first time, he looked afraid.

Aurelia turned in the thick, flickering light, searching the crowd as the sounds of choking and staggering feet rippled through the vampires. Another body dropped, convulsing. A wet cough echoed off the curved ceiling.

Aurelia began to panic. She searched for Helena in the chaos. She should've been here. She was supposed to spread the word—warn the others that the vials were gone. That the chains were broken. That they could fight back if Alain tried to force anything.

But she wasn't here, and neither was Florent. Aurelia's pulse kicked up. The back of her neck prickled with sweat. She twisted toward the guardians lining the perimeter, her eyes darting from face to face.

Still no sign of them. Her gut twisted. *Something is wrong.*

Even in the chaos, Alain didn't stop. He didn't so much as pause at the sound of the vampires choking at his feet. If anything, he moved faster now, his voice rising, sweeping into the old rites like wind through broken glass.

She saw the flicker of the ring again, held tight in his palm. He didn't wait for silence. He didn't ask for a witness. "The blood moon watches. Let it bind what was sundered. Let shadow drink from light and light temper shadow."

His hand reached for hers, and she drew back. *No—*

Theo moved. He lunged from the shadows like an arrow knocked and set free. "Alain!" he roared, but he never made it. A shock of air burst through the chamber. Theo was ripped backward mid-motion and hurled into the floor near the altar with a sickening thud.

Aurelia screamed and rushed forward. And that's when she saw her. Not in the crowd. Not at the doors. But standing over

Theo, a hand pressed to his chest, holding him to the marble by the throat.

Helena.

Only—it wasn't Helena. Her hair was unbound, her skin glistening. Her eyes were deeper, the whites tinged with violet shadow.

Her mouth was curled back as she pressed harder, forcing Theo to the stone. Aurelia's chest hollowed out. *She was changed. Alain turned her.*

Pain cracked through her, and she spun as Alain's frantic voice finally broke through her shocked haze. "The bond will be sealed in blood and will, under the eyes of the Goddess, who sees all things as one."

He lifted the ring, and she shoved forward. She dove, not caring who tried to stop her, not caring what it would cost. Her hand reached for the stone pedestal where the ring was now pressed, her palm slamming against it just as Alain finished the rite.

And then—

Snap.

The air left her lungs, blurring her vision. A rush—hot and silver—poured through her veins. It felt like water, fire, and hunger all at once.

Her knees buckled. A tether wrapped around her ribs, her spine, her throat, sealing tight. The bond. They were too late—it was done.

How had this happened? Why was Helena targeting Theo, and how was she so strong? Tears blurred her vision as her body hit the floor, and Alain's maniacal laughter rose behind her. Exultant.

33

Aurelia couldn't breathe. The bond coiled through her like wildfire through dry grass. It didn't slip gently into place—it *tore*. Her spine arched against the stone, hands splayed as if trying to hold herself inside her own skin.

It felt like a thousand threads anchoring her to nothing and everything at once. And at the center of it, a single, brutal truth: She had been bound. Not to Theo. Not by choice.

"No . . . " she rasped, her voice shredded. She writhed, trying to reach for something—someone—but her limbs were too heavy, her pulse too erratic. Every thought drowned in heat and a power not her own.

She rolled and cried out, "Helena!" What was she doing? How did this happen? Vampires couldn't turn guardians. Their venom would not engage at the taste of guardian blood.

Aurelia's stomach flipped on itself. Or was that another lie she'd believed? Another half-truth told to keep them unafraid and at peace as they made their offerings?

Helena dropped Theo to the ground and hissed, "You move

and I will make you regret it." She stepped back from him and reached into the pocket of her trousers, withdrawing a vial. Aurelia knew it instantly. She'd watched it pressed to her skin, sealed by Helena's hand.

Her blood.

Helena uncorked it with a flick of her thumb, tipped it over a small ceremonial dagger. The blood ran down the blade in a perfect ribbon. Then, with no warning or fanfare, she soared up the steps and plunged it into Alain's chest.

It landed with a wet thunk. Alain's body jerked once, his face frozen in shock, and then his knees buckled. He gasped like a man drowning and pulled the blade out, staring at the wound in disbelief.

Blood poured freely, too red, too mortal. "I don't . . . " he whispered, staggering backward. "It's not possible."

Guardians huddled together. Vampires roared in outrage, but Helena lifted her hands, her voice rising above the din. "Your immortality is over! The Goddess has turned her face. The prophecy is clear. This is the end of the curse."

Gasps erupted. Screams. Vampires lurched back. Guardians faltered.

Aurelia stared in horror as Alain collapsed, choking on his own blood. *On her blood.* Every conversation with Helena flooded her head. *Your blood is the key, I'm sure of it . . . Underneath? They're still bound to the curse . . . Be willing to sacrifice if necessary . . .*

The vampire becoming sick after the ball. The first death. The vampires drowning in their own blood on the stone in front of her.

Helena knew. She'd *tested* it. Weeks ago, in secret. The way she'd kept her distance, the information she hadn't shared. Aurelia had made excuses. She'd missed it.

Aurelia struggled to her feet, the bond heavy around her neck. "Helena. This was not our agreement—"

"Agreement? You *should* be celebrating." Helena's eyes gleamed. "We did this together."

"No! You kept this a secret!"

She laughed. "And you and Theo don't have secrets?" She kicked the ring from Alain's stiff fingers and it clinked across the stone. "The only balance is obliteration. The vampires will fall, and from their ash, the world will breathe again." Helena stepped toward her. Held out another dagger. "Join me."

Aurelia stared at it. Felt her stomach twist. "Helena . . . " She couldn't let this happen. Theo sat panting against the pillar, his eyes fixed on her. *No.*

Aurelia tried to push forward, tried to stop her, but Helena was already moving, already turning, her eyes fixed on the panicking vampires. She raised her blade, and a voice tore through the temple.

"*Run!*" Florent stumbled into the chamber, barely upright, pale and staggering, blood smeared across his chest. His voice cracked with rage. "She's stolen it! *She stole my power!*"

His eyes locked on Helena. "You lied to me. You used me!" Florent flung his arm, and something shattered. The tinkling of glass. A small cork rolling across the stone.

Aurelia's blood ran cold. *She didn't destroy the vials.* Helena didn't just test Aurelia's blood. She used the venom on herself.

Vampires and guardians scattered, the chamber a blur of motion and panic. Theo ripped her up from the ground, one arm around her waist, the other grabbing her hand as she stumbled. "We have to go."

"We have to help them!" She searched for her father, for Clémentine.

"No time," he growled.

Helena turned, and Theo ran.

34

They crashed through the trees, branches slapping at Aurelia's arms, her lungs burning despite the cool night air. The blood moon lit the forest floor in pale umber, and the leaves looked rusted in the glow.

"Theo, stop!" Aurelia gasped.

He didn't slow. His grip on her only tightened as he sprinted, his feet barely touching the mossy earth.

"They'll die!" she gasped. "Helena—she'll turn on them!"

"She won't," he snarled. "She wouldn't dare—"

"She has *my blood*, Theo!"

He stumbled to a stop. Silence fell so suddenly that it rang in her ears. The forest sighed around them, alive with a blustery wind. Theo panted for air.

"She has the vials," Aurelia choked out. "Florent said—"

"I heard what he said." Theo dragged his hands through his hair, then ripped something from his pocket. The ring glinted silver in the moonlight. "I was too late." His face twisted. "The bond—" His voice broke, and Aurelia fisted her hands in his tunic.

"I felt it, but Alain is dead—"

"Is it gone? Did you feel it leave?"

Aurelia dove inward, searching for some sign, some release, but it wasn't there. "No." Her eyes stung. "I don't understand. Helena used my blood—"

Theo roared in anger, throwing his head upward to the heavens. "We did as the Goddess asked. We studied the prophecy."

"I know, I know." Tears pooled in her eyes. What had they done wrong? She'd done everything she could. Endured, studied, and sought with all her heart. She followed Theo's gaze upward and blinked.

Her eyes trailed along the sprawling branches, the freckled bark. This was her tree. She put out a hand, pressing her palm against the trunk.

How had Theo found it?

Her feet had felt that moss a hundred times before. Bare toes catching on the ridges, knees scraped raw from climbing too fast, too high.

He'd carried her here. *Home. To safety.*

She closed her eyes and, for a moment, she wasn't the girl who had run to the tribes for adventure. Wasn't "she who was born on the Day of Light." She wasn't the chosen one, or Alain's prize, or the girl who offered her blood in gilded rooms.

She was a daughter. A sister. A girl who climbed this tree to see the stars. Who laughed when the wind caught her hair. A girl who fell asleep in the crook of those limbs, sunlight warming her skin.

Aurelia sucked in a breath as heat spread through her fingertips. Not warmth—*heat*, alive and deliberate. It pulsed along her palm like a heartbeat, and she opened her eyes with a gasp. She flipped her hand, and there beneath her skin on the inside of her arm, something shimmered.

She peered closer, holding it out to Theo. Two chains twisted together—one barbed and jagged, the other smooth and unbroken. Both looped into a perfect ring that never closed.

"It's a rune." Theo's voice was ragged. "Proof of the bond."

Aurelia's heart lurched. "I don't understand." If Alain were dead, why would the rune remain? Why—?

Aurelia gasped, clinging to Theo and her tree as her mind lit up. The dream she'd seen in the manor house surged back in full. Not in fragments now, but in full imagery.

She stood at the edge of a river, the sky suspended in twilight. The water shimmered with light beneath the surface —reflections not of the world, but of herself. The girl with fire cupped in her hands. The silver-haired woman holding a blade. The child cradled in another's arms.

She understood now. *All versions of her.*

Blood lifted from Aurelia's arm and scattered above the river. Where it touched the water, new reflections bloomed. New lives. New beginnings. The current pulled them forward, the reflections sinking and surfacing, changing and reforming.

But then the current faltered. The water grew still in places, stagnant. One by one, the shadows within the river winked out —glimmers of dark that once swirled beside the light now sputtered and vanished, like stars devoured by dawn too early. A harmony unraveled.

One reflection—half shadow, half light—shivered and cracked, splintering into nothing. Above the river, the sky began to shift. Not into night. Not into day. But into the void. Balance undone.

Without shadow, light flickered wild and aimless—too bright in places, extinguished in others. The river began to churn, confused, unnatural. The Goddess had shown her the cost.

Blood floated up from Aurelia's arm once more. Not as an offering, but as an answer. It hovered in the air, burning with gold and crimson, then arced downward, falling not into the river this time, but into the sky above it. The droplets shimmered, bright as stars, then winked out one by one.

And as the last drop disappeared, the sky stilled. The current smoothed. The void recoiled.

Her blood had vanished to make space. To fill what shadow had lost.

Aurelia understood then. She wasn't meant to stay. She was the measure. The weight placed on the other side of the scale. She was the offering. The light submitting so shadow would not be lost.

Again, Aurelia came to herself, dragging air into her lungs. "She doesn't measure time in seasonrings."

Theo cupped her face. "Aurelia—"

"She sees time differently, Theo." Aurelia staggered back from the tree, clutching her ribs as understanding struck like lightning. "This isn't the end," she whispered. "It's the beginning."

The prophecy wasn't an ending. It was only the start. *And when she who is sent to bind appears, they will follow.* Theo reached for her.

She took his hands, tears streaking her cheeks. "I have to get rid of the blood."

"What?"

"The vials. The bond. If Helena has me, she'll become Alain. Or worse. This is only the beginning. We need another chance—"

"No." Theo's voice was steel. "Aurelia, you need your blood—"

"You promised to protect me." She pressed a hand to his cheek.

"I am protecting you! We need to run, we can find a way—"

"No." Aurelia dragged in a breath. "You said anything, remember?"

Theo's jaw clenched. "Not this. Not yet."

"Theo, she will kill you. All of you. Helena doesn't understand. We have to make her understand."

Aurelia reached for the ring. She stepped close, curling into his warmth. "Do you trust me?" He didn't answer, but he didn't have to. "Then make me yours, Theo. Bind me."

His lips parted. "Aurelia—"

"Please." Her voice cracked.

She lifted the ring. Placed it between their palms. She didn't know the words, didn't know if it mattered. She only knew what was in her heart. "I give my will freely. My strength, my light. That it might temper the shadow." The words tumbled from her lips—sacred and raw.

The air around them stilled. The moon flickered above the branches.

Theo closed his hand over hers. "I give my will freely. My strength, my weakness. I give it all to her. I beg of you, leave her with me—" His voice cut out as a film stretched tight, snapping into place.

Theo's breath left his chest in a shudder. His knees buckled as the ring flared with soft gold between their joined hands. The mark on Aurelia's forearm dulled, and a new symbol was scrawled into her skin.

Aurelia stared up at him, his eyes desperate and pleading. He didn't understand. Not yet.

She reached for the dagger Helena handed her, folded into the pocket of her cloak. "You will find me."

"Aurelia, please—"

"You must protect them. Keep them safe until I return." A

sound growled low in his throat, and she dragged her fingers over his lips. "Take my blood. Take all of it. Leave nothing—"

"I can't. Don't ask it—"

"Destroy the vials—"

Theo kissed her, tears wetting his lips. "I only just found you," he murmured against her skin. He clutched her against his chest, burying his face in the hollow of her neck. "If I could love—if I knew how—"

Aurelia's hand shook as she lifted the dagger. It was good that it was here. At the base of her tree. At the place she most belonged. "I give you all, Theo. Body and soul." She tore herself back and, before Theo could stop her, drew the blade across her throat.

35

Her blood splashed over the moss as he caught her. Theo dropped to his knees, arms out.

Too late.

The dagger clattered beside them. "Aurelia—" He gathered her to him, felt the slick warmth pulse between his fingers, soaking her robe, slipping down her spine. Her throat was open—deep, ragged, too wide. A mortal wound.

"No, no—*no*." He pressed his palm over it, tried to stop the flow, tried to hold her together. "Don't leave me."

Her eyes fluttered. Her lips trembled, twitching as if she might smile.

He leaned in, shaking. "Stay with me. Please."

The memory of Dara flashed in his mind's eye. Him crawling in the dark. Her skin cold and lifeless. The stillness. The silence.

Not again.

Not *again*.

Aurelia wasn't breathing. Her chest rose shallow, fluttering. He shook her once, gently, his mouth against her cheek. "You are *mine*, Aurelia."

Still no response. Only her last breath, and then nothing.

Her rune—the twisted chains—glowed softly at her wrist. His hand brushed over it as her body went still.

Theo's world stopped spinning. He held her, Aurelia's blood still warmed his hands, but it wouldn't last.

He pressed his forehead to hers, sobbing now, the sound gritty and raw.

Barteron screamed ahead. The trees opened into flame. Smoke rose from their homes. Theo had carried Etanos on his back. They were too late. They were always too late.

He kissed her mouth, still warm, smearing her blood across his lips.

"Forgive me," he whispered. "I wasn't strong enough." He bent forward, pressed his mouth to her neck, and drank, not for power, not for pleasure, but because it was hers.

And no one else would have it.

———

The shattered temple reeked of blood. Theo stumbled through broken columns, his mind blank, his body thrumming with fury.

Florent lay behind the altar. Theo collapsed beside him, grabbing his shoulder. "Florent—gods—look at me."

His friend opened his eyes, blood seeping from his ear. "Theo . . ."

"She used it," he whispered. "She used my venom."

Rage bubbled up in him a second time. Helena. A guardian turned.

Florent's breath caught, hitching. "She found it, all of it."

Theo swallowed, his throat dry. "I know."

Florent blinked. "She might use yours. You have to find her."

He couldn't tell his friend the truth. "I will. Thank you."

Florent clutched his sleeve as Theo rose. "Don't let her use it. She's not trying to balance anything. She wants us dead."

Theo stood. "I know."

"Where are you going?" Florent rasped.

Theo's eyes gleamed gold. "To finish what she started."

———

The manor loomed, half-lit by a slivered moon. Theo took no care to hide his movement. He burst through doors and hallways until he reached the hall, then barreled down the stairs to the cellar.

He followed the scent. Aurelia was everywhere. Her skin. Her sweat. Her blood.

His throat ached as he pushed open the door. The table was in the center. The chair she sat in. And there. Dozens of vials. Neat. Stacked in rows.

It was enough to start a war. Theo forced himself forward, his hands outstretched.

"Don't touch them." The voice snapped through the chamber. Cool. Measured. Poison.

Helena strode through the door behind him, radiant and monstrous, her new power thrumming in her veins. "These belong to the Goddess now."

Theo turned, every muscle vibrating with fury. "You are not a goddess. And they belong to *her*."

Helena smiled, stepping toward the table. "Well, then. Let's see what you're willing to do to keep them."

They circled the table. Theo kept his hands loose at his

sides, his body hunched like an animal ready to lunge. "She trusted you."

"I never lied." Helena watched him, eyes aglow. The power of a newly turned vampire was wild. Unstable. Ravenous. She hadn't learned control yet. "You can't stop this," Helena said softly. "Aurelia gave us the end of the curse as the prophecy said."

"Don't speak her name," Theo growled.

She laughed. "She was *never* yours."

Wrong. So wrong. She had been his from the moment she stood trembling in the candlelight, extending her arm beneath the shroud. From the first flash of her fury. From the way she made him feel again. Ache. Hunger. Hope.

Theo struck first. Faster than breath, he launched across the chamber, driving into Helena's ribs. She flew into the wall, stones cracking behind her.

She didn't stay down. She spun, snarling, and slammed into him with unnatural speed, her claws raking across his chest. Pain exploded through him, but he welcomed it. He needed it.

They crashed into the table. Vials scattered. One shattered on the floor, the blood draining over cold stone.

Theo roared and flung her off him. Helena hit the far wall, but landed on her feet, laughing through the blood streaming from her mouth. "You never wanted to live forever, isn't that what you told me? You wanted release."

Theo lunged again. They tore through the room, cracking the stones, denting the walls. His knuckles split. Her lip burst. She moved like a beast with nothing to lose.

But *he* had already lost everything, and that made him unstoppable. He pinned her to the ground, fangs at her throat.

"Kill me," she breathed, smiling. "I showed you how."

Theo glanced over at the vials, and in that split second,

Helena twisted, her blade cutting his side. He reared back, and she slipped through his arms, vanishing into the shadows.

Theo surged forward. He could chase her and finish this, but his eyes fell on the shelves. The vials.

He didn't hesitate. He grabbed a bottle and smashed it. The next. Then another. Glass and blood spilled across the floor, soaking into the stone.

He didn't stop until every vial was broken. Her blood destroyed. Her sacrifice protected. He stood, chest heaving, the last of Aurelia's scent fading into the air.

Then he ran. Out of the chamber, through the halls, and into the night.

Theo didn't stop until he found them near the tree line. A dozen guardians huddled in a knot—torn cloaks, scraped faces, wild eyes.

Raya turned at the sound of him. Her face was ash-gray. "Theo?" He slowed, taking them in. What had happened while he was in the woods? In the cellar?

"We must go. Hide." Raya held up a tool he'd never seen before. "This masks our blood."

Theo stalked closer and inhaled. He frowned. He couldn't smell a thing.

Raya beamed at him. "Hellebore. A smaller dose so it doesn't make us sick." She glanced over his shoulder. "Where is Aurelia?"

Theo gritted his teeth. "Not here." He started to walk. Helena must've left a trace somewhere. Something he could use to follow her.

"Theo, do you know of a place we can go?" Raya's voice was small. She motioned at the children huddled by the tree.

Protect them. Theo drew a breath and exhaled. "Come with me."

He turned, then gasped as white hot pain flared across the inside of his arm.

"Theo?" Raya stepped closer, but he wrapped a hand over his arm and stumbled back. He sucked in a breath and forced himself to look.

A mark etched into his skin. An oval, tilted, divided cleanly in two—half light, half dark, joined by a single swirling line that was unbroken.

Relief and gratitude flooded through him. They were bonded. She was still there, somewhere. All he had to do was find her.

He led the guardians further into the trees, and in the rhythm of their steps, one thought rooted in him, unshakable.

He would find her.

The prophecy would be fulfilled, and his curse would end.

And Helena would burn.

EPILOGUE

Theo

1403 A.D.

Montmorency, France

Rain clung to the eaves of the manor like breath to glass, gray and cold. The roof leaked in three places, and no one cared enough to patch them. Outside, the orchard rotted quietly, pears split open in the mud, fermenting in the leaf-littered soil.

Theo sat in the ruined parlor, fingers wrapped around a glass of wine he couldn't taste. The fire had long since gone out.

Clémentine stretched on the floor by the hearth, her head in a stranger's lap, humming an off-key tune while her fingers traced the curve of his collarbone. The man was already half-asleep, glamoured, blinking slow and stupid as she toyed with him before sinking her teeth into his neck.

She didn't even close the drapes.

Across the room, Florent sat slouched in a threadbare chair, face pale, eyes hollow. He hadn't fed in days. Maybe longer. He watched Clémentine with the look of a man who had once believed in gods and now only wished for endings.

No one spoke anymore. Not unless they had to. Sixteen centuries had beaten conversation out of them. Or maybe it wasn't only time. Maybe it was loss.

Theo set the cup down. He hadn't had a drop of blood. Not in five days, maybe six.

He stood.

The floor creaked beneath his weight, and Clémentine lifted her eyes, already bored. "Don't go far," she murmured. "But if you're interested, there's a tavern in the village with a woman who sings like an angel."

Theo didn't answer. He wasn't interested, and she knew it. He had no interest in cheap pleasure as she did.

He slipped on his coat—black, wool, too fine for this place—and stepped into the rain.

The night opened around him like a wound. The trees bled mist. The village below flickered with garish lamplight.

He didn't hate the humans, but he didn't mourn them, either. He fed when he had to. Sometimes too hard. Sometimes not at all. He didn't *care* anymore.

He'd watched kingdoms rise and fall, plagues burn through cities, oceans devour shores. He'd seen the bones of the Colosseum, watched Viking ships catch fire under green sky, stood at the gates of Constantinople when they screamed and never stopped.

And through it all—

She didn't return.

He had waited. Believed. Raged. Wept. Prayed.

But belief rots in the body like anything else. The prophecy faded to rumor, then myth, then silence. Only the mark on his arm remained. The signet—oval, tilted, half light, half dark, joined by a swirl—sat beneath his sleeve. The only thing promising he hadn't made the entire thing up.

Helena had vanished. No trace. No whispers. Not a flicker of scent on the wind. He hunted for years, scouring every lead, interrogating anyone who claimed to know where she'd gone. But it was like she had blinked out of the world. It was the one failure he couldn't forgive.

Theo ducked past the fence, then stuttered a step. He clutched at his chest, throwing an arm out against the wrought iron to brace himself.

A flicker.

A *spark*.

No warning. No sound. No reason.

Just light, sudden and sharp, slicing through him like a hot knife.

Theo staggered, then dropped. His knees slammed into the wet earth. His vision went white.

The signet blazed, searing into his skin. He pulled up his sleeve and stared at the mark as his breath caught. As tears stung his eyes.

Aurelia.

She was alive. Awake. Reborn.

His heart, dead and dry for centuries, slammed against his ribs with a force he hadn't experienced in sixteen hundred years.

He dragged himself up from the ground. She was alive. He didn't know where she was, but he would find her. He would burn the world to find her.

And this time—

This time, he would never let her go.

WATCH FOR THE SPECIAL EDITION OF BOOK #3 IN THE LE SOMBRE
SERIES

ALSO BY CINDY GUNDERSON

Tier Trilogy

Unreal Series

The Blessing Giver Series

See romance and women's fiction by Cynthia Gunderson at the link below

www.CindyGunderson.com

Instagram: @CindyGWrites

Facebook: @CindyGWrites

www.ingramcontent.com/pod-product-compliance
Lightning Source LLC
Chambersburg PA
CBHW061643190726
48289CB00006B/1729